FIRST POSITION

FIRST
POSITION

MELANIE HAMRICK

BERKLEY
New York

BERKLEY
An imprint of Penguin Random House LLC
penguinrandomhouse.com

Copyright © 2023 by Melanie Hamrick
Readers Guide copyright © 2023 by Penguin Random House LLC
Excerpt copyright © 2023 by Melanie Hamrick
Penguin Random House supports copyright. Copyright fuels creativity, encourages
diverse voices, promotes free speech, and creates a vibrant culture. Thank you for buying
an authorized edition of this book and for complying with copyright laws by not reproducing,
scanning, or distributing any part of it in any form without permission. You are supporting
writers and allowing Penguin Random House to continue to publish books for every reader.

BERKLEY and the BERKLEY & B colophon are registered trademarks of
Penguin Random House LLC.

Library of Congress Cataloging-in-Publication Data

Names: Hamrick, Melanie, author.
Title: First position / Melanie Hamrick.
Description: First edition. | New York: Berkley, 2023.
Identifiers: LCCN 2022045374 (print) | LCCN 2022045375 (ebook) |
ISBN 9780593638149 (trade paperback) | ISBN 9780593638156 (ebook)
Subjects: LCGFT: Novels.
Classification: LCC PS3608.A69657 F57 2023 (print) |
LCC PS3608.A69657 (ebook) | DDC 813/.6—dc23/eng/20220916
LC record available at https://lccn.loc.gov/2022045374
LC ebook record available at https://lccn.loc.gov/2022045375

First Edition: June 2023

Printed in the United States of America
1st Printing

Book design by Kristin del Rosario
Interior art: Ballet shoes © Stephen Orsillo / Shutterstock.com

To my love,
thank you for your endless support and inspiration
😉

FIRST POSITION

PROLOGUE

I can hardly see. I'm hot and freezing all at once and I can already tell I won't remember a lot of tonight. I'm glad that I won't. I look at the bottle of Xanax on my bathroom counter and want to throw it off the hotel balcony. I am better than this. Or at least I was.

I still am, right?

I get out of the bathtub and peel off my drenched dress, walking nude out of the bathroom and over to my bed. I sit with splayed legs for a second before looking at the zipped compartment in my suitcase. I can't believe I even still hide my old diary. Everyone knows what's in it. I can't even believe I've *kept* it. It's humiliating to revisit.

All these pages admitting to wishing I was a famous ballerina, looking forward to it. Believing in myself *and* the world around me so deeply, like life was going to be fair. Happy, even. I'm not a bitter old jaded hag now or anything, but I'm sure not that naive girl anymore.

I unzip the pocket and pull it out. What *ever* possessed me to buy a pink diary?

On the first page, there are the rules.

Oh, the rules.

I read them carefully, though my eyes are seeing double. Maybe it's less reading and more viscerally, instantly remembering each and every one.

THE RULES:

1. Be good. Be very good. Beyond reproach.
2. Do not reward yourself—dancing with the NAB *is* the reward, not dessert.
3. Sleep.
4. Drink rarely, and only a delicate glass here and there. Do no drugs.
5. Do not have sex with *anyone*. Not unless it is *truly* meaningless—which is very unlikely—just avoid it altogether. (Sidebar: when they call you a prude, tell them you're not but that you just don't want the drama—it's true and it's respectable.)
6. Put no shit talk in writing. Ever.
7. Do not let friendships get ugly. Better to have no friends than to get involved and risk the drama.
8. Befriend the staff without being a brownnoser. Just be above all the pettiness—they'll eat that shit up.
9. Dance as Juliet by the time you are twenty-one.

I laugh and shut the book. Jesus. I've broken every single one.

CHAPTER ONE

WASHINGTON, D.C.
NOW

Sylvie

I used to love the word *encore*. It meant everything. It meant I want more. It meant they wanted more, more of what only I was able to give. It meant I was good. Too good to stop.

Encore meant, *I don't want you to say goodbye—not just yet.*

Once upon a time I yearned to hear it. Now the word fills me with dread. I'm a weary traveler under the hot sun, exhausted, desperately thirsty, and achingly hungry; and I'm being told that the end is only a mirage—there are more miles yet to go.

"Encore!" Diana's voice screams the word. "Again!"

I take my position and repeat the phrase for the hundredth time. Sweat is running down my forehead from the exertion under the hot stage lights. I can feel a blister beginning to swell and bloom on my heel. I know that's going to mean pain, and that the more I ignore it—and I will ignore it—the longer it will take to heal.

I smile. Not because *it's all worth it* or anything like that. I smile because I must, and if I don't—and if I don't *convince* Diana that the smile is effortless—I'll just have to do it again.

Again.

Again.

Encore.

Diana is the ballet mistress, which means she is basically like the coach, and we're her players to prep for the big game. She begs *more* of every position, straightening every line in our physique, making us bend until we nearly break—all while managing to look as peaceful and easy and effortless as a weeping willow.

Diana is who yells *encore* until the word starts to feel like a whip through flesh.

Last rehearsal, Diana's command of *encore* meant doing a *piqué arabesque* fifty-seven times in a row. My feet bled at the end. No one cares when your feet bleed here. Honestly, to see a track of bloody footprints down the glossy floors of the halls is no more suspicious than grass and dirt in the locker room after a football game.

The week before that, *encore* meant doing *échappés* until the entire bottom half of my body went numb.

If beauty is pain, then becoming art is torture.

Never-ending torture too. It has taken me twenty years and counting to hold my hands correctly, and every single day I am *still* told that a finger is out of place. Usually it's my thumb, jutting out just a bit too much. I catch a glimpse of it on a rare moment when I am *not* thinking about the stage and my body, and the relationship between them. I hate my thumb. I hate it like it's out to get me. And in a way, it is. I'm supposed to have control of it and yet . . . I don't.

My fucking thumb.

And, of course, it doesn't stop there. I privately sneer or glare at every inch of my body. It's not just me who does this. It's every dancer. We glare and find fault in the mirror and in one another—like predators looking for weaknesses in prey.

I loathe the extra millimeter around my hip bones that forms when I'm retaining water before my period. The greyish-blue discoloration beneath my eyes from practicing too late into the night and waking again too early. And later I will glower at my heel for daring to grow a blister when what I need is calloused, tough skin that looks as smooth yet still as hard as a porcelain doll.

We wait for our entrance music. Diana is already poised to dislike the performance and ask for another before we have even begun.

I join hands with the three other swans. None of us groaning or letting on to the others that we are worn too thin to go again. They smile just as placidly as I do and stand as upright and solidly as ice sculptures.

The combination we are being told to do *again* is, I must admit, absolutely essential to get right. It is the Dance of the Cygnets, also known as the Little Swans. The beauty of it lies entirely in its hypnotizing synchronicity. The four of us dance in complete unison for a little more than ninety seconds, our feet moving so effortlessly that we almost seem to float. Our gazes moving at the same rate, the effort and concentration never appearing on our smooth, placid, pleasant faces. And it ends with a final *arabesque* to the knee.

An *arabesque* that must be hit by all four swans at the exact same moment, nothing short of mirror images. The height, the balance, the momentary suspension between the leg and the floor must be *exactly* the same.

The music has still not begun, so we wait.

I think of the half-empty box of Sobranie cigarettes in my bag. I want one so badly I could almost run off the stage and go to them like a comforting lover.

Dance of the Cygnets is a crucial lesson for a ballerina, not that all of us get the chance to dance it, much less dance it until we are filled with rage. It's a lesson in humility. The goal is not to stand out, or even to be seen as an individual beside other individuals. The aim is to become part of a moving machine. A four-part monster with many limbs moving together. A machine with pistons, not four girls with minds of their own and even tensions and feelings between them that should prevent them from something as intimate as touching, or as cooperative as being synchronized.

I used to yearn to be singled out. The old me would be craving individual celebration for being the best of the four. And so I recognize it in my fellow dancers, I can see that that's what they want.

It's such a difficult balance of trust and faith in the others—if one of us indulges our need to be *seen*, then the dance is ruined and we all look bad. But logic is not involved when they fantasize about Diana's bark turning to cooing praise, acknowledging and celebrating the dedication, talent, the fine lines, and the beauty. It's the craving not just to be lauded but to be elevated above the others.

"Stop," Tess bites at Alicia. "You're squeezing my hand too hard."

"I wouldn't have to if you could keep up," Alicia snaps back.

"We could all be done with this shit if Tess would stop holding her *arabesque* longer than everyone," I say.

"Seriously, it's so obviously on purpose," says Alicia.

"I have no idea what you're talking about; I'm simply doing it right."

Tess has the nerve to sound truly dismissive and patient with us. It's obscene. We all know what she's doing, including her.

"*Shh!*" Inga hisses.

The music begins, and our cue approaches.

Inga begins to quietly count under her breath to help us move as one.

The music and her counting fade into my periphery as I count along in my head.

I must be perfect. But not because I want to be praised. Only because I want to get off the stage. And perfection is the only way to be free.

We do seven *piqué passés* across the floor.

1 and 2 and 3 and 4 and 5 and 6 and 7, fifth hold.

Then right into sixteen fast *emboîtés*. Inga's count quickens as my own does.

1, 2, 3, 4, 5, 6, 7, 8, and . . . *piqué arabesque* to the knee.

Hold . . . release.

Then Tess releases. A little late. Again.

"Encore! As one! *Allez!*" says Diana.

We all breathe and release for the few seconds we have.

"Tess, I swear to god—" I begin, not even sure how to end my threat.

Tess blinks a few times and looks down.

Alicia looks shocked. "Are you going to cry?"

There is an invisible shadow of anger in Alicia's question—if someone is going to have an emotion besides silent seething or whispered sniping, then we will be set back even further.

"No!" A tinge of rose appears in Tess's cheeks. It is so sheer that I might be the only one among us all who can see it. I know what she's feeling because I *know the feeling*. She, like I would be, is offended at the very idea that she might cry in front of the company.

I roll my eyes at this. How do they have time to *give such a shit*?

And we go again, the familiar words pulsing in my temples:

I have to be perfect.

I *have to be perfect*.

I don't even hear the music. I only hear the counting.

1 and 2 and 3 and 4 and 5 and 6 and 7, fifth hold.

1, 2, 3, 4, 5, 6, 7, 8, and . . . *piqué arabesque* to the knee.

And . . . release.

As one.

"Yes, at last! Good," says Diana, who turns from us to talk to Matt Martin, who is saying something about Paris. She nods and looks at something he shows her on his iPad.

"Finally," says Alicia, relaxing from moving statue into human again.

"Was that so hard?" I ask Tess, my voice sharp staccato.

"I don't know, Sylvie. Was it hard for you to keep that constipated look on your face the whole time?" Compared to me, her voice sounds like honey. Toxic honey.

I laugh. I don't care.

And again . . .

"*Encore!* Again, get it right this time, but I want *less*, please!" Diana's hand is on her waist and she begins to pace. Tired of us. Tired of us for not being perfect.

I begin to protest, but Inga shoots a look at me.

She's right.

One complaint will buy five more repetitions.

"Let's go," Diana says, and the music rises.

We cross arms, join hands, smile, and begin again.

1 and 2 and 3 and 4 and 5 and 6 and 7, fifth hold.

1, 2, 3, 4, 5, 6, 7, 8, and . . . *piqué arabesque* to the knee.

Diana claps her hands once and emerges from beyond the dusty rays cast by the stage lights. All four swans brace for impact as she floats toward us. Her face is serene and inscrutable. It always is. I feel a dewy drop of sweat run down my breastbone to seep into the fabric of my light pink leotard.

I rest my hands on my hips, trying to calm my nerves and appear to be *not the problem*.

"Did you not hear me?" asks Diana, with that quiet, murderous tone she is so famous for.

There is a brief, *almost* funny moment when all the swans look around at one another, feigning innocence. Not me, I stare right at her. I know who she is talking to. There is a certain, poisonous je ne sais quoi that Diana reserves just for me. My humiliation at being identified as *the problem* is made worse by the utter confidence I have that if it had been anyone else, I would have felt relieved and even agreed. Like I'm sure the other three swans are feeling and doing right now.

"I asked if you heard me," she says, sinew in her tone as she removes all doubt that she is asking me.

"I did."

I know I am not the problem. I know, even, that Diana might be picking one of us at random to direct her criticism at, but it does not matter. Because she always picks me.

"Then why did you not listen?" She grins at me, her eyes void of any light.

The other twenty-five dancers who wait on the stage are absolutely silent as Diana's verbal blade cuts through the air.

As Diana takes her time closing the gap between us, I smooth down my blond bun and tighten my hair pins. Just in case I need to repeat anything. I swallow my pride and put a smile on my face.

"I am listening. I must not understand what you mean by *less*."

I used to look to Diana as the perfect version of a retired ballerina. I've seen her dance. She was brilliant. And now she is elegant. Now she doesn't need the validation from beyond the stage lights.

She moves toward me, her light linen blouse hanging on her delicately, sweeping through the air as she moves.

She steps close enough for me to smell her rose water perfume. I wonder if that floral scent is a modern perfume like Le Labo's Rose 31 or something older and more classic like Chanel Coco Mademoiselle Eau de Parfum. I can see the lines around her eyes that somehow make her more regal, the light strands of grey hair in her dense, brunette chignon.

"What happened to you, Sylvie?"

A question simple on paper that sends glacial shivers down my spine.

"I don't know."

"You don't know?"

She repeats my words. The twisting of her French accent makes my words—in my *simple* American accent—sound even more foolish than I could do if I were kidding.

I look for words, hoping I can find a way to avoid the dismantling of my delicate psyche. "If you could just be more specific. About . . . about what it is you want more of. Or . . . or less of—"

"Less of this. Less"—she glances at my sweaty chest—"less *Sylvie Carter.*"

I start to answer, but I have nothing to say. When you have already been carved out like a jack-o'-lantern, your guts thrown in the trash, your frame hollowed completely and turned into something only to serve a temporary purpose, just how exactly *does* a person remove themselves any more than that?

I am empty, here to hold within me the fire lit by someone else, *for* someone else.

Diana goes down the list of all the ways in which I have disappointed her during the rehearsal. I remain poised and still, nodding a little every time I think I should.

"You are *stuck*"—the micro-raising of her voice almost startles me—"in your head. You've been told this for how long now?"

I swallow. Give a small nod.

"Here," she says, putting a palm to my temple.

She doesn't move quickly, and yet I still flinch as if I am about to be slapped.

I see her notice, and her cheekbones twitch a little. Her version of a scoff.

"Leave the stage," she says simply. "Figure it out. And we will move on to"—she looks at her open notebook—"act three with Jocelyn. Somebody find her, please?"

I shake my head and go. Jocelyn, Diana's little princess.

As I grab my bag from the wings and walk off stage I run directly into Jocelyn, practically chest to chest. I *feel* her before I even see her face. The heat from her body comes at me like an assault. Her energy is always like that, no matter what she's doing. I feel like prey in the wild. When she's around, I can feel her there. As if she's waiting to pounce.

Her dresser, Kate, trails behind her. She's like a saddled pack mule, weighted down with anything and everything that Jocelyn might need during her rehearsal. On her shoulder hangs a bag stuffed to the brim, and I can see that she has leg warmers, warm-up pants, warm-up booties. She's also weighed down by Jocelyn's dance bag. In a clear plastic tote on her other shoulder, I see Vaseline, ChapStick, a neatly kept sewing kit, mints, eye drops, a phone charger, and more. She's also clutching a steaming, powder-blue Hydro Flask and a Nalgene water bottle with Jocelyn's name written on the side. Every girl has one, so we're like veritable kindergartners with our names plastered on our things. Kate struggles to close the lid with full arms and hands and Jocelyn doesn't pay any attention to her.

I look at Jocelyn and immediately regret it. When the two of us make eye contact, it's like a lit match meeting gasoline.

She's the flame. I am the gas.

She burns bright and hot and fast, often burning those who aren't afraid to touch her. And those who are. I feel as though I am merely the toxic environment that erupts and explodes when it crosses her fire.

I try to move past Jocelyn, but she shifts very slightly before me. I hesitate and then step to the left.

When her stare doesn't stop burning into me, I look at her, determined not to let her know how much she rattles me.

I raise my eyebrows and try to look like I don't care what she thinks about me. "They're starting act three. You should probably"—I gesture—"go."

Her shrug is so small I wonder if I imagined it. "They won't start without me."

She's right.

"There's that team spirit," I say, finding my own water bottle at the bottom of my bag. Mine is a Nalgene, too, same color as hers. A coincidence that used to be cute.

Jocelyn tilts her head a little and opens her mouth before shutting it.

"What?" I imbue the single syllable with as much poison as I can.

She smiles and looks down. "You dropped something."

I look down too. So does Kate.

It's a small bag with a few pastel, oblong pills.

I look up to answer, but she is gone, already having flown onto the stage and into the spotlight, leaving me behind, standing in the wings.

CHAPTER TWO

WASHINGTON, D.C.
NOW

Sylvie

I push through the outer stage doors and begin my walk of shame up the grand, red velvet aisle of the empty theater.

"Let's go, let's go," Diana says, with snapping fingers. The pianist begins the music and I hear the gentle shuffle of the dancers' feet as they scramble to places behind Jocelyn.

Diana's voice wafts through the theater like smoke that hangs instead of drifting away.

I pull on my sweats violently and tug hard at my bun to let my hair fall loose down my back.

I think of Giselle, the namesake of the ballet, and how she went mad over a guy.

I can't help but laugh as I pull out my phone to numb myself with pointless scrolling. I pick a row without looking and take a seat. I am not yet allowed to leave. I have to wait until the end of the act before I go. It won't take long, not nearly as long as our section. If Diana wants to see Jocelyn's solo again it will be to merely applaud her perfection and only because she liked it so much.

"Is something funny?"

There's a figure in the row behind me.

"What?" Then I remember that I had laughed out loud. Like a crazy person. "Oh, that. No. Nothing is funny."

I clear my throat and look back down at my phone. I am grateful to have it as a shield. It serves as a DO NOT DISTURB sign. It serves as an escape without the energy of reading or watching something that takes attention. It serves as relief without hangovers or withdrawal. It's just *nothing*. That might be everyone else's problem with it, but it's exactly what I appreciate about it.

"May I?" He is silhouetted at the end of my row.

Nerves surge in my chest. I gesture: *Sure, why not?*

He makes a noise that may be an exhale or a laugh, but I can't tell. I have to resist sarcastically echoing his own words back to him. *Is something funny?*

He stops a few seats from me and watches the stage. Maybe he isn't actually joining me. Maybe he just wants a better view.

I squint at his profile and my body tenses before my brain can react. It's been a long day—my eyes are bleary from performing so intensely, my brain is scrambled, my body worn, so I'm not sure I trust myself, but something about him seems *too* familiar. Something about him—his frame, his profile, his *essence* or something— is ringing a bell somewhere in the back of my mind.

He turns away from the stage, toward me, and he comes closer, stopping two seats from me and sitting down. He has so much confidence, he's so at ease.

He looks like the artistic director of the NAB, Robert Graham, in his younger days, but with a better hairline. He has a mischievousness to him. A playfulness in his eyes.

Ballet doesn't have time for much of that.

He pushes up the sleeves of his black sweater, eyes back on the stage. He exposes unexpected, winding tendrils of a tattoo with lines as fine as thread. He rubs his fingers together absentmindedly, and a muscle twitches by his elbow.

I can tell by his form that he is a dancer, but I only know because I'm in the world. A girl at a bar would just think he has an amazing body.

He gets up, and for a moment I feel a plunge of regret that I didn't say anything interesting and instead sat here dumbly. But then he moves to the seat directly beside me.

I take a small breath of distance back from him, afraid—idiotically—that *he* will feel crowded by *me*.

"She looks to be a bit tough on you," he says, his voice low but not quite a whisper.

It takes me a moment to realize that I'm embarrassed by what he has said.

"Diana?" I ask.

He gestures at her. "Your mistress?"

"Yes, her—yes, her name is Diana."

He nods and considers. "You were upset by what she said, no doubt."

He has an accent. At first it seemed light enough that it could have been regional or just the low volume and the big room. But now that I am practically in his lap, now that the heat from his skin is punctuating every word by wrapping itself around the different parts of me, I can tell that he has a somewhat strong accent. I would guess Italian or Spanish. And definitely sexy.

For some reason, my default is to defend her shit as reasonable. "It's rehearsal—she's got to be hard on us."

"Seemed she was only hard on *you*." He looks at me. "Right?"

"Yes, just . . . then she was, but it's fine." I open my mouth to say more but lose all conviction one way or another. I shrug, not sure if I am actually defending myself or Diana.

"She must see something more in you. If I had to guess, I'd say there's a lot more to you than what I just saw."

My eyes shoot to him. I'm not sure what to say. Is he being a dick?

I look back to the stage, where Jocelyn is performing beautifully, and where Diana is nodding in time to the music, watching her. Ugh.

The stranger and I sit there for minutes. I feel tense, suspended in air.

Finally, I say, "I don't think it's fair for you to say anything when all you've seen is— I don't even know how much you saw."

"I saw enough."

I'm not going to say anything.

As is becoming more common these days, my anger drags me back into the fray like a haggard doll in the care of a sadistic child. "Look, ballet is my life. It has been since I was four years old." I waver, suddenly aware that he has not asked for an autobiography and I'm sounding like a babbling fool. "I have passion." Who am I trying to convince?

"She did not tell you that you don't have passion. Not at all. And neither did I, by the way." He remains expressionless. "She said you're in your head. This is not a damning insult."

"Well, I don't know—how am I supposed to read that? In my head? Whose head should I be in?" He doesn't answer before I rail on. "Maybe it's just that she hates me, and it's really that simple."

He laughs. "You're doing it now."

I think he will elucidate, but he doesn't. He just gives a little grin and then runs his hand through his hair. It's that amazing, thick, shining chestnut color with loose natural waves.

"I am *not* all in my head." I turn away from him, away from *his* head, focusing back on the stage. *This conversation is over*, I think. But instead, I find myself turning back to him, words falling out in a hissed bravado before I can catch them. "I have to be in my head! If I'm not, then my form falls apart. Or it would. I *have to* be on the stage, in the music, and *I have* to be thinking *in my head*. Of course I do."

"It's hard," he says simply.

I am now deeply offended that this stranger thinks he has any right to tell *me* why ballet is hard. Ballet is blood, sweat, and tears—all of which are to be hidden at all costs. Ballet is hard, yes, but he—whoever he is—is not going to tell me why.

I sit back again. This isn't a conversation I need to have. I don't owe this guy anything. He just pushed on a bruise that was already sore and I reacted. I'm not going to give him the satisfaction of any more reactions.

My body is a coiled spring.

"I can tell you have passion," he says easily, clearly unaware of—or undeterred by—the turmoil of reactivity thirteen inches away from him. "I watched you for only a little while up there, not even alone, and I know you can be much better than you are. *Even* better, I should say."

At first his eyes stay on the stage, even as he turns his head toward me, and then with a slow blink, he looks me in the eye.

I can smell him. Is it cologne or just him? The notes are clean, maybe a little woodsy or smoky but not aggressively so. It could be soap and body heat.

The softness of his sweater—is it cashmere?—lightly touches the skin of my upper arm and I find myself not wanting to move.

"I can tell you have passion in the worst way," he goes on, oblivious to my mental argument. His consonants slur together slightly from his accent. "The worst kind of passion is the kind that is fighting to get out but is being barred by something its owner thinks is necessary. As if to be passionate is to be weak, or to be foolish, or to be uncivilized. As if passion is not the only thing that has ever made it possible for brilliance to be translated from one to the other. Passion is not a detail of talent. It is the synthesizer, the vehicle, the translation, the magic drug that makes it possible for talent to not only be seen but to be *felt*."

My god, maybe he's brilliant.

I stare at him. I wish I had a recording so I could transcribe his words, because I suddenly feel dumb and empty, like half of what he said has gone completely over my head.

So, as I tend to do when I'm afraid of being seen for who I am, I resort to being flippant. "Do you always speak like this?"

"Like what?"

"Like some quote, unquote *inspirational* caption you might see cut and pasted under a filtered picture of some ditzy girl's Gramercy rooftop cocktail."

He laughs. "I don't always need to."

His laugh is something sparkling and easy, and it makes me want to hear more of it.

"And now you do?"

"Maybe you need me to."

My heart squeezes tight. Foiled at my own game. "Right," I say, sinking into my seat with crossed arms and deciding that he is impossible to impress and therefore no longer my responsibility. Although when exactly *had* I decided to impress him?

"Ah, you're hurt again," he says, as if observing a missed return at Wimbledon.

Irritation rises in me. I can't believe how long this guy has been able to keep up my ire.

It's because he's right, a small voice inside me says.

I bring a knee up to my chest and become aware that I'm a therapist's field day right now. My body language is a tell-all.

I put my foot back down. I must be confident. I must be a *statement*, not a response.

He stares at me, and I think of those tests everyone talked about for a while, where you stare at your *lover* for four straight minutes and it's supposed to . . . I don't remember, do something to you. Create love. Create a lifelong bond. Promise them your firstborn. Something.

I think of this because as his eyes bore into mine, I start to wonder when the last time someone really looked at me was. Jocelyn's challenging stare doesn't count. Neither do the laser beams cast from Diana's pupils. This is something I didn't realize mattered to me. When was the last time someone looked at me, really?

Me. The me I have to shovel out in order to be an adequate vessel for Diana's instruction. For the *feeling*. For the *art*.

And even so, if he *is* the first in a long while, he's not even doing it with that much warmth—more just with this cocky amusement. How starved am I, if this feels like a meal?

Everyone looks at me and wants to change something about what they see. Even this stranger, who has apparently sat down next to me in order to be a fucking asshole and that's about it.

"What are you feeling now?" he asks. When enough time passes, and I say nothing, he gets more comfortable in his chair and says, "You're going to really have to crack yourself open somehow."

"Yeah? Is this the moment where I overcome my vague fears, jump out of a plane, and sign a new lease on life?"

"Maybe. Or maybe you just need to find a way to stop thinking. To . . . how do you say it in English"—he clicks his teeth and shuts his eyes trying to remember—"*resa*."

He lets his hand drop to our shared armrest. His fingers curl around the wood.

I don't know the word and yet it makes the hair rise on my arms. I feel my body reacting to him in a way that feels . . . like something I used to understand.

Familiar, but forgotten.

"*Resa*." He looks at me and leans a little closer. "*Resa, resa*."

There's a rush going through me now, like champagne with tiny, sharp bubbles, perfectly chilled and flowing right beneath my skin and intoxicating my very veins.

His jaw drops open a little and he looks from my eyes to my lips and back again. I recognize that glance from a distant past, one that is coming back to me in ephemeral gusts of imaginary air—or maybe it's just him. He exhales and I find myself leaning closer to him completely of my own volition.

It is dreamlike. No choices are being made: it is human magnetism.

It's the sort of moment that in retrospect you cannot believe. You cannot believe you had the guts to be so forward. You can't believe you correctly interpreted someone else's insane body language and responded to their chemistry with your own. And yet . . .

I reach a hand out to him, and momentarily lose my nerve.

He blinks and says, "Close your eyes."

He has not lost his nerve.

I smile and look sideways at him.

"Do it, close your eyes. If you want to. Of course."

And for some reason, I do.

He takes my hand, the one touching his sweater. He lightens my touch, taking it from a grip to something more akin to a hand sifting through sand. He runs it slowly over the fabric on his arm. "Just feel it, do not worry. Do not think. Send every thought to your fingertips."

The words release me further and I feel the soft, fine fabric. I also feel his hands and the warmth of them on my narrow bones and thin, cool flesh.

It's like some strange meditation or hypnosis.

I keep feeling this and he lets me go, and I spread my palm over his shoulder and then his back, which brings me closer to him. I am lost in it for the briefest of moments and then open my eyes, feeling odd and foolish. And very young. What am I doing? This is—

"Don't close up again," he says. Then he whispers, "Stay open."

His face comes close to mine and then I feel his breath on my neck as his forehead touches my jawbone. My head falls back, exposing my neck and chest to him as if he were a vampire who could suck me dry—and has my permission to do it. It is literally intoxicating. I don't know how a voice or a touch can do that, but it does. I am powerless against it.

"What do you want, little swan?"

Chills run through me. "I don't know."

"Yes, you do. Tell me."

I think again about apologizing or saying I don't know, but then decide to be honest. "I want you to touch me."

I feel like I'm on hard, deadly drugs. My inhibitions have vanished.

He draws back almost imperceptibly, and I feel a reprise of fear.

"How do you want me to touch you?"

I nod. "Any way. Every way."

I am breathless.

I am so suddenly stolen away into the night of this feeling, and I don't even know how I got here. I can't remember the last time I felt something like this, and yet I am also feeling this ache with the skill of someone who has done it a million times over. My mind is hesitating, but my body has not a slice of confusion about what it wants. And the only reason my mind is hesitating is because I am truly afraid I have lost my mind.

"I want to give you what you want," he says, a slight rasp to his voice revealing that he isn't quite as in control as he was a few minutes ago. "Are you sure of what that is?"

His hand is on my waist. I take it and guide it quickly, feverishly past the waistband of my training sweats and don't stop guiding him until his fingers are winding around the sudden wetness of my leotard and nudging between the fabric and my skin.

"Mm." He makes the noise by my ear, crippling me yet further. "I believe you that you want it now."

A gasp escapes me as he touches me.

I glance half-heartedly around, making sure there is still no one near us, but honestly even if there was, I wouldn't have the power to hide.

The feeling he is giving me is a little like drowning. I'm losing myself more and more, feeling more and more deeply submerged in it, and losing the ability to do anything but give in with every gesture.

In my past, when I have been more prepared, I have often found sex to be as performative as the stage; I move my hips this way, toss my head that way, arch my back now, and fold before my audience. But this is making me forget I can even be seen.

I believe it's not just him, this man whose name I do not even know, but also how badly I need to feel free. In this moment, I don't care about anything but this.

I raise my hips and he takes the sign I can't believe I have communicated effectively and pulls down the sweatpants and moves aside the thin cotton of my leotard.

"Again!" barks Diana on the stage. "But very good, Jocelyn. Very good."

"Yes?" he asks.

"Yes, *yes*." I touch his hair, that *gorgeous* hair. It's even more perfect to the touch. I pull him by the back of his head, and push him where I want him. He moves out of his seat to crouch in front of mine.

The heat and the wetness and the surprise of it makes me feel desperate. My heart is pounding and everywhere I am throbbing and clenching and releasing. There is no longer a past or even a future. All that matters is *now*. And it is intense. It is taking everything in me to remain silent.

He exposes my thigh and runs his hand down the muscles of it, chasing his own touch with his lips, kissing, biting, and sending me into quick convulsions.

"This—yes, that, do that," I whisper throatily, my voice wild and quiet and nearly primal.

He squeezes my thigh and then smacks it. The sound reverberates through the auditorium and my head lurches up and he forces me back down and puts his mouth on me and begins to do something I do not even have a guess for. Sucking, kissing, licking, flicking, I have no idea whatsoever; all I know is that I am suddenly plunged into an ecstasy I have scarcely, if ever, felt.

My hips begin to twitch, I feel my insides throbbing and

responding to everything he does. I let out a moan and he some-how does *more* of what he's doing, and I squeeze his arm to indi-cate that he's doing the right thing.

"*Resa*, swan, *surrender*."

In the moment of relief from his touch so that he can speak, my body yearns so desperately that when he goes back to it, it is too much. I let out a gasp of air and convulse into him, then again, again, and . . .

"Yes," he breathes against me.

I grip into his body as if I trust him with my life and surrender completely to him.

He doesn't disappear as soon as I am through. Instead he lin-gers on my thighs, kissing and touching me lightly. I lie my head back with my eyes shut, certain that my legs would go out from under me if I were to try to stand. I could sleep or slip into the devastatingly soothing heat of a warm bath.

But almost a moment too late, I register the sound I have just heard: the stage manager, Mike, clapping his hands and yelling at the theater at large. This is the moment when the dancers are summoned to the stage over the god mic for notes. I know what comes next.

"He's going to ask for the houselights up," I say, patting the stranger on the back, though he is already off me. "He's going to ask for the houselights up!"

I scramble into my sweats just as we both hear, "Houselights, please!"

With the dancer's grace, I swing my leg over the stranger and twirl a few seats away, crouching silently behind the backs of the seats in front of me just as he leaps covertly over the other rows.

I catch my breath and register that Robert Calvo, our director, has joined Diana onstage. His shock of white hair is lush against his dark skin and he still moves like a dancer, even though he has not been on the stage in more than twenty years.

"Everyone gather round," says Robert, clasping his long fingers in front of him.

I stand and adjust my warm-ups as I prepare for the walk down the aisle. My inner thighs are weaker than they've been in years and I'm afraid there are telltale signs on me that I cannot see.

Robert does not wait for the full company to arrive before saying, "I want to introduce to you all, our newest principal dancer, the great Alessandro Russo!"

The entire company erupts in gasps and applause from the usually impermeable girls. And I see a man begin to walk down the aisle. Chestnut hair. Broad shoulders. A perfect frame.

He glances at me as he walks by. He takes his right hand and touches his lips and nose. To anyone else it would look like a human gesture that meant nothing at all. But I know where that hand has just been.

"God . . . dammit," I utter.

He winks.

I have just made a huge, huge mistake.

CHAPTER THREE

Sylvie

I walk down the aisle behind Alessandro the Great. It's as if everything that's happening to me is through a film of some kind. A memory, a dream, something surreal. My ears ring like I've cracked my head on asphalt. Everyone sounds far away and through the muffle of cotton. The floor beneath my feet feels a fraction of a centimeter more distant than usual. My body, which I am usually so conscious of, seems suddenly not quite right. My arms a little too long, my weakened legs moving with unearned confidence. I feel like I might come to at any moment, like everything will crash down in a tidal wave of lucidity, and I, the Fool in the Leotard, will simply collapse where I stand.

He takes the steps two at a time, and I follow him, moving quickly but keeping as much distance between us as I can. He moves like a ghost compared to me. I move like shattering glass.

I take a deep breath and count to five before joining the ballet company as they celebrate and welcome Alessandro.

He is not just famous for being good. In fact, he is not just *famous*. He's . . . what's the word?

Ah. Right. *Notorious.*

Alessandro is a notorious bad boy. Unreliable, aloof, temperamental, and often rude to his partners. An unapologetic playboy.

But he gets away with it, because he is simply the best.

And because, by all accounts, he's incredibly charming. He has a million-dollar grin that has disarmed countless offended interviewers. While everyone seems to agree that he's difficult to work with, no one seems to have a bad word to say about him. Just one of those guys who gets forgiven for everything.

They say he's like Baryshnikov and Nureyev combined.

He's good, he's straight, and he's hot. The kind of attractive that transcends personal taste. There is probably scarcely a soul alive who wouldn't admit that they're at least just a *little* attracted to him.

But how had I not recognized him? It's marginally concerning that I didn't.

I decide that it's a combination of a few things. Most girls have probably pored over his magazine shoots, but I never look at that stuff. I've only seen him dance. In those videos—which of course, I used to consume as eagerly as if the clips were milk chocolate—he is all business. He completely folds into the characters and succumbs to his perfect form without losing any attention to detail. He moves with an energy that seems to come from its own orbit, its own galaxy. And everyone within sight of him can feel it too.

It's also been a long time since I've watched any other dancers or even really thought about *the greats.*

I used to, but that was an old life.

A chill runs through me as I think of his hands, his form, and his beautiful face and how close to me they were only a few unbelievable moments ago.

Up close and extremely personal, there was more to him, his frame, and his features than I could have imagined. He emanates something wholly distracting, like a pheromone effect. Maybe that's what it was. A musk so thick and intoxicating that I could scarcely see through the fog to recognize his face.

"Can you believe this?" Alicia asks, startling the shit out of me.

I shake my head and answer truthfully. "I really cannot."

"He's way sexier in person, don't you think? YouTube and *GQ* really do him no justice." She silkily strokes the side of her water bottle. The top is loose and a few drops spill out onto her hand and the floor. "Oh, what do you know"—she smiles—"*I'm all wet.*"

A shiver runs me over, and I mask my memory with an eye roll. "You're *so* vulgar, Alicia, *really*." I say it in my best Diana impression.

She snorts.

She's only a year older than I am, but she has already danced in three major ballet companies. A soloist at the Royal Ballet, principal at the San Francisco Ballet, and arriving here at the North American Ballet just last year. Here, she is a soloist, like I am.

"You're always *just saying*," I add.

She shrugs.

I jokingly glare at her and then smile. She leans into me and then looks back to Alessandro, sighing.

It would blow her mind if I told her what just happened.

"His debut in America, which he has so rudely avoided making for so long." Laughter. "Press photos will take place Wednesday, right before our opening night. We are just simply *over the moon* that Mr. Russo will be our Siegfried, *this* Saturday, so please give your absolute *all* this week, all of you." Robert looks back at his star. "We're absolutely *over* the *moon*!"

He claps wildly and applause follows from us. Alessandro scans all our faces, lingering not even an extra second on me.

He smiles graciously and holds up his hands, shaking his head and looking embarrassed. "Please, please," he says. He speaks low, but it's enough that all of us quiet our hands.

"I am grateful for the chance to dance with so many talented artists. I look forward to getting to work with each of you. Truly, with all of you."

"I would believe any word he says," says Alicia.

I would too, I think.

Robert closes out announcements with a few mundane details, and then, practically blushing in his presence, gives one more round of applause up to Alessandro.

Once dismissed, all the little ballerinas twinkle across the stage to him. They shake his hand, wax rhapsodic about his talent, congratulate him on the position, flirt with little laughs they would never conjure up just for the appreciation of their peers.

Alicia and I don't make the slightest movement toward him.

"Oh, hey." She turns to me, looking concerned now. "Are you okay, by the way? I heard Diana shouting at you. And did you get into a thing with Jocelyn? Again? When are you guys going to just let the past go?"

I let out a tense breath as the memory—briefly eclipsed—comes back to me.

"I'm fine."

She makes a thin line with her lips and says, "Okay, that sounds healthy!"

"I'm good, really. Diana's just Diana. And Jocelyn just takes every opportunity to be a bitch now that she has proof that she's the better dancer."

"She's not a better dancer than you. Really, she isn't." When I give her a look, she says confidently, "She might be *as good* as you, but she is certainly not better. I mean that—you know I have no filter."

"I hate when people say that."

She inhales deeply. "Whatever, I'm just saying you know I'd be honest with you if—"

"If what? You'd be honest with me if *you thought I could take it*. Or you'd be honest with me if *it would help anything*."

"No, you horrid cow, I would be honest with you if *that* was what I believed, I would tell you. I would be honest with you if you asked me to be honest."

"Be honest," I say, bracing but not letting it show.

"The truth is you got fucked. You're good but no one cares anymore."

I was right to brace. I knew it was true, but hearing her say it out loud somehow made it even more real. I laugh. "Well, there you go."

"You just have to make them care again."

I get suddenly hot. "How am I supposed to do that when I don't even care anymore?"

She raises an eyebrow. "Yeah, that'll be pretty hard." Always wanting to move on from the heavy stuff, she adds, "Let's go get a drink, huh? On me?"

"Do you think they're all over his body?" A male voice with an English accent arises, and we turn to see that David has walked up, setting his dance bag at our feet.

"Jesus, you need a bell around your neck," says Alicia.

At the same time, I ask, "Is who all over his body? Those sycophants? Clearly." I gesture at the company.

"The *tats*," he says. "So hot. I love a guy with tattoos, just love 'em."

David's smooth skin glistens with sweat from the rehearsal he's just finished. Even sweaty and gross, he looks like he could have been right next to Alessandro on the pages of any of those magazines. He's one of those gorgeous gay men who look at once more beautiful than most women and more handsome than most men. It's offset by the charming, but strong—as he puts it—*just south of posh accent*.

"Yeah, I was in Royal Swedish Ballet when Alex guested there," David says.

"What?" Alicia says, jaw dropping. "And you call him Alex?"

"Absolutely, babes. He's a nice enough guy, if you can look past his ego. Easy enough for me, since I think people are not arrogant *enough*."

I watch Alessandro—Alex—and wonder why he just did what he did with me. Was it because of me, or is that just his MO? Both? Had I just been ensnared in his trap?

Maybe that was his version of a handshake.

"Sylvie?" David asks. I get the sense that it's not the first time he has said my name, that maybe I've been zoned out longer than I realize.

"You okay?" asks Alicia.

"Yes, yeah, sorry, lost in thought." I breathe in deeply. "Rehearsal is over, meeting's over, our introduction to god is over." I glance at Alessandro. "Shall we get the hell out of here?"

"Let's *do*," says Alicia.

"Hotel bar?"

"Yes, I have to drop my bag in the dressing room first," says Alicia.

"I'll go with you. I left my sunglasses in there, I think," I say.

We make our way there, and I rifle through my bag just to make sure they really are missing. But when they aren't in the dressing room either, I realize where they must be.

In a darkened aisle toward the back of the theater.

"I have to find them. Why don't you guys just go on ahead and I'll catch up?"

"Honestly that's better. That way I can take a shower, and I think everyone would be more grateful to us if we all did."

"Oh my god, did I tell you I got this Diptyque soap that is just *to die*," says David, already moving on from my missing glasses.

To be fair, the lost glasses would be a lot more interesting to them if they knew what had made them go missing.

David's voice fades away and I wait a moment before sneaking into the empty aisles. No one is watching me. I'm not doing anything wrong now, but I feel like I am.

The stage manager is setting the lighting cues and the lights go up again, as if someone is not only watching me, but reading my mind.

Bathed in big lights, it looks completely different. It makes the whole affair seem even more dangerous and unbelievable than it already is. I get on all fours and look up the slanted floor beneath the seats, trying to spot them.

"Like this? All these lights? In front of everyone?"

I turn and see Alessandro standing over me. Over me, who is, of course, on all fours.

Begging for it.

"These what you need?" He pulls a leather case from his back pocket. My beloved Yves Saint Laurent glasses.

"Thank you," I say, taking them.

"I was going to hand them to you, then the lights . . ." he says.

"It's okay, yeah, don't—don't worry about it."

He smiles. Damn.

"Why didn't you *mention* who you are?" I ask.

"My manners." He shakes his head, as if he is a rascally child, always forgetting to be polite. "Alessandro Russo." He extends his hand, grinning. "Nice to meet you."

A smile tugs at my mouth, despite myself. "Sylvie Carter." I take his hand, and his fingers—*those* fingers—curl around mine.

I feel a buzzing, and for a moment I think it's my nerves but then I realize it's my phone. We unentangle, and I pull it out of my bag. It's Alicia. I hit the button on the side to stop it buzzing. "I have to go."

"See you around, Sylvie."

I nod stupidly, and then give a dumb little wave and run toward the doors.

I'm hoping they are unlocked. I swear to god if I take off like that and then slam my body, cartoon-like, into a giant locked door, I may actually just burst into tears and tell him to forget we ever met.

I hesitate and then press on the bar, and blessedly it opens. I glance back and he's still there.

"You thought it was going to be locked, didn't you?" I ask, grasping feebly for an upper hand.

"It would have made for a more interesting exit," he says.

"Sorry to disappoint you."

"You," he says quietly, "did not disappoint."

And there goes that upper hand.

I smile, a thrill running through me, and continue out into the lobby. Alicia texts me: **Oops, didn't mean to call! See you in 45!**

I walk the ten blocks back to the hotel, from one grand lobby to the next.

In the shower, I let the hot water run over me, touching

my whole body, wishing, a little, that I could keep a trace of his scent on me. Since I can't, I just shut my eyes and let the water hold me.

Despite the heat, a chill runs through me every time I think of Alessandro's unfamiliar hands on me.

Every time, I turn up the heat a little more. It turns my skin red.

Hotels. Hotels and their endless supply of hot water. I could stay in it all night.

And I nearly do, before realizing I'm about to be late for drinks. Something about today seems to have ruined my sense of reality.

The bar is old-school, hidden behind two heavy, closed doors. It's sort of like The Oak Room, which I was enchanted by in *North by Northwest* with Cary Grant, when I saw it only a few years ago for the first time. I had been disappointed to learn that the real one had closed.

This bar has the same feel. Dark wood; plush, overstuffed, and upholstered furniture; and a bartender who looks like he's been there longer than I've been alive. It's dimly lit, and the wallpaper is heavily textured and dark. It's quiet, windowless, and there's a piano player in the corner. Some of the guests are dressed to the nines, clearly on their way to another event or coming from one. They're the types who will come to the ballet, but for now they have no idea (and I'm sure, no interest) in the fact that three of the dancers are in their immediate vicinity.

My eyes land on Alicia and David. They're already tucked into a lush, deep blue banquette right next to the fireplace, which is burning, despite the heat outside and the heat in my thighs—which may be coming from rehearsal or what happened directly after.

"Sylvie!" Alicia calls out, waving her hand madly, as if I could ever miss her.

I nod and wave at her and then smile politely at a group of middle-aged men leaning on the bar and looking appreciatively at me.

There's another table I notice watching me as I cross the room. Young guys. The "young professional" types that are so far from my world I can't begin to understand them.

I don't even give them a smile.

"What took you so long?" asks Alicia as I settle in. They've ordered a bottle of Veuve and it's resting on shaved ice in a copper bucket. I take my glass and fill it.

"I walked back. And I actually ran into Alessandro on my way out. He's charming—you were right." I nod at David. "Sweet, actually."

"You walked, that explains it. You're such a slow walker. Remember the time we saw that *brilliant* exhibit at the Tate. Holy shit, I've never been through a museum more slowly. Seriously. I bet I didn't burn a single calorie."

"I like to look at everything! Should I have just skated by it all at top speed? What's even the point in going if you're not going to take your time? Museums are meant for meandering."

Alicia laughs.

"There's a happy medium, babes," says David. "And also, did you really just call Alessandro *sweet*? That's honestly got to be the first time anyone has ever described him that way. I said charming, but sweet . . ."

"I think you're into him," says Alicia, biting her bottom lip.

I roll my eyes showily. "What am I, some horny high schooler?"

Kind of.

"A bit."

"He seems fine."

"He's more than fine," says David. "Wait until you actually spend any time with him. He won't remember me, I'm sure—we barely talked and he's so on another level. And of course, regrettably, straight. But he's just got this draw to him, I'm telling you. He's kinda quiet, but everything about him is so . . . *big*. Like, his talent—when he's dancing, he's the only one you can see onstage. When he wants to be charming, or get his way, he gets what he wants. And when he's mad or frustrated, his bad mood takes over the whole room."

"Wow, he sounds like a monster," says Alicia, laughing. "Are we supposed to think those are good qualities? Sounds like toxic masculinity."

"I know, but it's just so hot," says David.

"I can't help but agree with you," Alicia says.

They laugh and clink glasses.

It's fucked up, but I can't help but agree with them both.

David's phone buzzes on the table, and his face lights up.

"Is that *Chris*?" Alicia asks, nudging his knee.

"It is," he says, distracted. "I hate this part of touring, being away from him. His rounds just ended at New York Presbyterian so he's about to get on the train home."

"You're so lucky you found each other," says Alicia. "You guys are seriously perfect. But can we forget about *true* love for a moment and go back to how Russo is the *perfect* distraction for Sylvie? And also I'm being generous here, because I would *not* turn down a night with him myself, oh my god. Those *legs*, for real, those thighs could crush you. Really pin you down. Totally control you—you know what I'm saying?" She sighs. "I tried dating nice guys, they're just so boring. I mean the one I'm seeing now is . . . fine."

"Who's the guy you're seeing now?" David asks her in a way that implies he already knows who it is.

"Who is it?" I ask.

Alicia cringes. "I hate his name."

"Say it," says David teasingly.

She pouts.

"Say it," I say, David's smile catching.

She hesitates and then says, "Bill."

The name is dripping with so much distaste that it cracks us all up.

"Yeah, you guys are destined for a long and happy life together," I laugh, taking a bubbling sip of champagne.

"Do you, Bill, take Alicia—" says David.

"Oh no! Mrs. Bill!" I almost spit out my champagne.

Alicia cuts David off. "Oh my god, *stop*." She looks to me. "So are you going to do something about it?"

I consider telling them about what happened, but then shy away from it. I don't want him to find out I told anyone. And I'm almost afraid it didn't really happen.

My smile fades and I take another sip. "No."

"Why *not*? He was really eyeballing you. I think he'd go for it."

Just then, one of the *young professionals* comes over to our table.

"Excuse me," he says, looking at Alicia. "But . . . are you Zoë Kravitz?"

Alicia lets out a deep sigh of irritation, but her lips curl up in such a way that betrays the fact that she actually *loves* that he asked.

"No, I'm not," she says, tone dripping with irritation.

David looks to me and does a gagging motion.

The guy apologizes and Alicia says, "It's fine, happens all the time."

This is true, but it makes it no less annoying to witness her false irritation.

"Oh, don't act like you don't love that shit," says David.

"I do not!" She sips her champagne and then says, "Okay, I totally do. Zoë Kravitz is so gorgeous."

"Which makes you insufferably vain," says David.

"Okay, can we get back to the point at hand?" Alicia gestures at me.

There's a pause, and then David asks, "Is this about . . . the one we do not speak of? Speaking of toxic men?"

"As you said, we do not speak of him."

"We agreed not to say his name," says Alicia.

I roll my eyes. "It's not about . . . *him*, it's just . . . Oh my god, I mean I haven't even talked to Alessandro. Just a few words."

That, at least, is true.

A sick feeling rises in my stomach, replacing the thrilling glee of the forbidden rendezvous. I was sobering up—emotionally, because I was actually getting drunker—and realizing I'd done something really, really dumb.

Again.

"But this is different than with—" David stops when Alicia raises her hand. "This is different than with *him*. He's not going to ruin your career and damn you for all time like he did."

I raise my eyebrows. "Wow. For all time."

"Shit, I didn't mean it like that. Sylvie . . ."

"No, it's cool," I say.

I suddenly feel overwhelmed, uncomfortable where I felt safe only moments ago. My heart begins to pound. A panic attack is starting, my heartbeat racing beneath my rib cage. If I don't get out of here, I'm going to convince myself I'm dying.

My hands are sweating and my breath feels suddenly too shallow.

My body is saying *escape*.

"He didn't mean it like that, Sylvie, you're *not* damned, your career is absolutely *not* ruined." She glares at David, who looks guilty and awkward. I can tell he doesn't know what to say.

"I'm fine. Seriously."

There is an uncomfortable moment where the two of them share a look. They do this all the time and I hate it. It reminds me that I'm the third of three.

"Ooh, I know, let's do *sushi*. Huh? Sushi and sake? Do they have a Nobu here? What fucking city are we touring in right now? Oh, right, the capital. I'm an idiot," she says, laughing at herself.

"I'm down for sushi," says David, finishing his champagne.

Alicia downs hers too.

I finish mine. The two of them stand, Alicia staring into her phone, looking for Michelin-starred fish in walking distance.

"I think I'm good," I say.

"No, come!" Alicia whines. "David's an idiot."

"I'm an idiot!" he says.

"No, it's fine. I'm actually just sort of worn out. It's cool—I'm not pissed." He looks doubtful and a small part of me doesn't want to reassure him, but I try anyway. *"Really."*

My heart plunges and I take in a sharp, deep breath.

"Okay, if you're sure . . ." says Alicia.

"I am. Bye, guys." I sound normal.

I start to go, and David says, "You know, there's a chance that fucking Alessandro might actually help your career. You know? Maybe you break even. Bang the big shot once, get fucked. Bang the next one, maybe you're back on top. Even steven. But, hey, it seems like you don't even care anymore. About success, about living up to your potential—"

"David!" Alicia shrills.

"No, I don't care! Maybe what she—maybe what you *need* is a little tough love. The kind you can get from a guy like Alessandro, or maybe this kind: Sylvie, one day you're going to look back and see that you gave up everything just so that you don't get embarrassed again, and it'll be too late, and you'll be sorry."

"Dude, David, what the fuck?" says Alicia.

I wait for hurt or anger to appear in my chest, but I feel nothing.

He hasn't hurt me. In fact, all I've done is decide on the burger from the room service menu while he talked.

"Yeah, maybe you're right," I say.

David calls another weak apology out after me, saying something about *trying to help*, and I trip on a small ripple in the carpet and catch myself. The table of young professionals rushes to save me, the damsel, but I escape them with a polite, forced smile.

Jocelyn is at the mouth of the bar, waiting for her own friends to leave. "Wow, is there anyone left on earth you still even get along with?"

"Can you stop, Jocelyn?" I can't believe she always has the energy for this bullshit. "You don't even know what's going on."

She purses her lips and considers me. "If I had to guess, I'd say that your friends said something you didn't want to hear, and now you're storming off. Because you are completely without the virtue of patience. Or forgiveness. Or really anything that makes a good friend."

I sigh, breathing through the pounding of my heart, hoping to look bored instead of seen. "You have no idea what you're talking about, so just give it a rest for once."

She gives a small shrug. "I will if you will. I can't believe you still have the energy for being Sylvie Carter. Especially with all the . . ."

She mimes shaking a pill bottle.

Everything in me tenses. Somehow, I manage not to slap her in the face and get past her. I want to. I want to hit her.

I get in the elevator and then get all the way up to my floor before pressing the *L* button again and going back down.

All the dancers have left the bar. It's just middle-aged politicians paying too much for whiskey, girls taking pictures of their drinks, and the young professionals laughing and flirting with the cocktail waitress.

"Bozal on the rocks, please. With an orange."

I lean on the counter and look toward the table of guys. One of them looks at me, the one in a perfectly tailored suit that's probably off-brand, but made-to-measure. Indochino, not Armani. That's the highest end for guys like this. The one who thought Alicia was Zoë Kravitz is next to him.

I smile at him and then look away coquettishly.

Out of the corner of my eye, I see him whisper something to his *buddies*, and then he stands to come over.

"You can put that on my tab," he says, with a wink to the bartender. "I'm Philip," he says to me, holding out a hand.

"Sylvie," I say. "You didn't have to do that."

He shrugs as if to say, *I can afford it*.

"Want to do a shot?" he asks.

Guys like him always want to do *shots*.

"Sure."

"Of what?"

I say what he wants to hear. "Whiskey? I'm a big whiskey girl."

This piques his interest just as I knew it would. "Damn. Okay. Excuse me." He raises his voice to the bartender who is handing someone else their check. "Excuse me."

The bartender comes over, and the guy orders two shots of Buffalo Trace.

We do them, and then he asks what I do, and the blah-blah-blah begins.

He's never met a ballerina before. He works for his dad's IT company, but it's expanded by more than five times since he started. He mentions a Fourth of July keg party from the last year, which he looks a little too old for.

He shows me a picture of him holding an enormous fish. He's in Chubbies shorts, wraparound sunglasses, and a Vineyard Vines T-shirt, and he's standing with a man he looks exactly like. He tells me that's his father, and I'm in no way surprised.

"Want to go to my room?" I ask, just as he starts to talk about college, which he left eight years ago.

"Absolutely."

He goes with me to my room, where he picks up a practice tutu and says, "You really wear these things? That's crazy."

I decide to cut the foreplay; he talks way too much for me. I grab a condom from my purse and pull him to the bed. I get on top of him and say that I need him inside me. As I'm saying it, I feel him hardening underneath me.

He says, "I bet you fuckin' do," with all the confidence of a man who does not know that he is a compromise. "You like that, don't you? Oh, yeah. I can feel you getting tighter on my big fucking cock," he says, sliding into me.

He finishes after half an hour. I don't finish, but I do forget about my life for a while.

After, he asks for my number.

I say no.

When he leaves, I realize I don't even remember this one's name.

CHAPTER FOUR

Sylvie

Here I am, I think.

It isn't that I haven't been here before. I have been. I've stood on this street corner a thousand times, staring up at the building, tourists and locals passing by me on either side. I've lived here all my life, and yet I've always felt like the core of the city has not been unlocked to me. Like I was skating around the perimeter of what Manhattan *really is*.

Until today.

The acceptance letter isn't enough for me. It's only today, when I walk through the doors of the North American Ballet, the NAB, that's when I'll believe it's real.

I can't stop myself from openly smiling up at Lincoln Center. Lincoln Center, home of ballet, opera, and the philharmonic.

Despite how cold it is outside, people are sitting on benches and at little tables everywhere. The cold fashion of New York hiding underneath chin-to-ankle Canada Goose jackets.

I walk along the uneven cobbles, looking into the greenery of Dante Park.

When I open the stage door to the North American Ballet, I'm hit with warm air. My face is like an icicle, and I know the pale skin on my cheeks is probably blooming like two red roses. Always has. If you look at pictures of me as an infant, I was a total Gerber baby. That's what my mom and dad have always called me. I had a button nose, little bow lips, blush cheeks, shiny blond hair.

The man at security takes my name and my picture and tells me my ID will be ready on the way out. He tells me to take the elevator to the fifth floor, so I do.

The floor bell rings, and the elevator doors open to a mostly empty hallway. A few chairs sit outside closed doors. A window looms at the end of the hallway, casting a figure in silhouette.

Me. A *real* ballerina! As if the years and years of practice had not counted, and only now was I really *a ballerina*.

I walk down the hall, toward my reflection. The first door is marked COMPANY MANAGER. I'm supposed to wait here. I'm early, as usual, so I spend a few minutes scrolling through my phone, unable to focus from the nerves.

When I hear music, I follow the sound.

To my left, the music is coming from beyond an almost-shut door. A glow of golden light is seeping out around the edges.

It's a big, beautiful rehearsal room with a grand piano.

I peer into the room.

Three girls take their places as the music begins again.

"That's right, remember your chin, Jennifer," says a man's voice.

I can see countless reflections of the girls, who themselves look like mirror images of each other. The man turns and I see his face.

"And one, two, three, one . . ." His voice fades as he watches the girls, his eyes scanning each of them, looking for errors in their form or technique.

It is Sebastian Alvarez. I almost gasp.

There are lots of people in the world of ballet that I would love to meet, living or dead, and Sebastian is in the top three.

He's not just talented; he didn't just dance exceptionally. He changed ballet. It's hard to describe how it feels to watch him dance, as I have done countless nights. On nights when my stomach churns from having nothing more than plain chicken and boiled spinach and water for dinner, and I need to satisfy my hunger some way, I would consume old footage of the greats.

He has always been my favorite.

I knew he was supposed to be here. Knew he was the NAB's assistant director, which—though an intensely coveted position—was still not good enough for him. Not in my opinion. He was one of the greats.

I knew he'd be here, but I don't believe anything until I see it with my own eyes.

His eyes land on mine through the crack in the door.

I gasp and move out of the doorway, feeling caught. I haven't done anything wrong, really, but I have always been like this. I scurry back down the hallway and to where I am supposed to be.

"Excuse me," comes a man's voice down the echoing hall, from where I just was.

I turn. It's him.

"Oh, I—I'm sorry, I heard the music and . . ."

He narrows his eyes. "Are you new?"

That Spanish accent makes my skin run hot. I am always a sucker for a good accent.

There is a ding at the end of the hall. I look to see a girl wrapped in about ten layers of Antarctic-worthy thermal gear.

"Christ, it's cold," she says to herself, not even having noticed me yet. She walks my way, and says, "Oh, hi. God, how do you stand this weather?"

I look back at Sebastian Alvarez and say "Sorry" again.

He shuts the door and I hear the music begin.

The girl looks between me and the shut door, trying to parse out what she was walking into.

She seems to give up, then stands across the hall from me, leaning against the wall. Without hiding it, she looks me up and down. Evaluating me. I am being more subtle about it, but I'm evaluating her too. It's impossible not to when everyone is competition.

The company manager door opens.

"Sylvie Carter, come on in," says a man, without looking up from a clipboard. He turns away from the open door. "And . . . is that Jocelyn Banks?"

"Yeah," Jocelyn says as we follow him in. "Let me just get out of all this."

What happens then is practically a comedy sketch. This girl, Jocelyn, takes layer after layer off, unwinding her scarf, removing a hat, removing her coat, then a sweater, then leg warmers. Until finally, she is like a cored apple, all thin and strong now that she is nearly bare.

The guy with the clipboard is staring at her with undisguised horror. He looks like a George Michael—statement earring and all. He looks like the sort of guy who knows some shit, has seen some shit, and takes no shit. He also looks like he is rarely struck silent.

"Sorry, I'm from the South. I can't with this weather," Jocelyn apologizes.

The guy looks at her. "What are you?"

"What . . . am I?" asks Jocelyn, looking confused.

"Mm-hmm, are you Puerto Rican? You look like you might be, and I'm gonna let you pass for all this shit if you're Puerto Rican because we gotta stand together, but if you're just another cold-ass white girl, I have no time for this."

She cringes. "I have no idea. Never met my dad. I'm just a cold-ass white girl as far as I know. With great hair that may or may not come from my dad's side."

She lifts up dark locks and gives a charming half smile.

Clipboard Guy looks reluctantly amused, but quickly clears his expression and looks important and stern again.

"All right, I'm just going to start off with this little bit of advice and then we can just move on." He shuts his eyes and drops the clipboard on a table before clapping his hands into prayer position. "Please fucking God, don't waste my time. Girls like you are *so* fucking replaceable—and that's serious, it's not even a threat, it's just that you really *are*—and every time you *do* get replaced, I have to take time out of my day to start *all* over with some other girl just like you. So just—" He waves his hands, looks me up and down, then lets his hands drop and sighs, defeated.

We both stare at him. He turns, rolls his eyes, and gestures for us to follow him. We fall in line, moving feverishly in the wake of his long, purposeful strides.

"Damn, someone's sassy," says Jocelyn, leaning toward me.

I say nothing.

"I'm Matteo Martin, you can call me Matt, but also don't call me. I'm in charge of company life outside the studio. I do hotel sign-up, payroll questions, health insurance, all the stuff that you"—his hand twists in rumination, the corner of his eye almost cast on us again—"*creative types* can *literally* not handle without someone like me. I am not the one to go to if you can't get your little pirouettes right, or whatever. But if you need a place to live, I'm your guy. The only thing I know about what you all do is that you do not take a spot at the barre unless you are sure it's available."

"Why not?" I ask.

"I have no idea, I just know it's a huge faux pas. All I know about dancing is that I shouldn't do it. Unless it's after midnight at the Rosemont and I'm really feeling myself."

"Ha!" Jocelyn laughs.

The two of them exchange a *you know what I'm talking about* look.

Girls like Jocelyn are always making instant friends like this. It never happens like that for me.

Matt gives us more and more tidbits of disjointed advice, pointing left and right at things we might need to know. It is very clear he's done this a thousand times, and any of the not strictly related information is more like him venting than responding to our being here.

He shows us where the studios are and then—oh my god, *then*—he shows us the wardrobe department.

Wow. Just . . . wow.

This huge room is filled with more pointe shoes and ballet slippers than I have ever seen in my life. They are stacked in cubbyholes from floor to ceiling. Rows and rows of them. On racks in another, smaller room, there are hundreds and hundreds of tutus.

Oh, I could stay in here all day.

There are champagne-colored ones, rose-colored, periwinkle, bloodred, wedding-dress white, true black—and on and on. I can tell from the doorway that they are the good kind. Of course they are. The not-so-itchy, soft kind with hand-sewn embellishments.

There is a mini stage in the room and pictures upon pictures of famous dancers covering the walls. It looks like my bedroom.

Matt calls for a woman named Soon Ye and introduces us. She's the assistant wardrobe director.

Brian, the head of wardrobe, evidently doesn't "deal with newbies" and we have to "earn that privilege."

I honestly think she is joking at first, so I let out a small laugh.

They look at me. Jocelyn gives me an amused, approving look.

"Sorry," I say, baring my teeth in apology.

Matt breathes deeply. *"Jesus."*

Soon Ye then goes on to say that she has ordered us each *a hundred* pointe shoes, based on the information we sent back a few weeks ago. She says if we ever change sizes, styles, or brands to let her know and that if we want to customize them, she'll arrange the appointments. I spot my cubby, with my last name marking it. Each pair of shoes costs about a hundred dollars.

She says that corps dancers, which is where everyone starts, are permitted to take ten pairs of shoes with us a week, but we also shouldn't, apparently, or Brian, the Absent Wardrobe Manager, will be furious. Corps de ballet girls should really only be taking five, it turns out.

"Then just say to take five," whispers Jocelyn.

Again, I say nothing. Even though I'd been thinking the same thing.

Then Soon Ye says, "You are not as important as principals."

"Oh, of course," I say, finally speaking up, only to degrade myself. Well, to degrade me and this Jocelyn girl.

Either way, five pairs a week is enough for me. As a student, I only got three a *month*.

Soon says we can get custom ribbons if we become principals. I feel myself inflate with the idea.

"Okay, take it all off—time to measure," says Soon.

Matt answers his ringing phone and walks out of the room.

I strip down and hold out whatever limb I am told to. I have always been told that I am the perfect size for ballet. Long of limb without being too tall. Slender, but I still have a subtle, feminine shape. A long neck, but I don't look like a giraffe. It's so easy for girls to be thin but also shaped like a diving board. Long limbed but also too tall. Shapely, but . . . too shapely for ballet. Right now, I am a perfect balance. I make a shorter male partner look taller and a taller male partner appear stronger. I am like an optical illusion: the stage warps around me.

I know it may not seem like it, and I'm not trying to sound vain or into myself or anything like that; it's just true and extremely important. It's a huge part of why I am good. Not only because my frame makes me more appealing to those in charge, but because it makes it more possible for me to be a good technician and partner. Like having the right tools for the job. The right canvas, paints, and subject.

And I know how unusual it is. In this world, you find your spot by finding how unique you are. Because everywhere you look, there's a girl who has trained harder, more intensely, more successfully than you have. And everybody has legs up on each other—not just literally. One girl might have the kind of muscle that learns extremely quickly but also becomes sharp and makes her look angular. But her competition might have a body that doesn't take on technique as fast but remains as soft as cream no matter what. And then they are both replaced when someone comes along who has the best of both their worlds.

What would *that girl* have that I do not? What do I have that *she* does not?

I find my eyes landing on Jocelyn as these thoughts run through my mind.

There's so little space, and our peers are also our competition.

As Soon Ye measures me, I stare at the cubbies, scanning the names, wondering what these mystery girls have that I do not. I would do anything within my power to rise above them.

On my way out, hours later, I feel energized. Buzzing. Electrified. It is all here for me, this whole world. Well, here for us.

Once outside, Jocelyn stands beside me, having returned to her Gore-Tex and down cocoon. "Do you want to go get a drink or something?" she asks.

I send a text to my family. The group text photo is an almost objectionably Nordic display. My mother, sister, and me, all blond hair and blue eyes. Though my dad's hair is silver, and now speckled with grey.

First day in the books, it was AMAZING!

I smile down at my phone as the celebratory emojis come in immediately from my sister, Anna.

"Sorry—a drink?" I say belatedly.

"Yeah, you know, like . . . alcohol?"

The door pounds open behind us.

"I hear you—yes, I am listening, love, I'm not— Of course I want you to express yourself. I tell you that all the time."

Sebastian.

I want to walk away. I am walking home anyway, but if I do it now, it will be rude to Jocelyn.

I send a quick text to Anna.

Call

She calls instantly.

"Hello?" I answer.

"Trying to avoid a creep?" she asks. It is our usual custom to send a text like that when walking down sketchy streets or being chatted up by weirdos.

"Oh, no, not at all," I say.

"Did you actually want to talk?"

"No, no."

"Oh, so you're just trying to look busy."

Jocelyn looks at me with raised eyebrows. I shake my head and point to the phone as an excuse.

"Yes, absolutely, for sure," I say.

"Ah, okay, well, I can just bore you then and talk your ear off about how much I hate this place, and I'm sick of working here. We've had three customers all day and they're just sitting here like the cast of *Cheers* and I just *know* they're not going to tip well . . ."

I hear a man laugh in the background.

"I'm gonna go—it was nice meeting you," says Jocelyn, not looking like it was nice to meet me at all.

I wave and mouth *bye*.

"Gotcha," I say vaguely into the phone, looking out of the corner of my eye at Sebastian.

He is lingering on the sidewalk, too, nodding into the phone. He glances at me. I look away.

"Anyway, yeah, I don't know, the good news is I'm absolutely about to order some goat cheese fritters. I don't know how you go your whole life without eating, it's really . . ."

She carries on and I zone out, listening instead to *him*.

"Listen, I've got to go now, love. Yes—yes, okay. Goodbye."

He ends his call and walks toward me. I hang up the phone, panicking.

He cocks his head with a smile, looking at my phone. "No goodbye?"

"Oh." I hold up my phone and think fast. "She had me on hold anyway. I hate when people do that."

He puts his hands in his pockets. His coat is beautiful, double-breasted thick wool with solid-looking buttons. It looks like Amiri to me. Gazing at beautiful clothes online, in shop windows, and in stores is one of my few hobbies that's not ballet.

I can't quite look him in the eye.

"How was your first day?"

"It was amazing," I say candidly, unable to stop myself from smiling. "I love it here. It's been my dream my whole life."

"Yes, you and everyone else who comes through those doors."

I feel a little wounded but smile anyway. "No, but for me—"

"You're different?"

I laugh, uncomfortable. It isn't in my nature to brag. So instead, I blush. "No, probably not."

He narrows his eyes at me again. "Listen, would you like to go get a drink?"

I feel completely different when he asks. When Jocelyn asked, I felt immediately stressed about what I would talk about with a complete stranger. But when he asks, I ache to say yes—what would come of spending time alone with *him*? A hero of mine. In the flesh. It kills me and embarrasses me to say, "I can't, I'm . . . I'm eighteen."

He smiles. "I didn't ask your age. I asked if you'd like to go get a drink."

I'm confused, but with a pounding heart, say, "Okay, yes."

We step out into the city, already shrouded in the first blue darkness of the coming nighttime. The street is surprisingly empty. A few bicycles speed by, flickering in and out of the pools of light emanating from the streetlamps above them.

"It smells like snow," I say.

"Hmmm. So tell me, Sylvie, what's your story?"

"How did you know my name?"

"I asked Matt before leaving. Before getting that call from my lovely, beautiful, soon-to-be ex-wife."

"Does she know that's what she is?"

He laughs. "Yes. We sign the papers this Friday."

Thrown off by the sudden collision of the man I knew on paper with the man who stands before me, I remember who his wife is—Vanessa Larchmont, a former heroin-chic It Girl from the nineties.

"So. Your story. Why are you special, Sylvie Carter?"

"I don't know if I am. I just love ballet."

"You love it?"

"Well, I suppose that's an understatement. It's my whole life. It's all I've ever done. My family would have been fine with me just being a normal kid, like my sister is. Or was. I mean, not *was*—she's not dead or anything." I'm rambling. "Uh, anyway, my parents let me do what I loved. It was all I could talk or think about. They were always trying to get me to like other things as well, not that they didn't want me to do ballet—they did everything they could to make it happen. But they wanted to make sure it wasn't all I had. Nothing else quite took, though. It's all I want."

"Here, this is the place." He lets me in ahead of him.

It's loud and busy. I love it.

We sit at a cramped table in the window. Everything around us smells like cinnamon and apples and burning wood. Lemon, butter, vanilla. People eat crème brûlée and ice cream and truffle fries and chicken piccata. They drink bright-red drinks with smoking cinnamon sticks and explosions of aromatic mint.

That is another hobby of mine. Enjoying food from afar. I've gotten extremely good at it. It's like taking away a sense, and how it improves the others. Since I never taste anything but the plain stuff that is great for me, I have become positively professional at peripheral appreciation.

While I ogle everything around us, he orders two glasses of something in French.

A surprisingly fast moment later, the server returns with two glasses of bubbling, pale pink champagne.

"Sylvie Carter. To your first day as a real ballerina. Salud."

It is like he'd read my mind. Blushing yet again, I clink my glass with his, and take my first sip of champagne.

It bounces on my tongue and warms and cools me all at once. It's like drinking a starry sky.

No wonder it's in so many songs and served at only the most glamorous events.

"My goodness," I say, sounding even more coquettish than usual.

"It's nice, isn't it?"

I nod. "Yes." I take another sip, and then realize how little is in the flute. It's already half gone.

"It's not your first glass, is it?"

How did he know? "No, of course not."

I am a terrible liar. The corners of my lips turn up and he's clearly onto me.

"I'm not surprised. Years at ballet school, only practicing, day in and day out. You have a lot of fun to catch up on."

There is something mischievous in his expression, and it makes me nervous. In a good way.

"Well, we still had some fun. We splurged on popcorn or having a little ice cream every now and then. I know some girls got into other stuff, but . . . I just danced. I mean, we all took sleeping pills to go to bed. So we could fall asleep early, at like eight, and wake up fully rested. The fewer hours we were conscious, the more we could restore and the less we would eat. Don't tell my mother that."

He laughs. "I'm not in touch with your mother."

"Sorry, yes, I know. Of course not." I take another sip of champagne. "Plus all the supplements they would try from dubious websites that suppress appetite or repair muscles or whatever."

"And you didn't get into that?"

"No. Just melatonin and Tylenol PM. And coffee. Lots of coffee. Not that I didn't love it. But we didn't go out or do anything. You had to sign up in time just to go get some fresh air. I once went a month without going outside."

"Well, hopefully you feel like you've landed in clover at the NAB."

"It is amazing," I say.

"Seemed like Matt was in one of his moods today."

"He was fine!"

"I have a secret for you," he says, leaning closer to me. He smells like firewood and iris. "And it's that Matt is *always* in one of his moods. Don't let him scare you off. He doesn't know what's going on around here. All he knows is numbers and arguing on the phone with various hapless concierges all over the world. I hope he didn't make you think it was going to be the hell I believe it is for him."

"It sounded pretty intense," I say. "But it should be. I mean, I expect it to be hard. I'm ready for it."

"Well, what do you think of going to a spot nearby here for some dinner and I can tell you a few of the secrets for your survival."

My stomach lurches. Sebastian Alvarez wants to take *me* to dinner.

"I'll have to text my parents and let them know."

"Are you still living with them?"

I nod. "Yes. I'm really close with my family. I was away a long time at boarding school, so I don't mind being there."

He nods. "Do what you want, of course. But if you want my advice, I'd say try to get your own place. Matt can help you find one near the theater. You're going to want your autonomy."

"I'll think about that."

He nods. "I remembered your audition now, by the way, once I heard your name. You are very talented."

My heart soars. "Thank you."

"But we have a lot to work on."

I don't know why, but *the* Sebastian Alvarez is taking an interest in me, and all I want to do is say *yes, yes, yes*.

He hands a fifty to the server as he walks by, and says, "Shall we?"

"Yes." I nod eagerly and smile. "I'll text my mom on the way. And just run to the restroom really quickly."

I go to the bathroom, and while I wash my hands, I look in the mirror and can't help but grin. Maybe it's the champagne. Maybe it's just that life is getting better.

When I exit the restroom, he's already outside.

It's beginning to snow. Glimmering, drifting snowflakes are falling suddenly, landing on the cars and the heads of passersby. I think of *The Sound of Music*.

"Snowflakes that stay on my nose and eyelashes . . ."

Under the newly falling snow, Sebastian is talking to a young man who seems to need directions. Sebastian points left, toward a line of red brake lights.

I walk out, the noise going from crowded, buzzing restaurant to tires on wet asphalt and car horns in the distance, snippets of conversations in the air as people bustle by.

The guy talking to Sebastian nods and leaves, thanking him.

"De nada." Sebastian smiles.

I look up at the sky between the buildings. It's violet and the snow is coming down like . . . well, like the flecks in a snow globe. I breathe in. I love the city when it snows.

I can tell it's going to stick.

CHAPTER FIVE

Sylvie

The days leading up to a performance always feel different. The late nights in the hotel bar come to a crashing halt. The viperous sniping is set aside. Flirtation is postponed. Enjoying a meal is a fleeting memory.

Life is nothing but dance. It is nothing but sucking it up and working hard. For me, it's a vague memory of something I used to love. I don't think any of us even choose to change or slide into work mode like this. It just kind of happens. A natural switch, like one of those old analog kitchen timers hitting zero—lazy ticking stops, and screaming intensity commences.

And also, just screaming. Mostly from Diana, sometimes from Mike Laren, the stage manager, and of course the glare of Robert, the artistic director. It's seven o'clock on the night before the run of performances begins. At seven, we are finally free to stop, but we are not free to go. We all sit in the front rows of the theater. We all smell like sweat and hair spray, and a good number of us have a hint of rose water thrown in the mix, due to the damaging nature of the heavy makeup and the remover. Most of us are in sweatpants and holding empty or just-refilled bottles of water, and all we want is to go home. But, no, we are at least one long lecture away from that.

I'm alone, which is not unusual, but this time it's with the haze of vague animosity after how I left things with Alicia and David. It's not as if I even talk to them every day or anything, especially on days like this, but it's different when it's because something *happened*.

I glance around and notice Jocelyn is alone too.

And Alessandro is nowhere to be seen.

There is a loud *ca-chuck* sound and the houselights go up.

Robert, the director, walks out soundlessly, like he always does.

He is joined by Diana and some of the other staff.

Diana is wrapped in an expensive-looking, cashmere cardigan. It's pulled closely around her; the theater must be chilly to anyone who hasn't spent the last eleven hours on their feet, constantly moving.

"Okay," he says. The theater is utterly silent; no one has the energy to chat, so he doesn't have to do the usual work of cutting through our conversations to get our attention. "It's been a long week, as always."

"For all of us, trust me," says Diana. Her French accent is always stronger at night. It's the only sign of wear she ever seems to show.

"You are good, you know," he says. "Let it show. Have *fun*, for god's sake—let these shows be special. And let's keep the energy up, don't get tired; we don't have time for this. Dance with the skill you know you have."

Diana steps in. "You all know you can be better. I have seen some of you for many years now, and I am frankly stunned when I see how unwilling you are to push yourself to your full potential.

It is as if you have a key in your hand and stand before a locked door and still you refuse to step through. You hide the key, swallow it, throw it away. Why will you not *use it*?"

The last words are shouted, and they ring through the hall.

I am staring at my toes, bending them and stretching them. When Diana doesn't go on, I look up at the stage to see she is looking directly at me.

My gut drops, and I'm sure I blush, but I still stare right back at her.

"You must know you still have it. You can be so much more than you are now." She has moved away from me and back to the company at large. Her tone has also gotten softer, and I wonder if maybe that's not a coincidence. "I know how it is to be onstage the night of a run of shows, trust me. I still remember even though it's been, oh, what, a hundred years or so?"

There is a light chorus of laughter. Suck-ups.

"I know that when you get on the stage tomorrow, there is something inside you that will awaken." She grasps at the air. "There is something inside that will light up; there will be a fire, and it will drive you. But I beg you to do *more* with that than usual."

Actually, for Diana, this is about as close to a pep talk as you can get. All in all, pretty cheerful.

One of the side doors opens, and as if choreographed, every head turns.

It is, of course, Alessandro. He does not raise the obligatory apologetic hand or give the *I know I interrupted, sorry about that* smile that anyone else would. He just walks forward and leans on the stage.

"Here is someone now who understands how to dance with everything in his possession."

Alessandro does not look at any of us. I find myself staring at him, baiting him, and hoping for his gaze, but I get nothing.

"Now go, get sleep, be restful, do whatever it is you need to do so that this week, when you are performing I see what I believed was in you when you started here. Because I cannot look at . . . *this*"—she gestures with disgust at us—"anymore," and then walks off the stage.

Alessandro pushes off the wall of the stage as everyone around stands up and hoists their bags onto their shoulders. Everyone is saying things about sleep, their bodies, or the upcoming week of shows.

Alessandro leaves. I am not far behind him, hoping to run into him, but he is already gone.

I am always wired on nights like this when I shouldn't be. When the day before me matters most, I toss and turn and stay awake, watching the time on my phone or the hotel alarm clock get later and later.

I turn on the dim light on the nightstand and look ruefully at the mirror lying flat on the desk, where this morning's white powder residue still sits. I don't do coke that much. I really don't. But sometimes. Lately, it's all that works to get me up.

Looking at it now, as I wish I could fall asleep, I'm drenched in a hot, smothering guilt. There's still a good girl inside me who can't believe I'd *ever* do that kind of thing.

I get up and blow the coke off the shining surface, letting it float in the air. It's easy now, like tossing leftovers when you're already full. I know I'll wake up tomorrow and regret it.

I shut off the lights and lie there for ages, trying to breathe calmly, trying to get myself to sleep. I can tell it's going to be the kind of night where I lie awake the whole time, anxiety about my consciousness leading to more of it.

It is after midnight when I decide that there is only one thing for it.

I put on my hotel slippers and my embroidered robe over my silk nightgown, which is such a pale blush pink that it is almost the same color as my skin.

I love hotels at night. I love the plush, ornate carpets and running my hands over the wallpaper. I even love the room service trays outside the rooms: they make me think about other people leading other lives. This hotel is new, so everything smells like new cars and new beach toys. It's chic and modern, and I know if I were to go to the bar—which I considered—there'd be that ultra-mod, pointless, beginningless and endless music with bass thrumming like a telltale heart. It's the kind no one can dance to, but only sidle and sway. It's music made for people to be attracted to other people and that is all.

I read the panels on the side of the elevator buttons and hit the button for the roof. I stand and wait, my body propelled by some mania that has no basis in reality. I should be asleep. I find myself yawning and think some derisive thoughts about my body for pretending it could *really go for* some sleep right now. I am momentarily considering going back to my room when there is a soft ding.

The elevator doors open right to the night air, which I didn't expect. I can't believe I haven't been up here sooner. The lights of D.C. are different than the lights in other cities because, mixed in with all the streetlights and the late-night taxis and glowing restaurant signs, there is also the smattering of important buildings and monuments, all of which are grandly uplit. It's like they are on a stage too.

I pull out my pack of cigarettes and the pack of matches I got from the Kimpton Fitzroy in London. I light one and inhale deeply.

Another habit I've picked up over time, trying to impress some guy. Another habit the good girl in me feels guilty about.

There is a pang in my stomach, and then I realize it's not just guilt. It's hunger. I never did have dinner.

I walk toward the rail and look out at the city.

The reflecting pool, the Washington Monument, the Capitol building, the Lincoln Memorial—they are all quiet and ominous. Their un-ancient, unfeeling architecture mixed with the ideals they're built to represent . . . it's all a bit . . . well, I can't say breathtaking, that never really happens to me. But it's bizarre. And it is beautiful, in its way.

Washington, D.C., is definitely a city that sleeps. Especially in this area, which is distinctly political and far removed from the sexy, clandestine freedoms of other cities.

I lean on the railing for a moment and look down. I imagine falling. It's dizzying. Maybe I really am more tired than I realized.

"Tell me you're not going to jump," says a voice behind me.

I do jump, but not how he means.

I smile when I see him, the door to the elevators falling shut behind him.

I find myself hiding the cigarette, though I know he'll notice. "Tell me I've got reason to live, won't you?"

Alessandro walks toward me. "I know I teased you the other day, but that's no reason to end it all."

"You know it depends on which ending you believe in. Does Siegfried jump after Odette? Does he save her or sacrifice himself? Or is it all a happy ending?"

He chuckles. "I appreciate the symmetry."

"Thank you."

"I guess if you don't jump, those things will kill you eventually." He gestures at the cigarette I'm hiding behind my back.

Guiltily, I bring it to my lips. "I know."

He comes over to me and takes the cigarette. I think he's going to take a drag, but instead he extinguishes it on the railing and then tosses it over.

I'm ashamed to admit that I find this a little sexy.

"I wasn't hurting anyone. But now you've littered."

He gives me a look. "I came up for a dip in the Jacuzzi. Would you join me?"

"Well, that's why I came up, too, actually."

"Can't sleep?"

"I can never sleep when I'm supposed to."

"Going to be a long week. I'm glad to see that you care."

"I care," I say unconvincingly.

He shrugs. "It is hard to tell. I'm sorry."

I squint at him. "You are insufferable."

I walk toward the hot tub. He stops at the bar.

"I'm pretty sure it's closed," I say, looking at the empty bar with its covered computer and absolutely no lights.

He raises an eyebrow at me and then opens the counter flap and walks in.

"What are you doing?" I ask, suddenly hissing. The well-behaved ballerina from long ago suddenly making an appearance.

"I'm sure they've left something behind."

He opens the ice well and finds several bottles of liquor. He makes a face. "Too strong—we don't need hangovers." He opens a cooler and smiles. "Jackpot."

He pulls out a bottle of Cloudy Bay Sauvignon Blanc.

"We can't just take that," I say, but realize my hand is already extended.

He just laughs at me. "I'll ask them to charge me later."

We both go to the hot tub. He turns on the jets, and the lights come on. They undulate from red to pink to purple to blue and back again.

"This is like a hotel out of *Blade Runner*," he says.

I nod, but then when I see he's looking at me, I shrug. "I've never seen it."

"Really? Huh."

"Really. I don't really watch movies. Or TV. I used to read a lot, but not much anymore."

He takes off his shirt and walks into the Jacuzzi in swim shorts.

Shrugging off my robe and stepping out of my silk nightgown and in only my pale thong I join him in the Jacuzzi.

"I like this style," he says. "No swimsuit."

I blush. "I wasn't sure I'd get in. It's practically the same anyway."

He twists the top off the wine. He smiles and says, "Fancy."

That million-dollar grin. It makes me melt.

"Very," I agree.

He hands it to me and I take the first sip.

"Cheers," he says.

I hand it back. "I hate when people always think you have to cheers to something. You know, you say *cheers* and then someone halts everything and says *cheers to what* and then everyone has to find someone to celebrate or something to clink glasses to. You know, just take a drink."

He narrows his eyes at me. "You *hate* that?"

I feel suddenly stupid. "I mean I don't hate it, I just think it's . . ."

"What a lot of time people like you spend thinking in this way. Who cares?"

I can't think of anything to say, so I take another sip and then set the bottle down to expertly gather my hair into a bun and keep it out of the water.

A few moments of silence pass, in which he seems completely at ease, and I am bubbling with eagerness to get it right and I can tell that I'm not.

"So you don't watch anything and you don't read. Usually the ones I meet who are this way are also scratching each other's eyes out, trying to get ahead. But not you. You seem perfectly content."

"How am I supposed to be?"

"Well, not *supposed* to be any way, really. I just find that usually it's one of two ways. The ones who want to bite and claw their way to the top are almost monk-like in the way they starve themselves of the world outside. They eat plain chicken and salmon, drink only water, listen only to Tchaikovsky, and they use the Internet only to watch these old ballets. They will do anything to taste their dreams. Then there is this other type. A kind who stays in the middle. They're happy, usually nice people. And they stay connected, a foot in both worlds. They see movies and they let themselves have a piece of birthday cake. They usually marry some nice doctor or bar owner or something, and eventually leave the lights of the stage to live a quiet life. Ballet becomes only an interesting tidbit for their new friends to learn. Most interesting mother on the—ah, what is it—yes, on the cul-de-sac."

Some of that sounds a little too familiar.

"What's your point?"

"You are not either of these."

"No, I'm not. I could never be like that. Ballet is all I know."

I take back the bottle and have another swig.

"You intrigue me," he says.

"I do?"

I want to say that it's obvious, considering that within a few moments of meeting me, he had his tongue where my leotard ought to be. But I don't. I never say what I want to.

"Yes, you do. You are different from all the rest."

"How can you tell?"

His eyes briefly glance down at my body and then he controls himself. It makes me tingle and want to force him to lose control.

"How could I *not* tell? The girls talk about you. Diana singles you out. You separate yourself. Always alone."

"None of those are good things."

He takes the bottle back. There's something hot about him drinking after me, me drinking after him.

I take a deep breath.

"Did you like what we did the other day? Or was that very bad of us both?"

My heart rate rises, but this time not from panic. I want him.

He knows it. There is a devilish look in his eyes that makes me burn.

"I liked it."

We watch each other for a few seconds too long for the moment to be ignored.

Ding!

The elevator.

I break the gaze and look at the intruders.

"*Whoa*, dude, look at that fucking view, man. Babe, stand over there and let me get a pic."

A girl in a tight, short, unflattering dress and with thick thighs teeters over to the rail and does the boring Insta-girl pose: hand on the hip, one popped knee, a raised eyebrow, and a curious jut of the jaw.

Who could care about a picture like that? It's like some people only take pictures to prove to themselves that they're hot. But then they try to look as little like themselves as they can.

I realize then that one of the guys is the one who was in my hotel room the other night. In my hotel room, fucking me.

And now he is posing for a picture with a girl in an engagement ring. They kiss, and he does not notice me.

I look away from them.

"Did something happen?" asks Alessandro.

"Happen?" I think at first that he's talking about the guy, but then realize he must not be. "Happen with what?"

"I get the sense of something with you. With the company. With your"—he searches for the words—"unmet potential. It makes me think something has happened."

"Something happens to everyone."

"Yes, but you know what I mean, don't you? I'd say it's something normal, a feud with another girl, an eating disorder, a drug problem. But I don't think you are that simple."

My eyebrow arches. "You're right about that."

He squints at me and I'm suddenly overcome with the fear that he's going to figure it out.

"What time is it?" I tap my phone. "Mm. I should go. I think I'll be able to sleep now."

"Just like that?"

"I may not have mentioned it, but I've got this big performance tomorrow." I get out and pull my slip on over my wet frame. It clings. He looks. I like it. "I'd say thanks for the drink, but I don't think a stolen bottle counts."

"Then maybe I can owe you one."

I nod. "Yes, I think you do."

It's not until I'm on the elevator alone that I realize my heart is still pounding. Was it that way the whole time?

When I get back to my room, I am as loose as an untied satin ribbon and I am warm from my core to my skin. I take a little nibble of Xanax just so I can really feel calm.

I step out of my slip and slide into the sheets of my hotel bed and let my hand slide down to my thighs. My nipples are hard, my heart is pounding, and I wish those fucking tourists hadn't interrupted whatever would have happened between us.

I think of the smooth feeling of my thighs on his strong torso. His lips on my neck. I think of his hands on my back. I breathe in deeply and then open the drawer to the nightstand beside me. Beside the Bible, which was there when I checked in, lies my small pale pink vibrator. It looks so innocent and almost like it might be a beauty tool.

I bring it between my legs and let it begin to hum against me. Immediately, I feel myself contract and feel almost as if I could finish right away.

But I don't want to. I want to revel in it.

I don't have that much to go off of with Alessandro, so I think of the time in the theater earlier that week. The way he moved and touched me like he'd been doing it for years.

The way he hit all the right spots, inside and out, with expert ease.

But I need more. I try to imagine him fucking me, but can't—don't know what it would be like, so my brain starts searching for other memories.

Much as I do not want it to, my mind sends me to the bathroom at the InterContinental Hotel in Los Angeles four years ago.

I went to the bathroom and *he* followed me in. *He* locked the door. Seventy stories above the city, he pulled up my skirt and kissed me from behind, kissing my neck and my ear and whispering, "You're the only one I want. The only one in the whole fucking world."

The words were as much of a turn-on as the way he forced my legs apart, touched my tits, and the way I was dripping wet for him. I never thought it was possible to *really* care about the size of a man, but his dick was the kind of perfect that just looking at it made me go primal for him.

Even now, as I tried hard to reroute my brain back to Alessandro, I found my stubborn mind lingering on *him* instead.

Him. The one we don't discuss. The one who shall remain nameless. The one I want to pretend never existed.

I think of *him*, deep inside me, where I had once so badly wanted him to stay.

CHAPTER SIX

WASHINGTON, D.C.
NOW

Sylvie

Cracking a sole of a pointe shoe for the first time makes a distinctive snap that sounds like a bone breaking.

Snap! The left.

Snap! The right.

I put them on, and my feet feel at home.

I sit meditatively lost in my ritual while beyond the heavy velvet curtains, the historic theater fills with the type of people who can afford to come to a show like this. It's very old-world out there—fur and pearls and preshow champagne. These people come to be seen just as much as they come to see us, the romantic creatures who twist and fly on the stage before them. They want to be carried away to another world, one more surreal and magical than the one in which they live. It's the same for us. The whole event is defined by this transcendence. The rules are different here. This world is different. Higher.

There is not a drug on this planet that could replicate the

feeling of being backstage before a performance. I know that once I am out there, it will feel completely different. A pulsing, organic high that will buzz through my veins and under my pale skin. The stage lights will hit me, hot and glowing. Countless eyes will watch us from behind the inky curtain of the darkened theater.

I am not on until act two. But I've gone ahead and gotten ready early to watch act one, Alessandro's grand entrance as Prince Siegfried. I sit silently in the buzzing hum of the wings and wait.

Settled on the cold floor just next to the rosin box, my white tutu flaring around me, I am wrapped in a black puffer jacket to protect the intricate bodice underneath, as well as to keep me warm. The thick stage makeup makes my face itch, and the feathers from my headdress tickle above my ear. I have reached monklike peace with such discomforts and distract myself with deep breaths and bending my legs so that my forehead presses down on my shin bones. Prince Siegfried (Alessandro) doesn't make his entrance for a bit, so I fold and stretch, exhaling as I curl over my legs and I repeat my mantra:

I am in the right place at the right time. I am in the right place at the right time. I am in the right *place at the* right *time.*

"Well, what the fuck does he need, then?" a voice barks, echoing, shaking me from my reverie and breaking the usual quiet.

The voice is that of Mike Laren, the stage manager.

You never want to piss off the stage manager. I lean back covertly, to see beyond the curtain beside me. I want to know who is risking it all by enraging Mike in the middle of a show. It's Cressida, Alessandro's personal dresser. She whispers something.

"I can't hear you. What are you saying to me?" he says.

"He got some kind of phone call and now he won't come out.

He was speaking Italian, I can't . . . I don't know, up until now I didn't get why he had the reputation he—"

"What is the *upshot*?"

"He won't come out!"

"What the fuck do you mean, he won't come out? He was fine five minutes ago at warning to places!"

"I mean I am holding Siegfried's costume and right now we have no Siegfried."

Cressida holds up his act one costume, the forest green velvet tunic that our star is supposed to be wearing right now. Cressida is clearly at her wit's end. Behind her glasses I see tears starting to form and her skin is all blotchy and pink and red. I can practically hear her thumping heartbeat from here. Cressida frequently looks as if she might burst into tears, but this is different. She looks like she might storm out of the building after knocking over the sets with a roar of expletives.

And if Alessandro isn't about to get onstage, she may as well; the whole show will be shot, and she'll be out of a job.

I continue stretching to look busy, but I keep listening.

"Shit, fucking goddammit. Where the fuck is his understudy then, that Dave, Daniel, fucking—*fuck*, whatever his name is. Come with me, *now*. We have maybe ten minutes until his entrance."

"David," she mutters, her voice small again.

"I don't fucking care." He leads her away to find David. He's the alternate who will disappoint the three thousand people in the audience who came specifically to see the Great Alessandro Russo's American Debut. It could never matter how beautifully David dances—and he does, he is an incredible dancer. It could never matter because most of the people out there came to see a living legend. An icon.

A god.

My eyes land on the velvet costume, which is slung over the chair where Cressida flung it.

Before I know what I'm doing, I've leaped up, grabbed the tunic, and am already halfway to the quick-change booth.

I step inside and find him shirtless and sweaty, pacing back and forth in the tiny room like an angered lion in a cage. I guess that makes me the possibly ill-fated lion tamer.

His eyes land on me. He scoffs and shakes his head. "Get out of here."

The relationship between us is brought into sharper relief with the time-sensitive intensity of pressure that surrounds us.

I am a little stunned to be snapped at after the few encounters we've had, but then again, what was I expecting when I took it upon myself to come in here?

I truly don't know what Alessandro is capable of. He might roar at me to leave, or he might ruin the show, make fools of us all—drop someone to injure them and ruin their career. Do I think he would do any of those things? No, I don't. But god knows he has performed unpredictably in the weeks since I first met him—and *how* I met him.

"You need to leave and take that fucking costume with you."

His accent wraps, seething, around his syllables and I'm as surprised as he is when all I do is take a step closer to him. Up until now, I—like Cressida—have only seen him on his best be-havior. This temperamental showstopper is the Alessandro Russo I've heard of but never seen myself.

"Do you need someone to talk to?" I ask quietly. My voice sounds small but soothing. "Maybe I can help."

"No. You're not going to *help* me."

"I love a challenge." I smile a little, and I can tell I've disarmed him. Just a little.

"How are you going to help me, little swan, when all you dream of is getting by? You don't even have dreams, do you? You just want to stay in the middle, be a part of this big thing we're all in. You don't care if you're remembered, don't know what it feels like to not just make any impression—though I don't even know if you care about making one—but to make *the right* impression? How can *you* help *me*, when instead of shooting for the moon, you barely shoot for the stage lights above your head?"

My emotional thermometer barely rises. He's trying to push me away, but I am so good at staying neutral these days. So good at stopping the feelings before they have a chance to breathe and bite.

He is breathing hard. Disproportionate to the activity. My eyes roam from his chest, rising and falling, to his face. He is biting the tip of his tongue. His hands tense into fists over and over and he turns from me. He is breathing shallow and fast.

And I understand completely.

"Breathe. Slowly. I know it sounds like nothing in the face of it all, but just do it."

He hesitates, but does it, breathing bitterly in through his nose.

"Hold it," I say, and then, "let it all the way out."

He nods, his version of telling me he feels a little better, I'm guessing. He keeps breathing.

"What's wrong?" I ask.

The clock is ticking. He must know exactly how much time he has—or doesn't have—before he's due onstage. We're cutting it extremely close.

"It's the same fucking costume. I felt this way at my costume fitting and thought I could swallow it. Green velvet, the gold shit all over it. It's the same, it's the same as the Bolshoi, the Royal Ballet, the Finnish fucking Ballet. This is why I didn't want to come to fucking America."

"Siegfried always wears some version of this—"

"But *I'm* the same in it," he snaps. He holds my gaze. I realize now why he wasn't wearing it at dress rehearsal yesterday.

I try silently to communicate that I truly understand.

I nod and the silence expands.

Ticktock, ticktock . . .

I am not nervous right now. I am not panicking. But I know the feeling so well that I feel as though I can reenact it in my mind. This isn't him being a diva. This is him freaking the fuck out.

I reach out and take his hand as if we've got all the time in the world. To my surprise, his fingers curl around mine.

"You're not the same, you're Alessandro the Great." I roll my eyes and do a gagging gesture.

This seems to take him by surprise. He laughs, thank god.

"Just breathe. Take it one second at a time. Trust yourself, there's no way you could disappoint those people. Unless you don't go out there. That's the only way to guarantee it. Your body remembers how to be good. Let your mind remember too."

The smile fades fast and he releases my hand. The music from the orchestra swells, and I can tell the waltz is almost over. The telltale shuffling, quiet chaos of a backstage preparing for the next scene change.

"I was going to come to America and it was going to be different. It was supposed to— *I* was supposed to be different." He points violently at his own chest. "It drove me, this thought. I thought I would get here and I would feel *it* again."

"And then they handed you this," I say.

"Then they handed me this. This symbol of"—he looks for the word in the air around us—"mediocrity. I get everything you're supposed to dream of, everything *I* dreamed of, and it's nothing, it's empty. *Hollow.* I gave up my childhood, training eleven hours a day, never seeing my family, I don't even know my brother."

A pang as I think of my own family, my own sister.

I nod. This is not about me. "I know."

"When you are a principal at twenty, where is there for you to go but *down*? Down, down, *down*. And I'm not! I'm *not* fucking"—he throws up his hand—"twenty, anymore. I don't know what to see in this future."

He slams his hand on the dressing table and I know it can be heard by everyone backstage.

I don't know what comes over me, but I put my hand on his face. Without being careful or fearful, I take his jaw in my palm, raise up on my tiptoes, and kiss him. After a second, he softens, putting his arm around me, lacing his other around my waist. He is not cautious about the beading on my costume as he presses the tutu up against me. He's crushing the tulle like delicate flower petals and neither of us care. He pulls me in toward him by the base of my spine.

Ever the intuitive partner, he moves closer and puts his mouth on my neck just when I want him to. He lifts me up with practiced ease and my legs wrap around him. His sweating, hot torso connects hard with my thighs and I feel him hardening, even through the tulle of my tutu. My skin tingles with his expertise, and I want to fuck him as badly as I want to be onstage with him. Maybe even more. I want him for myself. Briefly, I don't even care about what everyone out there wants with him. Fuck 'em.

I grab his back and his muscles flex. A quiet rumble of a groan comes from somewhere deep inside him.

I want to scream out.

Mike's walkie-talkie crackles outside the booth. He's getting closer.

Using all my restraint, I pull away, and hold up the velvet costume again.

"You know you'll regret this if you don't do it. You know how good you are: go show them. Don't throw a tantrum and risk losing it all. If you lose it all, you'll leave, and you'll never get to take me for that drink. And what a waste that would be."

I step away from him and walk out of the booth. Mike and Cressida are there. David is on the other side of the stage warming up. I know how he must feel, preparing to walk onstage to perform for an audience who will hate you simply because you are not someone else.

Mike and Cressida see me. Mike rolls his eyes and swears under his breath. Cressida looks aghast, but points at her own lip to indicate my makeup is smeared.

I run to the nearest mirror, just a few feet away, and adjust. It's a blessedly quick fix.

"Russo, it's now or never, what's it going to be?"

David from across the stage and Mike, Cressida, and I watch the door of the quick-change booth along with everyone else backstage, waiting to see what he will do.

Alessandro emerges from the booth and looks around at all of us. "What's the issue?"

Mike shakes his head and clicks on his walkie. "Russo is on in two."

He storms away. If this was anyone else but Alessandro, Mike would destroy them. But this will probably not even get discussed again.

His performance is incredible. After act two, once I've changed out of my costume, I watch the rest of the ballet from the wings. Everyone watches. I feel certain he will be glad he did it. Not only that, but I even harbor a small suspicion—hope?—that he will be grateful for me.

At the end of the show, when the curtain falls and the audience roars and applauds, I expect him to say something to me. He says nothing, just walks exhaustedly off the stage and toward the dressing rooms. As if I am not there.

Unpredictable men. I've had it with them.

The girls from the corps de ballet pass by me, eager to get to the dressing room and change out of the ballerina attire. Another *Swan Lake* ticked off on the never-ending performance schedule.

The corps girls never get a break. Never a show off or even an act off. They grind day in and day out and absolutely *live* at the theater. It's hard on the body, hard on the mind; it is practically a long-acting hallucinogen. Delirium, nightmares, quivering muscles, aching bones. It destroys you and anyone around you if you let it. I did everything I could to get the *fuck* out of the corps.

Ha. Did I ever. Not a soul in this company would deny that I did *everything I could*. For better or worse.

Most of the corps girls are still fresh, excited, and into everything.

I can't even remember what that's like.

They're all talking about his performance in the dressing room; I hear them when I go to grab my things.

"It was amazing. He's every bit as good as everyone said," I hear someone say.

One of the other corps girls says, "Well, I mean, of course we've all watched his performances, but in person and in rehearsal it's really something special. Some people are just born icons, huh?"

Once I grab my bag, I walk out of the theater. As usual, there's a gathering of people, mostly the youngest end of the audience, hoping to see the ballerinas on their way out. Alessandro is signing programs.

"Hey, little swan," he calls after me.

I stop, shifting my dance bag on my shoulder.

He holds up a finger and takes three more selfies with people while I wait for him. Yes. Of course, I wait.

He comes over when he's through and puts a hand on the back of my arm. His hands are big and my arm is small enough that one hand completely encompasses it. I picture him holding it down on a mattress as he—

"What are you doing tonight?" he asks. That silky voice and slurring accent. Ugh.

I shrug. "Was thinking about going to the hotel bar with the others." Not true.

He nods. Someone calls his name and he looks up and smiles at them. Then back to me. "Would you want to get a drink with me? If your plans are so loose. I think I owe you. Especially after earlier."

"Yeah, fine, I guess," I say. "Where?"

"Uh, well, I've got dinner with some patrons at Pineapple and Pearls, but that shouldn't go that late, or at least I don't fucking want it to." He sneers. "Maybe the Watergate, say eleven? Seems like a good place for a . . . ah, *clandestine* meeting."

"Is it clandestine?" I cock my head. "Is it a *meeting*?"

He laughs and then bites his bottom lip for just a moment. My mouth opens of its own accord.

"I should go," I say.

He's not even listening now, bending over to a little boy who has run over to him with a program and a Sharpie.

In my hotel room, in the rush to get there in less than an hour, I put in more effort than I'd like to admit and watch the clock as I obsess over my outfit, my hair, and my makeup. I look too done up, then too casual, then too done up again. I want to be subtly stunning and show a different side of myself than he's seen, and the effort to balance the two takes me until ten thirty. And half a Xanax.

I grab a book from my bag, even though I haven't read anything in almost two years. I borrowed this one from Jocelyn and still haven't read it but do still want to.

Getting there is a breeze, almost making the Uber feel like an overreaction to the distance, but hey, I'm saving my feet from extra damage.

I sit at the corner of the bar and put my clutch on the seat beside me.

"Just you tonight, ma'am?"

Ma'am? Well. I hate the bartender already.

"No, I'm waiting for someone." I desperately want to tell him who, want him to care so that I can brag about it, but resist. "I'll have a Nolet martini, please."

"Shaken or stirred?"

"Stirred."

"Rocks or up?"

"Up."

"Olives or twist?"

"Uh. Twist."

"You got it. Water?"

Jesus. "Yes, please."

I open my book, but he asks, "Sparkling, still, or tap?"

"Sparkling, please." I smile tightly.

"Pellegrino or Perrier, ma'am?"

Ma'am again. Wow. "Pellegrino, please."

"Would you like ice and lime?"

Would you like me to actually climb back there and make it my *goddamn* self?

"No ice. Lime. Sure."

There are, at last, no more questions.

Eventually, I have my Pellegrino sparkling water, with no ice and lime, and my stirred Nolet martini with a twist, up, and my open book. My tableau is complete. Now, all I need is to be come upon by Alessandro, who will see an off-duty ballerina with exquisite taste, independently occupying herself.

It's only five minutes until he's supposed to arrive.

I try to actually read, but it really is just a prop. I skip to a third of the way in, so that I appear not to be doing exactly what I'm doing.

Five minutes pass. Ten. Twenty. It's midnight. He's nowhere.

At first, I thought it was probably fine. That his dinner ran long, those things always do. And, like morons, we didn't muddy the informality of the "clandestine meeting" with something as silly as phone numbers, so I just have to wait. Like a lost child waiting at the agreed-upon spot.

And then I start to spiral. My anxiety is powerful enough to make me question whether or not we actually even *did* make a date or if I just imagined it. Now that I'm a little tipsy, too, and the Xanax is making the edges of everything a little fuzzy, I really don't know. And I'm so fragile feeling at the moment that insanity might be preferable to the idea of being completely ghosted.

The bartender seems to pity me, *winking* as he gives me an extra heavy pour on my rosé once I finish the martini.

Ma'am.

I'm honestly too tipsy to read and too frantic and frustrated to let it go. I feel like an idiot, as if somehow I invented the invitation.

Did I make it up?

No.

I finally leave, feeling no refreshing gust of air as I get out onto the D.C. streets. It's hot and muggy. I hate this city. Suddenly.

I decide to take a cab, catching one right outside the hotel where they sit and wait, presumably for stood-up women who just want to get the hell home.

The entire ride back, I chastise myself for being upset. One side of me asks *Who cares* and says *Honestly, it's probably for the best*, and wonders if I even really *like* the guy or if I'm just riding the high of our extremely hot first meetings and catching everyone else's viral obsession droplets.

The other side of me feels sorry for myself and refuses to tap into exactly how much it hurts because ninety percent of the pain is to do with other things in my past and not to do with him at all.

When I get back, I decide to stop into the bar and see if Alicia is there. I figure at least some of them will be, but Alicia is the one I want to see. Hell, I'd even make up with David if it meant I could get this off my chest and have someone get mad with me.

And there, leaning on the bar and holding court, is Alessandro.

You've got to be kidding me.

How embarrassing that while everyone was together here having fun without me, I sat a mile away, jilted at a bar. We never get over the childlike horror of finding out you are *the one not invited*.

Fuck this.

His eyes land on me and he says, "Ah, there's Sylvie! Where have *you* been?" He looks me up and down, taking in my outfit in a way I had not expected him to take it in.

"I had a date," I say.

"Ah, okay, well . . ." No recognition. He tilts his head. "I guess that's a good enough reason to ignore all your friends, ah?"

He is kidding, but it doesn't matter that he's kidding, because it is very clear he doesn't remember that the date was with him.

I don't stay to untangle the misunderstanding, add another drink to my buzz, or risk showing my embarrassment.

I just leave.

Once in my hotel room, I kick off my shoes. I drift out of my clothes. I step into the marble bathroom and I take another shower to wash off the embarrassment I feel. The hottest shower I can stand. The water runs over me and I feel too weak to do anything but stand there and revel in it. The steam soaks off the makeup I applied for no one. My skin turns red from the heat. I want to be wet to the bone. I almost wish I could sleep here, in the bathtub, under the pounding of the water. I let the water run over me like a waterfall, wanting to be cleansed of everything, cleansed of the humiliation, of the person I've become. There are people who are so powerful and effortless that they would never be blown off, never be forgotten. That's not me. I'm just quivering and messy and no fun.

I spent my life training to be a ballerina. The ballerina I trained to be, it turns out, is the kind who plateaus and can't get better. Simply is not good enough.

My panic attacks used to make me think I was going to die, but nowadays they just make me uncomfortable. I wonder sometimes if it's because I've stopped caring if it's a heart attack or not.

I'm shaken out of this aquatic hypnosis when there is a knock on the door.

My head whips quickly toward the sound.

"Sylvie." I hear his voice. I hear his accent.

I don't turn off the water. I don't grab a towel. I go to the door and stare through the peephole and see him standing there.

My heart pounds as I decide what to do.

Open it, lose all respect for letting him ditch me and then come in anyway? Walk away and let him think I'm an angry shrew?

Then I see the wine bottle in his hand. Optimism.

I open the door, completely naked and dripping wet.

His mouth opens when he takes me in. His hooded eyes look deeply into mine after he's finished scanning my body. His jaw tenses as he pushes off the doorframe.

When he starts to speak, I reach for the wine bottle. He lets me have it. He starts to smile and then I close the door in his face.

I will not make the same mistake twice. I already fucked up extravagantly for one man. I won't do it again.

I turn off the shower, walk over to my bed, and lie down the wrong way on it, my wet hair drenching the soft and delicate thread count of the cushy duvet.

How the fuck did I end up here?

In a movie when someone asks themself that question, I feel like they're usually in a slum somewhere. They're tearing apart an apartment looking for heroin or gazing into a mirror at a set of black eyes. They're not usually in a gorgeous hotel room, making good money for doing what they love, and turning away attractive men and looking toward a flight to Paris.

And maybe that makes it just as shitty. Because I look back and I see a happy childhood. I see a classic idealized American life with supportive parents. Tears fill my eyes and threaten to trickle down my face. I miss my family.

I look around me and *I* don't even believe my own despair and restlessness. I don't believe it, and yet that's not enough to turn it off.

I don't know what I want anymore, and I used to know exactly what I wanted. I know that I did.

Somewhere along the way that changed. And I know exactly when.

CHAPTER SEVEN

MONTREAL
FIVE YEARS AGO

Sylvie

The first few months are soul shattering. I have worked hard my entire life. I am only eighteen, and yet all I know is discipline. I know how to behave well at a dinner party, how to tell the difference between crystal and glass, can identify the aromatics in fine wine, even if—until recently—I never partook of any. I am polite and competent, never need to ask for help. I didn't need to be woken up as a child: I would set my own alarm or wake up when the sun first cracked across the powder-grey sky outside. I understood inherently the difference between good and bad, and wrong and right. Broccoli, good. Stealing, wrong.

And yet nothing was enough preparation for life at the NAB.

In some ways, school was harder. The girls in ballet boarding school were more unhinged, less restrained than the girls here. So they were meaner, less consistent, more likely to break a rule or veer from the course. Here, everyone is more professional.

But I have begun to learn that it is not that the claws do not exist here, only that they are more subtle, more controlled. They don't whisper and point and talk about you like they did back in school. They stare you dead in the eyes and say nothing at all. Or they ask innocent, unprompted questions like, "How long have you been dancing?" And then, when you answer, they say, "Hmm," and elaborate no further.

It's psychological warfare instead of throwing stones. Stones, at least, you can duck.

There's still the old, dependable conduct you seem to find in any group largely composed of females—they still talk or glance with secrets dripping behind the eyes. You still spot them out, all together, where you were not invited to be. Lines are always drawn.

I've just kept my mouth shut. I arrive early enough to rehearsals to avoid being late, but never take my place at the barre before seeing who's here that day. I'm fitting in enough. There seems to be some vague respect thrown my way because I have talent, but I can tell that the very same reason I'm gaining respect could be the same thing that could very well make me enemies.

Enemies seems like a strong word. But maybe it isn't.

I spend my lunch breaks alone. I spend my evenings rehearsing, practicing to get better and better. I go to the gym, I go to Pilates.

The closest thing I have to a social life is when we are in New York and I can spend time with my family. I've never appreciated them more than I have lately. Lately, I've missed them more than ever, and feel close to tears when I'm with them. Their easy, breezy ways. All of them are so happy and comfortable in life, even when things aren't quite right. How did I have the misfortune of being born the only restless one? The only one who needs *more*, always *more*?

They aren't complacent. It's not that at all. It's simply that when things go wrong, it becomes fodder for dinnertime or drinks on the roof terrace. When my sister has a bad date or has an uncomfortable run-in with some rude stranger at Starbucks, instead of feeling bad or small, she will just tell us and it will become a hilarious story. I say that she will tell us, but she's probably like that with her friends. My parents probably are, too, with their friends. They have friends over every other night, it seems. Especially now that neither Anna nor I live there, now that I have taken Sebastian's advice and moved into my very own place.

When I talk about my life, it is hard to have the same level of amusement. My life is hard work. And as featherlight as my family sometimes can be or seem, they are also very protective. They want to hear that everyone can see how special I am. That I am soaring through the ranks at record-breaking speeds, being discovered as a prodigy. Making friends with girls who are just like me, who understand the struggles I have been through.

They do not want to hear that I have never felt less special or seen in my life. They do not want to hear that I have found my place in the world, but that once here, I found that there are too many other versions of *me* here for the real *me* to stand out. They don't want to hear that Diana, the mistress, who had seemed at least marginally interested in me at first, is not paying me very much attention now and seems more focused on other girls.

Especially on Jocelyn. The girl who started on the same day as me.

She's not as good as I am. Or at least, she's not the same kind of dancer I am, and I think the kind of dancer I am is better. I dance with precision, with tight lines, my body moving with the fluidity of water and the sharpness of glass. Jocelyn is an emotional dancer. She improvises micro-movements. And instead of doing what I'd think a ballet mistress would do, which is to tell her to stick to the choreography or nail her positions with more accuracy, Diana heralds her for becoming the role.

This was not what ballet school told me to prepare for. I was prepared for endless nights trying to get everything *just right*, not trying to loosen up like Jocelyn always does.

No, my parents don't want to hear that I am in a one-sided feud with another dancer.

And they really do not want to hear that the only person who seems to think I have anything uniquely special is a man. Sebastian. Who spends late nights with me, training me, trying to get me to be the best version of myself. They do not want to know that he is the reason I am finally drinking wine with them these days.

My family truly, definitely, absolutely does not want to hear that I am falling desperately in love with my assistant director.

And so I do not tell them. I say nothing. When they ask about my life, I tell them in so few words that they can neither become concerned nor protective. The problem is that it also means I have nothing amusing, nothing exciting to tell them either.

So I have begun to feel *other*, even at home. Even with the only people on the planet who are cosmically bound to love me.

In a way, I have never felt closer to fewer people in my life. Even at school, I had friends. A little group of girls who all wanted the same thing. But we were all pretty different, at the core of it. I wonder if I'll ever even see them again. We've all joined different ballet companies or gone to college.

Now there is only one person I spend real time with. One person who is there, witnessing the changes that are happening to me as I grow into the next version of myself.

Sebastian Alvarez.

Wherever we go, we find a room. When others are around, sometimes he'll lock the door. He doesn't want them to know that I'm getting special treatment. It is like an affair, but the sex is just ballet.

On nights when we rehearse together, he will bring in a speaker and a gallon of water, and usually a bottle of wine. He likes Beaujolais if it's red. So I now *love* Beaujolais.

I really like Beaujolais nouveau, which he says made sense since it tastes the most like juice.

He also assures me that one day we will go to the Beaujolais nouveau festival in France.

When we drink white, it is usually a Chablis or Sancerre.

We order a lot of sushi and ramen. I usually skip the rice and noodles. It sort of becomes our *thing*. I start to notice that in the afternoon, I start to crave it. Just like I crave him.

On the nights when he doesn't pull me aside or gesture to get me alone, I feel positively rudderless. And he always does it without saying *not tonight*. No, it will just happen or not happen. And I'll spend the entire day wondering if tonight is a night when it will *happen* or not *happen*.

When it doesn't, I will wander whatever city I am in, looking for bookstores to peruse, or when in Europe look for wine bars that serve Beaujolais, Sancerre, or a good Chablis.

I know how it will sound if I tell anyone. It sounds like I am obsessed with him. It is particularly a bridge too far to seek out the wine we'd be drinking if we were together but drinking it alone.

I have always been an incredibly dedicated person. Driven toward singular goals. Also, he is the thing that makes me feel good. Ballet does not make me feel good anymore, not unless it is with him. The girls around me are cold. The cities are new and beautiful, but big and somewhat frightening. I don't know any other languages, and regret not learning Spanish or French at least, alongside ballet growing up.

It's safe to say that my life revolves around the nights with Sebastian. And not just because I have fallen deeply, desperately in love with him. But also because he is making me *better*.

Diana has begun noticing me again.

"Your technique is almost flawless," Sebastian will say. "It's the magic that you have to find."

And when I am with him, I feel the magic.

Just yesterday at rehearsal, Diana asked what I've done. "Something is different," she said.

"Just feeling it, I guess," I said with a shrug, trying not to smile.

She and the girls have noticed. But no one can say anything to me.

My secret, professional affair with Sebastian is well and truly hidden.

It is early spring in Montreal when it changes.

It has been pouring rain every night, but the streets are cobblestone and I feel like I've been transported to another world.

It's a little past six, when I'm getting my things together to go back to the hotel, when I get a text. My heart jumps into my throat, the way it always does when I get a text these days. It happens rarely, and it's about a split percentage chance that it is Sebastian or my family.

Tonight, it's him.

Him.

It thrills me.

He says: **Come back at eight.**

It's enough, but then he does the best thing. He gives us more time.

And bring something to wear after rehearsing. Something nice.

I want to scream. But instead, I can't even smile. These girls can smell drama like sharks smell blood.

I respond with a quick **Okay!**

I go back to my hotel room, shower, and wait for what feels like forever, and then finally, at 7:40, walk out the door. I have packed a simple black dress, some stockings, black boots, and a leather jacket. I haven't had an opportunity to wear anything but my ballet wardrobe in so long. I haven't even realized how much I want to go out. I grab some mascara and red lipstick. Last minute, I grab my bottle of Chloé perfume and stuff that in my bag too.

I see my reflection in the mirror in the elevator, and think that I look thinner than ever, despite the new addition of wine to my diet. Perhaps the constant fretting about Sebastian is burning calories. It certainly seems like it is.

When I get to the theater, I pull open the doors to the hauntingly empty auditorium. There are pale lights on the stage, but they don't provide very much illumination. The mirrors are up in the back, as there isn't much practice space, and some rehearsals are done here, with mirrors needed.

"There you are, my ingenue," he says.

"Here I am."

"Put down your things and let's get to work. I know it's dark, I can't get into the lighting, they use some sort of app or something, I don't fucking know. I like the analog way. I'm amazed I got these on."

"It's okay with me," I say.

"The music, on the other hand," he says, and then presses play on his phone. Music booms through the speakers.

I can hardly hear myself as I say, "Wow."

He smiles, and I want to die.

"Let's start with your favorite," he says. He changes the track, and I hear the beginning notes.

Prokofiev, the balcony pas de deux from *Romeo and Juliet*.

My heart plumes like smoke. "I can't dance it alone."

"No, you cannot."

And then my most private dreams come true. I am dancing to my favorite score, from my favorite ballet, with the dancer I have most loved for my whole life. And on top of it, I am in love with him.

Usually, in ballet, there is such a huge divide between the mind and the body. You don't think anymore, your body takes over. You separate yourself from the humanity inside you. The carnal desires, the primitive needs, they go away. When I dance, I feel like a vessel. I don't experience hunger or thirst. Pain and exhaustion take on a different sort of tolerable life. Carnal desire is set aside from the dance itself. The hands on you don't feel the same as they would off the stage.

But tonight, it is something different. I am deeply aware of the heat from his body as it touches my skin. I am unable to feel anything but him.

Which, I realize, is his objective.

We work on it for almost forty-five minutes. I am ashamed to admit even to myself that I am wet inside my leotard, and not just from the sweat. I hope he won't see it, and I wish I hadn't worn the white one.

Then he stops the music. "I want to do something different tonight."

I thought perhaps we were nearly through. "Okay."

"I want to play something else for you. Enough straight rehearsal. I want to see you feel something. Feel it so deeply that I can feel it as well just from watching. You're missing moving those around you."

"F-feel something?"

"Yes, I want you to really *dig*. Find something to feel."

He comes back up on the stage where I am and presses play.

"This is different," I say.

He nods. "Jonny Greenwood. One of his more erratic scores."

"What dance do you want me to do?"

"What dance? Just free dance, love. Dance was never supposed to get so structured that you should feel *nothing* when you do it. You should bring something *to* the dance itself, not the other way around."

I nod, becoming nervous. I'm not afraid to dance. I'm afraid to get it wrong, afraid to disappoint him. Something new is being untapped between us and I don't want to screw it up.

So I begin dancing.

He walks around me, watching. When the song changes, I stop, catch my breath, and then am told to keep going.

This goes on for nearly an hour.

I have already rehearsed for eleven hours today, just as I have done every day this week. My body aches and resists everything I tell it to do. It wants to rest. To fall down. But I can't. I will not disappoint him.

Finally, he comes over with a flask and tells me to drink. When I finish my sip, he says, "More."

I take it.

Another fifteen minutes passes.

"My technique is falling apart," I say.

"Let it shatter."

Another swig from the flask. More hysterical jazz. More pir-ouettes, more *arabesques*, more *fouettés* and *grand allegros*.

My body yearns, and finally tears streak down my cheeks as I keep determinedly doing everything he asks. When he says "*grand jeté*," I do a *grand jeté*.

At one point, he lights a cigarette inside the theater and watches me as he smokes. His white shirt is unbuttoned; he is sweating under the stage lights even though he isn't moving like I am. I am completely soaked, my skin is hot and red—I can see myself in the mirrors.

He comes over to me with the cigarette still in his mouth, clutches it between his lips and pulls me close to him and begins to dance with me.

I follow along, exhausted and flustered still from the surprise of dancing with one of the greatest danseurs of all time.

He pulls me to him, he pushes me away, he lifts me up, and he manipulates my movements with his.

I feel light as air. He feels sturdy as marble.

Exhausted, almost erotic sounds begin coming out of me as we dance, my worn-out body not able to contain itself any further, now that there is the added element of his body.

And then without warning, as the music hits a fever pitch, he pulls me in and kisses me hard, desperately, urgently. I kiss him back. Our tongues press against each other's again and again; his grip tightens on my waist, and my wrists, and my ass, and my neck, in my hair. I grab at him, too, feeling his body beneath his clothes. He is hard as a rock against my ass as he turns me around and looks at me in the mirror.

My chest is heaving as he races a hand down my torso and then touches me. I let out a cry and it echoes around the theater. He pulls my leotard down, exposing my small breasts to us both in the mirror.

His big hand encompasses one and almost both as he kisses my neck. I have never done anything like this before.

I've only kissed a few people in my life. The girls at boarding school. We taught each other how. We spent so little time around boys that we knew we would one day be out there in the world and we'd need to know how. So we learned on each other.

This is what we had been rehearsing for. This moment.

And I have never had sex. Never felt a man's hardness before. Never seen it, touched it, tasted it.

I have seen it, but never in real life.

Never like this.

My heart is pounding so hard it feels unsafe. I am so hot I think I might faint.

"Come with me."

He takes my hand and pulls me. We go into the principal's dressing room.

He locks the door and then walks across the room. "You want a dressing room like this, don't you?"

I look around at all the things and imagine they are my own. Imagine I am the principal and that Sebastian is mine.

"Imagine it. You are Juliet."

I am imagining it. My heart leaps and shivers in my chest and I am suddenly desperate, *starving* for that life. I will do anything.

I walk over to him and this time, I kiss him.

He pulls my face down so that his lips are on my ear. "You must dance like that *every* time. You did it. That was it. That was the dancing that would make you go down in history, love."

I moan. I want to fuck him. I want to fuck everyone else by becoming Juliet.

I decide then and there that it is my singular goal.

"I will be Juliet," I say, with his lips on my throat. "I will be Juliet."

"You are Juliet, you are Juliet."

I am reduced to some animal version of myself as I pull him up by the chin and kiss him again, tugging at the back of his head and reaching for the button of his pants.

"Do you want it, Juliet? Show me that you want it."

"I want it."

"More."

"I fucking want it," I say, my voice sounding unlike my own.

"You want me, Juliet?"

"I fucking want you. I need you, please give it to me. Now."

He smiles.

There is a frenzied removing of clothes. I can hardly keep my eyes open or my mouth shut as he touches me.

He slows down for a moment and then pulls me to the chaise longue in the corner. He throws off the silk robe and tutu that lie on top of it, and lays me down gently, naked, against the velvet.

"Tell me you want it, Sylvie."

"I want it. Please."

I pull at him, and after a moment, he is inside me. It hurts at first, but it is nothing compared to the ecstasy I feel.

When he comes, I feel it all over my body, and the sensation of his pulsing dick inside my throbbing vagina makes me have my first orgasm. It takes me over. I feel like I must be dying, it's so different from the living I have ever felt before.

This. This is what they're all talking about.

Afterward, he lies on top of me and kisses every part of my body and tells me over and over that I am perfect.

When the moment has passed, we get up and I put on my outfit, toss my tousled hair to the side and look at myself in the mirror.

I look older. Womanlier. My cheeks are scarlet. There is something to me that was not there a few hours ago.

I have never danced so hard, been so miserable and so happy ever in my life.

We go outside, and he lights another cigarette. Then he offers me one.

"I don't smoke," I say.

"It is customary after sex, you know. Which," he says, handing me one, "I'm assuming you don't know because I have a feeling that was your first time."

I nod, found out, and take the cigarette. "Yes."

"Well, it felt fucking incredible." He lights my cigarette. "Breathe in, yes, just like that."

I cough, but mostly try to hold it in as we walk. My head swims. I feel crazy.

We walk to a restaurant that serves cocktails like I have never seen before, and we eat foods I've never heard of.

Then, he says we're going to a speakeasy. As he pays the bill, he says, "You're still spinning around in my head, like a ballerina in a music box. That was the most incredible I've ever seen. And also"—he leans in—"I can still smell you. You're perfect."

CHAPTER EIGHT

Sylvie

A dancer's day off is a thing to behold. It's very self-care, very me time, but also often a foray into hedonism. It's like we don't know how to stop using our bodies to express ourselves. We don't lounge on the couch at home watching reality TV like some people do on their days off. We seek comfort in . . . different ways.

On the day off before we fly to Paris, I go to the Russian Bath House.

It's a pretty go-to idea someone always suggests at the end of a hard week of shows.

Every city has them and the clientele is fascinating. Bathhouses are part of the world's secrets, the world's dark corners. Business deals are finalized, affairs begin and end, committed relationships open up to let in a stranger, people hide where they think no one is watching. Closeted gay men ogle or engage with men who are fully *out*, who charge for services, or who are closeted themselves. Young girls find sugar daddies. And then, of course, there's the lost sliver of people who come just to melt and treat it with the same amount of intrigue that they might a hot shower at home. Those types come in all business, let all the fat and wrinkles hang out, and give absolutely no fucks about any of the Caligulan goings-on to their left or right.

I turn in all my belongings at the entry, not wanting to put valuables in a locker. After a quick *spasibo* from the Russian woman behind the counter, I descend the stairs that take me deep into the underbelly of the nation's capital.

It's admittedly a grimy atmosphere, but it's still got this weird air of sexiness that rings through. It's the humidity, the sort of sweet smell. Glistening bodies soak up murky water behind thin lattice screens which are, at absolute best, a *metaphor* for privacy.

People are flirting, decompressing, sweating out hangovers, or causing new ones by ordering from the bathhouse bar. Half are completely naked and half are wearing very little. Some sit on the floor; some are in the water, their heads at foot level.

I love it here. Dancers come to rejuvenate, to detox, to lose weight. I can walk out of this place tipsy, three pounds lighter, and with a plan for a date the following evening. You never know who you're going to meet—and sometimes you never know who you met. Anonymity is not uncommon. I bet it's absolutely rampant here in D.C. Surrounding me are probably countless important men I'd never know. Ambassadors, lawmakers, senators . . . I'm not going to recognize them, but I bet they fear everyone will.

But actually . . . do I recognize some of them? Careful not to let my gaze linger, I try to place the old white man whose ancient body appears to be slowly melting into the water around him. He's talking to a very young, thin, effeminate boy, probably only barely old enough to drink. I can't place the older man, but I'm fairly certain he's one of the guys who thinks, very much out loud on

Fox News, that *marriage is between a man and a woman*. There's a waning old-fashioned on the deck next to him.

I move on. It's far from the worst I've seen.

I've talked to people, completely naked, in a sauna for more than an hour. I've gotten to know them deeply, if not intimately, and gone on to see them in all kinds of various media. Some-bodies, hiding in the sweaty, secret guts of cities.

I change quickly into my skimpy white bikini, so sheer and bare that it would get me physically removed from any family-friendly beach.

I pass all the small rooms and go straight to the bar.

The bartender is the same one I always see when I come here. I go to order a shot of vodka and then ask for a vodka soda with lemon, but he is already pouring them for me when I open my mouth.

I use the shot to wash down a half of a pill I brought with me. It's not much. Just a little Molly. Practically a microdose. I just want to feel good.

I thank the bartender and pay him using my bracelet code, and then go toward the saunas.

As I walk down the long bridge of concrete that runs between the dimly lit pools of men, women, and warmth, I garner little attention.

That's the kind of place this is: an optionally participatory Go-morrah.

That doesn't stop me from looking around, though. There are other women here, lots of different body types. I look at them, and I wonder what they think of themselves. I've looked at myself and other girls like me for so long, I don't know if I know what beauty is anymore.

Is it her, with the curvy waist, the short hair, and the tan lines?

Is it her, stubby legs in the Jacuzzi, long wet hair thrown over one soft, round shoulder?

Or is it her, the small girl in a pool all to herself, a simple, wide smile on her face, flirting with a man who seems into her too.

Bodies are being whipped gently with dry palms. A couple has their legs entwined, bags of ice on the backs of their necks. There are usually so many dancers here on their days off. We call it the lazy workout. The workout where you do nothing but lose weight.

First I go for a dip in one of the pools, setting my glass down and doing several laps, doing a dead man's float, and letting my head bob in the water so that I can hear only muffled versions of everything around me.

After twenty minutes of that, I get out and dry myself, and move on.

I open the hydraulic door to an empty sauna and sit down on the wood bench with a deep exhale, and pivot to lie down, since there's no one else there. I stare at the faucet, slowly dripping cold water for us to lower our temperatures.

I reach into the pocket in my bikini top, usually meant for padding. Inside, there is a small baggie with the other half of the Molly I had taken earlier. I take it out and put it under my tongue.

It'll take maybe half an hour to kick in, but the way it begins to dissolve is the beginning of the relief.

Last night's toxins drift out of me, and the new ones come in, both sensations bringing Alessandro to my mind's surface. Vague feelings of embarrassment for being ditched. Irritation with myself for even caring rings a small bell. Reluctant attraction to his form, his body, and his talent swim up through me, wrapping smoothly around my thighs and slithering into my utter center, whether I like it or not. I can't stop the yearning for him even though I believe it extremely possible I will never even see him again.

I turn onto my side, needing some kind of deep human comfort. I feel the skin on my face squish against the slats of the bench. I assume I look silly, but no one is here to see me.

I haven't bothered to look at casting yet, so I have no idea if he's even supposed to dance with us on the next leg of the tour in Paris. He wasn't at ballet class on Sunday, so I'm assuming he's not.

Which is totally fine, because I won't have anything to do with him either way.

Hookups in our world are extremely common. No one cares who's fucking who . . . until they do. Would anyone care if someone hooked up with Alessandro? Only insofar as they might be jealous. There's rarely a casting of judgment for that kind of thing. But would they care if I did?

Fucking stupid *yes*. They would and it would help nothing in my life.

I'm still enough in a spotlight that people are watching.

My thoughts grow a little disjointed over the next half hour as I feel the drugs rising a little in my system.

I sit up and take off my bikini, deciding that's the vibe today, and sink back into my feelings.

Just as I remove the top and start to take off the bottom, someone opens the door.

"Sorry," I start to say to the stranger, but I find that it's . . .

"Alessandro," I say, somewhat breathlessly. Come *on*. "What are you doing here?"

"Same thing as you, I'm sure."

"I thought you'd left."

I suddenly regret taking the drugs. Being around Alessandro makes me want to be sharp.

I start to put my top back on, but I know it's too late, and it's lamer if I try to hide myself. I cross my arms.

"I wish you had not closed the door in my face the other night," he says, leaning back and looking at me.

"I—" I swallow my apology. "You stood me up. You deserved it."

He shakes his head. "You must know how it is, don't you? That onstage is not the only dance we do, is it? The sponsors, the big shots." He smiles at me. "We have to keep them happy, don't we? You know how much better my life is because of the—what is it—*schmoozing*, I've done?"

"No."

"I'll show you my flat in Paris. That should give you some idea. It's not as big as the one I have in Manhattan, but I prefer it."

My stomach does a small flip. He has a place in *my* city? I feel suddenly surprised I never saw him. I feel vulnerable. Like discovering a camera in my home and I don't know how long it's been there or if someone's been watching.

I say none of this, of course, and instead say simply, "I've never heard of anyone talking about how big their New York place is."

"This is my point. It's still small."

"Okay, so your point is that you blew me off because you have to keep acquiring homes in expensive cities? You're right, I'm no longer insulted. That's very valid, in fact I can't believe I ever stood in your way."

"Please," he says, "don't be like this. I heard that you were once quite close to finding your place on top. Don't tell me you don't remember what it's like when you *have* to allow the people of influence to romance you."

My heart stops. How much does he know?

Instead of letting it show, I smile. "I understand."

"And anyway," he goes on, "I didn't even think you'd show. You're so aloof, it was hard to tell if you meant it."

"Why would—whatever." I laugh. "This is what happens when you don't simply exchange numbers."

"I'd ask you for it now, but"—he puts his palms out—"I don't have my phone on me."

"Good thing we're not making a date, then."

There's something in his expression that makes me feel guilty. Have I hurt his feelings? Is that even possible?

I'm about to ask what I said that was wrong when the door opens again. It's the last person in the world I want to see. Especially now.

Jocelyn slinks into the doorway, completely nude. She arches an eyebrow at the two of us. "If I'm interrupting anything, please don't stop on my account."

Her eyes drift to mine as she lets the door shut behind her.

She moves like a cat. Not even a real, live cat, but an animated one from the sixties. Thinner legs, more arch in her back. Her green eyes are feline, even without the perfect black wing she applies at night when she's off the stage.

She walks past me, sitting on the bench above us, facing us, leaning against the wall.

"I'm going to get a drink and then have a steam," says Alessandro. His eyes stay on mine.

I let my gaze drop.

I feel disappointed that he's leaving, and don't realize until he's gone that it was an invitation. That's what that last look was.

I am definitely not firing on all cylinders.

"I have something to tell you," says Jocelyn.

I whip back to look at her. I can tell by the tone of her voice she's being herself, not the character she's gotten so used to playing.

"What?" I ask.

Even her face looks different. Less intense. Real.

It's such a sudden change that I am worried, and I can't even think what could be so bad.

"Sebastian is a ballet master at the Paris Opera now."

That's what could be so bad. I feel as though my flesh might melt off my bones, I am suddenly so hot.

"No," I say.

"Yeah. We're going to see him again."

She lets her head fall back against the wall behind her and I turn away to face the door, hoping to god no one comes in.

I can't even find the words for how little this information computes, how not okay it is.

"I hate letting a man get to me like this," she says. "He's not going to make it easy. For either of us."

"It's going to be harder for me. I don't have any idea why you even care."

I can practically hear her roll her eyes as she says, "In a way it'll be harder for you, maybe. But trust me. You're not the only one."

"Really?" I ask. "Because if you ask anyone else—"

"God, Sylvie, I know, okay—can you just not take your shit out on me? Maybe don't fight this battle. Everyone is going to make it hard enough for the next few weeks. Maybe you need an ally."

"Who, *you*?"

I'm becoming venomous—as venomous as someone for whom the Molly is about to kick in can be—and it's not entirely about her, but in part it is.

I want to remain calm but it's impossible. "After everything that went down I can't believe you have the guts to be such a bitch."

"The guts?" She laughs. "I am seriously stunned that you think you're the wronged party. Always! Always. You ask me how I have the guts. Fucking psycho."

I am seething like only she can make me seethe. "Yes, *the guts*, Jocelyn. You tried pretty hard to ruin me."

She arches an eyebrow and looks at me as if to confirm that I meant what I said. I don't relent, and she looks off, takes a deep breath.

"You and I remember the past *very* differently."

CHAPTER NINE

NEW YORK CITY

FOUR AND A HALF YEARS AGO

Jocelyn

H oly shit. I am finally free.

Thank god no one can see inside my mind. If they could, they'd think I'm desperate and delusional. I walk down the unfamiliar streets of New York using Google Maps and hiding my screen from everyone I pass, as if they care, as if this would make me pass as a local, as if it mattered.

This is it: the real world.

New York.

New Fucking York.

My tiny bedroom growing up had the walls plastered with magazine cutouts and posters of three things: famous people, ballet, and New York City. I didn't know what I wanted to do or be, but I knew I loved those things.

And now I'm *here*. Standing on a street corner among the mythical creatures known as New Yorkers. They probably have the ability to smell my awe, my fascination, my status as a foreigner to this place. I want with all my heart to have already lived here my whole life. What kind of person would I have been?

In service of this fantasy, I try with all my might to keep my eyes at street level, to walk with purpose. I feign certainty, try to give off the impression that I am *just as sick of tourists* as everyone else.

I try to imagine what the locals think of as they walk down these historic streets. I imagine myself, tenured and secure as a New Yorker, walking out of my building—greeting my doorman, I'm sure—and getting irritated with the bike lanes (too many, too few, whatever) and taking the subway—or do they call it the subway? The card, of which I'm now a proud owner, says Metro on it. And I swear I've seen movies where people just called it *the train*.

Try as I might to contain myself, to blend in, I know I'm not fooling anyone.

I'm here, I've done it, I've gotten where I wanted to be. Now all I need to do is to stay. I cross the street—I learned a few blocks back that you follow the *people*, not the light—and wander into a park. I try to find a sign so that I can refer knowledgeably to it later.

I'd been to orientation, met that weird girl Sylvie, and seen the place, but I knew it would feel different as soon as it was a real rehearsal day. And it is. I've been here a few months now, and no one has said a word to me. It's unbelievable. I've never had so little conversation in my whole life.

My first show is *Sleeping Beauty*. I'm dancing as a Lilac Fairy attendant. I can't believe that is the first show I'll be a part of—the odds feel too great. When I was a kid, my grandmother showed me the ballet since I was so obsessed with the Disney cartoon one. Since I was already twirling around the house in a tutu all the time, the pieces went together pretty naturally.

I call my grandmother—Mimi—and tell her as soon as I find out and she gets choked up, which makes me cry. There's just about no one on Earth who makes me more human than Mimi, so I should have known and waited to put on mascara until after the call.

It's when I talk to her that I realize I'm kind of lonely. Which I've never been in my life.

I mean I have. Growing up with my shrew of a mother, who put me in auditions since I was a toddler, all in the name of making *her* a buck—yeah, I definitely didn't have a life where I felt particularly loved and coddled.

I grew up in a hot, sweaty, nothing town in Louisiana. The fact that I have a cosmopolitan bone in my body is thanks only to the globalization of the world and the Internet. I sought out glamour, elegance, beauty. I did not care about bonfire keg parties. I wanted to meet a young Leonardo DiCaprio and kiss him in the moonlight. I wanted to be whisked to Oviedo by Javier Bardem. I wanted champagne from crystal glasses, to wear silken gowns and to throw my head back in laughter.

I lost my accent by the time I turned thirteen, because it turns out that it's a choice. I curated for myself a personality that I thought would bring me the life I wanted. It did not gain me many friends. So I guess, actually, I've always been lonely. This is just a whole new version of it.

Until today, when Sebastian Alvarez seems to notice me for the first time.

"Jocelyn," he says. "Come here for a moment."

I look around the quickly emptying theater. We have a day off tomorrow, so everyone is eager to get started on their freedom.

I go to him as Diana says goodbye and then adds something in French that makes him laugh.

I stand before him and raise my eyebrows. "Yes?"

"You're very good."

"I mean, yeah. I'm in the NAB, aren't I?"

This seems to stun and amuse him. I smile to show I'm kidding.

"You have a spark to you," he says. "Your technique is not perfect, but you're just fascinating to watch. It's really interesting. I can't tell what it is. Where did you go?"

"Where did I go?"

"For school."

"Oh. Northwest High School?"

He looks confused and intrigued at this, taking off his glasses and chewing on them. "Interesting. No ballet school? How did you learn?"

"My grandmother had a friend who opened a studio. Mrs. Willett's Ballet Academy. And then I got a private coach in high school. But I mostly just had to practice myself. Forever. I didn't really have access to anything more."

He shakes his head. "And this is all you've ever wanted, I suppose."

The truest answer is that I'm not sure what I want out of life, on the whole. But the correct answer is *yes*.

There is a sound behind me, and his eyes travel back to look, then mine do too. It's Sylvie, my orientation—well, not *buddy*. Acquaintance. Everyone seems to hate her. I can't tell if it's because she's so aloof or because she's talented.

For me, it's both. She was kind of a dick on day one. She's also incredibly talented. She's the kind of ballerina I've always wanted to be.

She is the only one left in the backstage area besides Sebastian, me, and a few stagehands working in the wings.

"Sylvie," he calls.

She moves her hair out of her face and sets down her bag to come over.

"Sylvie, have you met Jocelyn yet?" he asks.

Sylvie looks at me, and then holds out a hand. It's incredibly delicate, and once I touch it, I note that it's soft and cold.

"Yes, of course; we have rehearsals together," she says.

"Jocelyn," I say, with a warm smile. I want to disarm her.

"She's very good," says Sebastian. "You know, it's somewhat funny. You both have what the other lacks. But you're both excellent."

"Thank you," I say, not sure if that is the right answer.

"I'm thinking we should bring her in on our little rehearsals." He says this to Sylvie.

Her cheeks go pink. "Oh."

"Oh?" He gives a crocodile grin. "I think you can learn from each other."

Neither of us says anything.

"Tell you what," he says, leaning forward. "Tomorrow, go for brunch. I'll make the reservation. I'll take care of the bill. Get to know each other. Have some champagne, order whatever you want. Then come over to my place after, and we'll have a little meet and greet."

Sylvie looks scandalized, and I look—I'm sure—absolutely mystified.

But I'm intrigued. "I'm down," I say.

She looks startled when I say it, but nods and says, "Of course."

We exchange numbers, and then I walk out, leaving them behind.

Fucking weird.

Sylvie texts me in the morning and says that the reservation is for Waverly Inn at 1:00 p.m.

I make a point of taking my time getting up. I put on some Top 40 music—essentially the opposite of classical, what we hear all day long—and put on makeup and do my hair. It's a little like being a normal girl and not a ballerina.

We meet on the corner of Seventy-Ninth Street and Columbus near Sylvie's apartment and walk to the subway together.

It's positively dreadful outside. Manhattan in February is, as it turns out, very fucking cold. By day, it's truly like living in a snow globe. The sky is as white as an untouched canvas, and the line between that sky and its horizon is blurred at best. The tall buildings block the little sun that manages to break through the nearly opaque clouds. The air is cold, sharp, brisk. The wind is like getting repeatedly slapped from ear to nose by a refrigerated Edward Scissorhands. I'm really regretting my choice of a short skirt.

Time becomes irrelevant, and the world feels like it could never have been any different, any brighter, any wider than this.

The atmosphere is made up of the weirdly sweet smell of garbage and candied nuts, and the savory scent of falafel wafting from around every street corner. Every few feet on the Upper West Side, the chime of a deli's front door will pour heat from the fabled *Inside* out onto the sidewalk, making me, at the time, wonder if our reservations should just be ignored, if we should just get an egg-and-cheese sandwich at a deli.

I mean, most delis may have a C health code rating in a city where even getting an A only means you have the *fewest* rats, but . . . well, it *is* right here.

"New York is kind of hell," I tell Sylvie, "but I fucking love it."

We take the 1 train and then walk a few blocks to Waverly Inn, which is cuter and cozier than I imagined. Our table is in a brick-walled area with ivy, tile floors, glass ceilings, and a burning fireplace. The clientele is dressed pretty consistently in après-ski, and it reminds me of watching *Charade* with Mimi when I was little. I take a picture to send her.

We order oysters with extra mignonette; fresh ricotta with warm, toasty bread; and share a lobster bisque.

My white trash background led me to the now obviously flawed thought that brunch meant we were going for pancakes and sausage links. When the manager, apparently a ballet person, finds out we're there from the NAB, she sends over two glasses of champagne.

I eagerly accept, and hold my glass up to clink with Sylvie's, but she hesitates.

"What is it?" I ask. "Not the right year?"

She smiles bashfully. "No, no, it's nothing. Cheers."

Once the glass is drained, she admits that she didn't use to drink. In fact she only had her first glass a few months ago.

I can tell that this confession is about as open as she gets with people. Unsure what else to do, I say, "Well, you'd never know it. You downed that glass like a pro."

This makes her laugh, and it seems that for some reason, despite being so different, we are getting along. Maybe it's the champagne, or maybe it's just that there is some sort of natural chemistry between us. I feel like I've known her for a long time.

She's the one who knows who most of the famous people in

the mural on the wall are, though I'm at least capable of identifying Andy Warhol all by my lonesome. When my ignorance shows, she comforts me, telling me that she bought a book about this place, and, though she doesn't often find time for reading anymore, she has recently perused that one. "It's basically a picture book," she tells me.

It's like somewhere in my fragile ego I inherently believe that she's friend, not foe, and that she's someone to learn from, not to envy or resent.

By the time we get the check, it's almost four o'clock.

"So," she says at the end of the meal, "shall we go? To . . . Sebastian's, I mean . . ."

"Right. So what's the deal with this?" I ask.

She flushes again. "He's been training me privately. It was meant to be a secret, but then he told you, so I guess . . . just don't tell anyone else."

"Why is it a secret?"

"Oh . . . I—it just is, I guess special treatment and all that. He lives nearby if you want to go over."

"Does he train you at his house usually?"

"No."

I wait, thinking she might explain more. But she does not.

"I would have thought someone as . . . *whatever*, as him would be up on the Upper East Side or something."

She shakes her head. "No, that's all WASPs and Madonna up there. West Village is where, like, Annie Leibovitz had a thirty-million-dollar compound. If this is where he lives, it's honestly not a surprise at all."

"Ah," I say.

The server comes over with his hands behind his back and says, "Your check has been taken care of by Mr. Alvarez."

Then he walks away.

"Then why did he bring the check?" I ask.

She shrugs. I take the check folder and open it, expecting to simply marvel at a large number, but nothing. Just a little slip of paper.

The server's phone number, which notes at the top that it is "For the Blonde."

Damn.

I glance at Sylvie, who is texting, and shut the check folder, as if I haven't seen anything.

She doesn't notice, and instead just says, "Okay, let's go," and stands from the table.

I nod and get up. Why are we going to his house?

I don't want to end up being one of *those* girls.

But this *could* be really, immeasurably good for my career.

But I don't want to even *seem* like one of those girls.

Outside, it's started to rain, and she leads us expertly round the blocks until we get to his house. I envy her for knowing the city so well, and then wonder if maybe she has just been to his house a bunch of times and knows because of that.

Finally, after walking down an idyllic block that looks like something straight out of my dreams, she stops.

"Well, we're here." She looks up.

Am I crazy or does she look nervous?

The front steps are wide and have stone rails. It reminds me of the front of Carrie Bradshaw's apartment on *Sex and the City*.

When I say that, she just states, "I've never seen it."

I don't even ask how it's possible she's never seen the show, no matter what age—it seems like every girl has seen it. Like it's part of the curriculum of being a girl.

I don't ask Sylvie because I know the answer will just simply be the same as it always is when it seems like she has landed here from another planet.

Ballet.

Ballet.

It's always ballet.

For me, ballet was always the thing I snuck in, the illicit thing that was only mine, the thing I did even though my life didn't allow for it. For her it had been just the opposite—it was the only thing she did, the thing that eclipsed everything else.

It's like she grew up in the world of Manhattan and the world of ballet *alone*. Two things most people will never understand thoroughly, she knows them—and only them—completely.

All the things I'm suddenly gaining access to, they're all old news to her. It's like she knows the styles and trends of the next decade and then people like me have to just discover them in real time.

Juicing. Drinking broth as a *meal*. Little chews filled with sodium and amino acids to help with stamina and energy before rehearsal.

All these things are new to me and some of them are such old news to her that they are practically irrelevant.

It's already darkening outside and the two sconces on the front of the building glow gold against the brick.

"Come on." She rings the doorbell and I walk up the steps.

Some people walk by behind me, chatting.

The door doesn't open right away, and we stand there, not speaking. What is there to say? The last chapter of the day has closed and there is nothing to do but wait for the next page to turn.

And it does.

Sebastian opens the door.

"Ah! Girls, come in, come in." He steps out briefly with bare feet and then holds the door open wider. "It's cold and rainy out here."

"Thanks," says Sylvie.

She steps in and I quicken my pace to catch up.

Sebastian closes the door and I look around me.

"Holy shit."

I didn't mean to say it out loud, but this place is seriously *holy shit out loud* worthy.

"This is beautiful," I say. "I mean wow. Did you decorate yourself?"

"Ah." He looks humble, earnest. "Well, I inherited the house from my father's side of the family. And thankfully I am close friends with a woman with impeccable taste. I let her use my house as a guinea pig. If it was left up to me, the place would be in shambles. I really need all the help I can get. If you don't mind taking your shoes off, I'm sorry . . ."

I step off the rug with my boots. "Oh my god, I'm so sorry."

There are grey, wet footprints from my boots. Sylvie hasn't left the tile of the foyer, so it's only me who's fucked up spectacularly.

"Please don't worry about it. If I hadn't let Jenna pick out a handwoven rug made by an indigenous man in Tibet, I would hardly think it mattered."

"Jenna? Not Jenna Cordray," I say, pulling my feet out of my black leather boots.

"That's the Jenna." He smiles.

"Oh my god," I say. "I saved all the pictures of her loft from the article in the *Times*. You're friends with her?"

"She's even nicer and more elegant in person. Maybe the stars will align and I can introduce you. She loves the ballet. Always tells me I have the world's best job, but I mean, look who's talking."

"Are these floors . . . heated?" I feel foolish asking the question, since it seems impossible to me that such extravagance could be afforded by anyone.

"They are, being South American I need all the heat I can get in these New York winters. I hope it's warm enough for you. If not, I have a fire burning in here; that should help warm you up. Leave your coats there, Miles will give them a quick clean so they're dry when you're ready to go."

None of that makes any sense to me until a small, older man appears out of nowhere and gathers our damp, frozen coats and takes them away.

I give Sylvie a look, and she smiles with a shrug. As if to say, *This is just what it's like to be rich as hell.*

The living room opens with soaring ceilings that even I know are unusual in this city. There is a door to a porch completely encased in glass and supported with iron. It looks like a green-house, except all the lush plants are outside and the porch itself is like another cozy sitting room.

Music plays through speakers all around, unseen, embedded in the walls and ceilings.

The hearth is marble and a real fire with real wood roars in-side it. A large painting sits on the mantel, leaning against the wall. In a gold frame there's a piece of ivory paper with ratty edges. It looks like the page of a book. I step toward it immediately.

Behind me, Sebastian says, "What can I get you to drink? I've got everything. Red, white, sparkling. I have whiskeys, gin . . . I'm a pretty good bartender. Have you ever had a Vieux Carré?"

"No, what's that?" asks Sylvie.

"It's like an old-fashioned made love to a Manhattan."

"Yes, that's perfect," says Sylvie.

I cringe a little. I hate the expression *made love*, especially in a context like that.

"Me too," I say, stepping close enough to read the poem.

At the top, it says *Neal Bowers* in italics. The poem is called "The Dance." Below the title, it says *For Nancy.*

I finish reading the poem and am just about to read it again when I hear my name. I turn to see Sylvie and Sebastian both looking at me.

"Sorry, what?"

"Do you want yours on the rocks or straight up?" Sylvie—I guess—repeats.

"Oh, however you think."

"So Jocelyn, this is a New Orleans drink. You're from Louisiana, aren't you?"

"Yes, I am. But not that close to New Orleans."

"I see." He begins stirring with a long spoon in a glass carafe. "New Orleans is a wonderful city. People think it's all jambalaya and gumbo, but it's actually quite cosmopolitan. I remember hearing about it when I was growing up in Argentina and I just thought, what is *that*? Bourbon Street, I mean it sounded like a nightmare. Just bachelorette parties everywhere, people throwing up on the street. And to be fair, Bourbon Street is like that. When I went for the first time I was handed a beer in a cup shaped like a pair of tits, and almost got hit by an ambulance that was racing to pick someone up from the next bar over. But, ah, the rest of the city"—he shakes his head, pauses—"so much . . . *corazón.* Sorry, sometimes my English fails me."

He pours the drink evenly into three glasses, each with a huge ice cube.

"I've never been," says Sylvie. "It sounds exciting."

"It is exciting. Jocelyn, what do you think of New Orleans?"

"I don't really know it. I went once, but I was with my mom. I don't think you can really get an idea of what a city is like until you're going without your family. Maybe unless you go alone."

He pauses. "So is this your first time in New York? In Manhattan?"

He uses a silver peeler to remove the rind of a lemon and squeezes it over one drink, then repeats the process for the other two.

"Yes, coming here for the NAB was my first time here, ever."

"Wow," he says. "That must have been incredible for you. Very brave. You must be the brave one in your family, right?"

"I've never thought about it." I laugh a little self-consciously. "But maybe."

"And Sylvie? Born and bred here, right?"

"The world ends at the Hudson." She collapses elegantly onto the chaise. I wonder if I'm brave enough to sit without being invited to.

"And you are as singular about ballet, I know."

"Life dies on the stage," she says.

"Even her boarding school was here," he says to me.

"Yes, but of course my family traveled some," she says defensively.

He raises his eyebrows and hands her a drink. He takes his time answering, handing me my glass too. "My mother was obsessed with all things French, which is why she gave me a French name. She enrolled me in ballet early on as a way of honoring French culture, and she used to take me to Paris once a year until I was sixteen to see the Paris Opera Ballet."

Then he stands back and says, "I knew you two were special. It's not a surprise to me that you got along after I forced you together. You are both very interesting." He stares at us for another moment, looking from one of us to the other. Sylvie, recalcitrant on the couch, one leg stretched elegantly out on the floor in front of her. Me, standing on the marble hearth in my thin tights, one elbow on the mantel, warming my cold skin.

Then he holds his glass aloft.

We mirror him.

"To the start of something completely fucking new."

It is then that I feel the first pang of attraction to him. He's sexy.

He walks over to the leather sectional sofa and sits down. Sylvie gets up and moves, too, sitting a cushion away from him.

I'm not warm yet, so I stay by the fire.

"Do you like Manhattan, then?" he asks me.

"I do. It's strange to be here. I've always loved it, always wanted to come. Watched all the old movies that took place here—"

"Allow me to guess your favorite."

"Go ahead."

"Breakfast at Tiffany's."

I freeze. "How did you know that?"

He laughs and leans back, taking a sip and putting his other hand through his hair and then on the back of the sofa. "Don't take this the wrong way, but that is the first love of every girl who falls for Manhattan. Have you read the book?"

"Yes," I say. It's not true, but I want to seem better than I evidently am.

"Good. It is a wonderful film, by the way. Audrey was so good, so unusual. The Givenchy. That Eastmancolor world. It's all so good. Just about everything but George Peppard was perfect in that movie. But then, that was kind of the point, no?"

"I think so." Suddenly I'm too hot.

I step down and sit on the hearth, still not totally ready to leave the heat.

"I am surprised you do not imitate Holly Golightly more," he continues.

"Imitate her?"

"I just mean, if you admire her, there are some traits of hers you could really do with on the stage."

"I can see that," says Sylvie.

Her comment feels like an unexpected pinch.

"There are a lot of characters I'd love to see you imbue in your art. As you learn more, which you must do."

I nod tightly. "Mm-hmm."

"And you," says Sebastian, shifting his spotlight to Sylvie. Thank god.

"'World ends at the Hudson,' 'Life dies on the stage' . . . It's good, it's cute to be so narrowly focused. It comes from something very true inside you. You need it like you need water, maybe more than you need water. You know the rules, so you can win these games. But the problem is, you get on the stage and that shows. I never thought of a way to say it before this one came along." He gestures at her. "Sylvie, you're so young, I don't expect you to be or even to seem worldly. I might think you more interesting if I knew that the girl who sat before me, so calm, that little smile on her face"—he leans in briefly, pointing at her—"ankles in a . . . tangle, like that . . . if I believed that you were more than just your commitment to ballet. If I knew that this girl here was no girl but someone who had been offered the world and who instead chose to sit here quietly, listening. That any moment she might choose something, somewhere, someone else. But, if only for this moment, she has chosen this, here, with me. With *us*."

Sylvie seems a little different, suddenly. She puts her drink down on the table and sits up a little straighter.

"And if I was that . . . then, sure, you might think I was more interesting. But I can't do all that and be the *best*."

So, she's gonna be the *best*.

I wonder what that makes me.

"But when she dances"—he points at me—"I would believe any story about her. That she was plucked from obscurity, that she had trained her whole life, that she had spent time in the Red Light District in Amsterdam. That she had once been committed to a life in the church." He laughs.

I open my mouth to respond, but am elbowed out by Sylvie, who leans forward.

"When was I supposed to fly to Amsterdam and get fucked in a window?"

Whoa.

He stares, pauses. Then smiles, softens, returns to his drink. "Listen, the thing is—I tell you, no. No, I don't need this from Sylvie Carter. But I *do* need to feel like the soul behind a Giselle or an Aurora or a Juliet . . . I need to believe that *that* soul has wound its way around the planet and landed on the stage before me, and I am fucking lucky to see it. Seeing that soul is a *miracle*. You, this . . . seeing this soul is an *inevitability*."

I realize I'm biting the tip of my tongue and release it before taking another sip of my drink.

This feels like a conversation they've had many times, but which I'm suddenly an audience for.

"Ah . . . but that's just me," he says. "What do I want? I want to find the next ballerina or the next ballerinas who are going to change it. Be good enough to change something for real. I don't want technique and I don't want rebels. I want something deep, something dark, something beautiful, something familiar to everyone. I want the stupidest man in the room to understand himself better when he watches the talent that I have helped to mold. Do you remember the first time you saw Anna Pavlova dance *The Dying Swan*?"

"I've watched it a million times," says Sylvie.

"I—I remember the first time," I say, surprised to hear my own voice. "I was at my grandmother's house. My mom had left me there for the weekend but didn't end up picking me up for a week. It was summer, so I didn't have school or anything but I also didn't know anyone around there. It was hot as fuck and my grandmother was a penny-pincher, so she was sparing with the AC. It was too hot to be outside but I hated being in the dark house, especially doing nothing. I was like twelve, so I'd been dancing already for six years. But I started googling 'best ballerinas' and watching everything I could, and that one"—I breathe in deeply—"it was so different."

"Tell me why." He leans toward me.

He's really so, so hot. I don't usually notice that kind of thing as quickly as everyone else. But he has bone structure like a celebrity. This wavy, thick, shiny brown hair. Almond-shaped eyes with dark, straight lashes, and the deep Spanish accent is just melt-worthy.

"I thought she was like everything at once. She was light as a feather on her toes; she was balanced and sturdy but breakable. Like glass. She moved, not like a human, and not like an animal, but I saw that she was . . . the swan? I could see it in her choices, in her movements, but she was also . . . I don't know, she was like a . . . feeling. She was the incarnation of a swan. An incarnate emotion. From the tips of her fingers to her toes was like pure electricity."

Sebastian puts his drink down with a slosh and then claps his hands together once loudly and says, "*That's* it. It's transcendent. It's like synesthesia of the heart and soul, right? She was not only death; she was what it *is* to die."

I nod. "Yeah. That's how I felt."

Sylvie smiles. "So you're looking to . . . what? Change ballet and you need a star?" She laughs.

"I'll take more than one."

My heart is beating hard. "So . . . what do we do?"

Sebastian smiles.

Chapter Ten

Sylvie

Swan Lake is behind us and *Sleeping Beauty* lies ahead. It's not my first time dancing it; the first time was five years ago when I first got here and was just a corps girl.

There's almost no break in momentum when a company tours. We begin running the full ballet every day with the whole cast together. It gives the principals a chance to tighten their chemistry and increase their stamina. Which sometimes is exactly what it sounds like and extends beyond the stage or hours of rehearsal.

The rest of the dancers get a chance to see how much time they have between entrances. To see if there's time to change pointe shoes, grab water, and time the quick costume changes. Up until now, everyone has been rehearsing individually.

Today, the studio in the theater is buzzing with something like seventy-five or eighty dancers, four ballet masters and mistresses, an artistic director, assistant artistic director, choreographer, pianist, and three conductors. And like always, there are people running around the theater that I don't even recognize, and I have no idea what they do. This is usually because they are the type of miscellaneous support roles that are either transient or more than easily replaced and often are.

Not everyone is dancing at the same time, so the sweatpants-clad dancers sit around the studio waiting and watching. It's more intense, in a way, than even the ultimate performance. The dancers are educated, critical, not here to be entertained or to gape in awe.

We're here to replace each other.

"God it's packed in here. I wish we were downstairs on the stage," says Alicia, collapsing beside me. "I know we're not exactly talking right now but can we just move on from that because I think I may die."

"Yes, but shut up," I say.

She snorts and pushes my leg.

I scoot up, my sweating back slick against the mirror behind me. There's a tiny gap in the door letting the slightest breeze in. We always spend a day or two in the studios at the theater while the sets are being loaded in and the stage prepared. I sought this spot out before rehearsal, knowing it would be hot as fuck with everyone in here for the full run-through. I staked my claim as soon as possible with my ballet bag and water bottle. And sweat.

The only chairs in the room are reserved for the ten or so staff who are watching and taking notes for corrections. The corps de ballet master and mistress focus only on the corps, giving notes. The soloist ballet mistress, Diana, watches only her soloists. Another ballet master along with the artistic director watch the principals. The choreographer and assistant artistic director watch the whole, big picture.

And I watch them all.

The time I spent in the sauna at the Russian Bath House has become an intense blur, like trying to remember what happened in a sweat lodge on a peyote trip.

What I knew for sure was that I was done sitting in the wings. If Sebastian was really back, I couldn't let him know how fucked up he'd really made me. How much my life had been ruined. I couldn't be a shriveling mess.

Alessandro, Sebastian, no one would have power over me again. The problem was that when I gave it away, I never got it back.

Until now. At least that's my resolve.

And today is the first morning in three years that I have stayed completely sober.

And I intend to stay off it all. In fact, I have to. Because I threw it all in a dumpster on Pennsylvania Avenue before leaving D.C., and getting a prescription filled in a foreign country is either a bureaucratic nightmare or extremely sketchy.

So far, I feel okay. Just okay. But it's not been long enough to tell. I'm starting to fear that I might have been feeling a little too invincible when I decided not to wean off them. I feel tired and itchy from the inside.

I reach into my bag and crack off a piece of expensive chocolate from a shop beside the hotel where I bought my espresso this morning. I bought it as a treat and replacement for my sobriety.

Or at least, near sobriety. I brought *some* Xanax—just a little—and I've decided to avoid hard liquor and just stick with white wine (this includes champagne). This might not sound sober.

But for me, it is. Now.

Ballet sober.

Alicia gets up to dance her part, the Lilac Fairy, and I watch her.

When finished, she sits back down beside me, watching for the long while until her next entrance. And since I'm on the basic as the understudy for her role, I'm required to know the part, to be at rehearsal, to be prepared in case of injury.

The basic, also known as the god book, also known as the casting booklet, lives in the dancers' lounge or, on tour, on the call board and holds the casting to all the ballets the company will dance throughout the season or year. Sometimes a part will have up to ten people learning it. They have systems for telling us who is most and least likely to play the role.

I am very unlikely to play the role. But here I must be anyway.

If it sounds like they're making us unnecessarily competitive, then you're missing nothing. They want us fighting, hungry, starved for attention, scratching one another's eyes out.

This is part of what I've realized lately. That I am miserable because I am doing *nothing*. I am exhausted and worn out from the constant fight, but I am doing it practically for nothing. I've spent years just trying to keep my head above water.

This is what I want to change.

This is what I am *going to* change.

The prima ballerina dancing Aurora today is Sofia. She's thirty-five years old, dancing sixteen-year-old Aurora, though you wouldn't know she was that old just looking at her. Thirty-five is definitely aging a bit in the ballet world, yet Sofia moves with effortless grace, beauty, and youth. We are all bred to retain nymphet-like adolescence, and Sofia is one who has really done it. I looked up to her when I was young, and yet here she is, in the same room as me. It's no longer admiration, it is clean, green envy.

When I was younger, it was not just a wish; it was a plan: become better than she is.

I was that way about all the great ones.

The truth is, if I were only an admirer, I'd think the casting was perfect. Sofia is a bending willow-like Aurora to Alessandro's sturdy, yearning Prince Charming. If I were merely in the audience, I'd be in heaven watching them.

I love watching Aurora's first entrance. She's like a butterfly waking up in the spring sunshine. Everything is glorious and dewy like fresh wildflowers after a light April shower.

I pull my knees up to my chest and rest my head on them as I watch her flutter across the studio. The dancers around her step back to give her space for the last of her diagonal *petits tombé coupé jetés*. She turns to leap into the air again and again. Even for a ballerina, it's an incredibly difficult move and takes a lot of co-ordination. Unlike a basketball player, who has to jump and aim and then merely remain strong and prepared, she has to jump, land silently and gracefully, then do it again, again, again, as if the floor were a trampoline. When you properly land from a jump, your Achilles stretches like a rubber band to support the weight. If it goes too far in the wrong direction, the rubber band snaps.

You land from a jump with your weight unevenly tilted to the outside of your foot, and your ankle has to support your body, and then the muscles supporting the ankle bones have to strain. First they may tear a little, then they rip, then they shred, and then eventually when you land and your full weight makes contact with the floor, the support in your ankle has vanished and you have nothing. An ankle bone breaks.

I think sometimes the audience forgets that gravity, ostensibly, affects us too. And that's the point. It means our ruse is working.

As if in slow motion, as if I know it's coming and watch that ankle with omniscience, I watch Sofia go up, up, up . . .

And then *down*.

She lands on the side of her ankle instead of her foot and she can't do anything because of the height of the jump. I *hear* the snap and crack of bone as her Achilles loses will against the impact.

One of my heroes crashes to the floor.

Suddenly, the world stops. For these moments, Sofia was the center of it all, the only thing keeping this fragile machine from falling apart. Now she's broken, and so is the room around her. The pianist stops playing. Since we were all watching, we all stop talking.

And again, since we are not just an audience, we understand exactly what we all just witnessed.

Sofia, the professional, has not made a sound. She did not cry out in pain. Like a good little ballerina, she stays on mute. For better or worse, she has continued to let her body tell the story.

Robert stands and nods to the doorway for a dancer to get the physical therapist ready. He then walks over to Sofia, who is crumpled on the floor. He strokes her head like she is a small, stoic child. Her eyes are tight with pain but she does not cry.

The boys lift her up and she is gone.

Just . . . gone.

Maybe she will come back, but she won't come back as strong, and it won't be soon. And if she does not come back, then we have all just witnessed the terrible, silent extinguishing of a dream.

At her age, it would be fair to put money on her not coming back.

The worst part is that we've seen it before. Many, many times.

No, no, wait.

No. The worst part?

The worst part is that hearts lifted as her body fell.

The only way to really ignite our own chances comes from things like this.

This could be someone's moment.

"Is Jocelyn here?" asks Robert.

"She is in another rehearsal," says Diana. Her hands are on her hips. Stressed Diana.

"What about Sarah?"

"I sent her home to rest her knee for the run-through tomorrow," says Steven, one of the ballet masters.

"Well, do we have anyone else available? Fuck, who knows this role? Do we have to pull Jocelyn? When did we get so low on alternates?"

Robert looks *pissed*.

"We have only prepped three Auroras," says Diana.

"Well, why the fuck is that? We have eighty fucking dancers in the company. Go down to the basic and pull someone else in."

I'm so distracted by watching Diana get put in her place that I barely notice Alicia tapping me. When she smacks me, I pull my knee away and hiss, "What?"

"You!"

"You do it!"

"They're not gonna want me. You're a perfect Aurora."

She tries to raise my hand for me, and I yank it back to my side, suddenly envisioning offering myself up and then being told no in front of everyone.

But wait, this is what I've been waiting for. This is so stupid—what am I doing? I know the part, I can do it, this is a chance to skip eight slots understudying the Lilac Fairy and become what I should be, which is—

"Me," says a voice. "I'm here, I can do it, I'm on the basic, I know it."

It's a girl named Mathilde. No more special than I am. Not better. Not by any stretch of the imagination.

"Good," says Robert. "Let's go. We can take it from the Rose Adagio."

Mathilde steps frenziedly out of her warm-ups, showcasing her own slender limbs, and slides on her practice tutu. She smiles to the conductor to begin, as if she was always the one.

This is such an ice-cold world. Not five minutes since Sofia's body failed her and already, someone is in her spot. Even a psychic couldn't keep up with this shit.

Alicia shakes her head beside me.

"What?"

"You're not even helping yourself," she says. "That was your shot."

My heart is pounding.

Oh god, is this what it's like without my prescription?

"You didn't take it either," I say.

"I'm not right for Aurora. I'm still working on technique for something like that. You have it."

I feel like I might puke, even while I kind of respect her for knowing herself well enough.

Mathilde just bought herself a principal role for the cost of a moment of confidence. I made all this silent intention to go move forward aggressively, to take back what's mine. And the chance cracked from the heavens onto the ground in front of me and I did nothing.

Was I always this way? I think of myself as being strong and filled with power and yet these days I seem to have none.

What the fuck happened?

When rehearsal is over, I grab my things and go down to the stage. No one really notices me. Everyone is jet-lagged and burned out. It's the sort of night where no one even suggests a drink at the bar. Everyone wants to slide into their nice sheets, maybe order a tea or glass of wine to the room.

At least, that's what I want. I want to fall asleep with the balcony doors open and watch the curtains dance in the breeze. In

Paris, I never need the TV on to feel comforted. The city itself seems to hold me in its arms, and I never feel alone.

I want to order a glass of Sancerre or Beaujolais and take a Xanax, light up one of the delicate little prerolled CBD/THC combo joints I like, and be hypnotized to sleep.

But I won't. Because I am trying to be good.

I can't stop thinking about earlier. Sofia's shattered career, Mathilde's captured chance, my silence.

The theater is nearly empty. Or at least I think so until I see David in the wings, who is still not my favorite person right now. I ignore him. He must have come down here to try out the stage as well.

I go on to the stage with my small Bose speaker and my phone, and I put on Prokofiev's *Romeo and Juliet*—the balcony pas de deux.

The stage lights are off; there are only the working lights above the stage that turn on from a light switch. It doesn't matter.

I get into position and shut my eyes. When the music kicks in, I do something I haven't done in years.

I dance for no one at all, with no rules, no expectation, no choreography, only from what is inside me.

It's what I grew up doing. Making it up as I go, stringing together my favorite moves and embellishments.

"Need a practice partner?"

It's David.

"I'm still irritated with you."

"That was D.C. shit. We're in Paris now."

I am so tired that I feel completely out of my body. A thin sheen of sweat forms beneath the fabric of my leotard and tights. In my pointe shoes my feet hurt so much that they are simultaneously almost numb, probably the result of jet lag.

"Sure. Fine."

As we improvise the balcony pas de deux, I fly through the air, weightless in David's (admittedly) powerful strength, and land with soft grace on the dusty stage. My gaze is gentle on everything around me. I feel like I might laugh or cry, and in fact a noise comes out of me that sounds and feels like a single sob and also like a laugh, I don't know what it is, just that it's some deep emotion from a well in my core.

At the end of the piece, I nail the final position.

The stage lights come on suddenly, blinding and hot. It's so startling that it may as well be a bolt of lightning in the theater.

I squint up to the box to see who turned it on. I'm about to turn to leave, thinking they must be testing the lights or something, when a voice comes on the PA.

"Position."

The voice echoes so much that I can't tell if I recognize it, or even if it is a man or a woman.

I blink up at the godlike voice. Do I recognize it?

I decide to do as it says.

David and I look at each other.

"Shall we dance?" he asks.

I shrug and say, "Fine," again.

I take position and wait for . . . what?

The music begins from the theater sound system and from the first split second of the violin, I recognize it immediately as Aurora's Rose Adagio.

There are supposed to be four male dancers here, but I improvise with David to make something work.

I miss no cues.

In the first promenade, I am on one leg on pointe, and the other is (hip height) in an *attitude*. David moves me around and I have to do this four times without coming off pointe or lowering my leg. Between each rotation, I have to let go of David and balance by myself. The first time, I am shaky and let go of his hand only briefly. David looks in my eyes and gives me a calm, confident nod and whispers, "You're good."

When he promenades me for the next rotation, I let go, balanced, having no wobbles. And by the fourth rotation, my right leg is burning and my back is cramping from holding my leg up so long, but the confidence is there. I lift my hand off David's easily and balance. The balance goes on and on so long that David lets out a small laugh. I lift my chin to the light and a smile spreads across my face before I slowly, and with control, lower my leg. I *bourrée* forward and David is there to catch me for the next set of turns.

It's magical.

I use the whole stage, trusting in my pauses and my own abilities.

When I finish and the music ends, there is silence. Panting, I look up and wait for something. There is nothing, and then the lights go out.

I wait another moment, and then, feeling embarrassed, I gather my things and look once more to see if anyone has appeared.

They have. Two figures are walking down the aisle of the theater. Two men.

I put my bag back down and walk to the edge of the stage.

"Oh, shit," I say.

One of them starts to clap slowly as his face comes into view.

Sebastian. And beside him, Alessandro.

"Oh, hell no—this is messy," says David. And he walks away, leaving me virtually alone with the two men.

CHAPTER ELEVEN

Jocelyn

So . . . what do we do?"

I have asked the question before we even finish the first drink and before I've warmed from the cold New York streets.

When I ask, I don't know if I'm asking something silly or something huge. When Sebastian answers, he just laughs and makes a joke about another round. I don't really get an answer until a few drinks later.

I never feel drunk, only tipsy the whole time. Sebastian says that's the effect of good liquor. And I imagine that the intoxicatingly desirable water from the shining Big Berkey has something to do with it. I keep returning for refills in the gleaming kitchen that looks magazine ready and rarely used.

Around seven, he makes the music a little more up-tempo and a little louder. We shift to champagne—Moët & Chandon—and, the rain having stopped, we wind up on the rooftop deck looking out at the lights of the city.

My city.

New York City.

The lights in the buildings glisten out in the velvet darkness. It's odd, I notice, that it seems like we're nestled in a sea of comparative darkness. On one side, the city I've always dreamed of— the Empire State Building, the Chrysler Building—so much smaller than I ever thought—and the eminent glow of Times Square. On the other side, what feels to me like the *new* city—tall, heartless buildings with uniform glass sides, and that dominating, monumental obelisk: the Freedom Tower, and everything it represents.

And there we are in the middle, we three little people on a little roof. The clouds are cast in an oily grey glow by the paper moon above us. We're in the bottom of the valley of light, caught, perhaps as always, between one world and the next.

Sebastian turns against the stone balcony and faces us. Miles has just refilled our drinks, so they're cold and sparkling in our glasses. We stand wrapped in blankets, looking out at it all. Sylvie and I stand close. The air is wrapping around me, but I can feel it wrapping around them too.

I'm completely in the right place. Like sliding a box into a square hole just its size. That's where I am. I'm living in a memory. Living in a memory I will look back on in the future.

I will reflect on this moment as the one that defined the next part. The time in my life where I met the friend who stands beside me all those years later, and when I met the man who saw something in me and devoted himself to showing that gift to the world.

I will remember this as exactly when I stopped being the hoodrat in a tutu and became the New York ballerina drinking fine champagne on a rooftop in Manhattan.

I feel so at peace it's almost aggressive. Like the compulsion to burst into tears, only it's happiness, not misery.

I want to kiss them both. Climb inside both of them. Climb the Empire State like King Kong. Swing round the steeple like a career stripper. I want to wake up tomorrow as Sylvie. Wake up in the arms of Sebastian. I want to pick up a pink plastic kid's phone and call my mother and tell her I hate her.

That's when I realize that the drugs have hit.

Sebastian had mentioned that he thinks drugs could be essential in unlocking the best in any artist. Somehow, that led to him pulling out a small glass box, and Sylvie, a bit sycophantically if I'm honest, saying she'd do anything he thought would make her better.

He was hesitant, telling her he didn't want her to make any choices she wasn't sure about.

Didn't she hesitate over a glass of *champagne* earlier? Although, once in Sebastian's company, she loosened up. Or opened up. Or . . . something.

I sort of lost track of how it happened, how I ended up agreeing. All I know is that I had the *oh my god, do I do it* feeling that I would ordinarily associate with standing at the edge of a building.

He laid the pill on her tongue, her eyes shut. Then he gave me mine—which I took from his fingers and swallowed without his assistance.

"Guys, I think I feel them," I say.

They both crack up.

"What?"

"You just said that a minute ago!" says Sylvie. "I did it for the first time a few months ago. I was nervous too."

She glances at Sebastian and he gives her a wicked look of approval.

I feel suddenly very far away from them. Twenty yards maybe, and like I'm listening to them through paper towel rolls. My mind latches onto that image and I consider how the sharp cardboard would feel on my ear. I imagine stuffing my ear into the hole of it.

"I don't think I like this," I say.

"You are fine," says Sebastian, who has at some point lit a cigarette and now hands it to Sylvie.

Are they . . . babysitting me?

Am I a problem?

He puts his hands on my shoulders and I feel the warmth and weight of them. "Listen, querida, you are fine. You took MDMA. It's a drug. You're supposed to feel different. Don't try to hang on to your everyday reality or you're going to drive yourself mad."

"Literally?" I ask, my tongue stumbling over the word, becoming every bit the child I have just decided I would prove I wasn't.

"No, not literally." He moves behind me and starts massaging my shoulders.

Holy shit. His thumbs move around the muscles in my back and it feels amazing. "Is this what massages usually feel like for people?" I ask. "I feel like whenever I get a massage it feels like nothing, it doesn't hurt and it doesn't feel good, but this—*unh.*" An almost pornographic noise comes out of me and I slap a hand over my mouth.

I expect them to laugh, but neither does. Sylvie is leaning against the banister and watching me with interest.

Sebastian, behind me, puts his cheek against my ear. Through my hair I can feel his breath and it sends a shiver down my spine.

"This is the drugs, that's all, Jocelyn. Everything always feels like this, but you don't take the time to notice. You're getting access to more of yourself. That's all, don't—"

My heart suddenly jumps and my hand shoots to my chest.

"Hey, *mi ángel*, hey. It is just adrenaline. Feel like you just avoided getting hit by a bus, right?"

I nod. "Mm-hmm."

"You're just afraid of losing control and your body is trying to protect you because this is new. But you and your mind and your body will learn together if you simply breathe. When was the last time you really breathed?"

He puts his arms around me, a hand over the hand still on my chest, and another on my stomach. "Breathe in . . . and out. In . . . and out."

I follow along, becoming calmer and more and more aware of his body heat behind me.

I nod after a few moments. "I feel better."

He lets me go slowly, my hair clinging to his stubble.

I put a hand on his arm, not thinking twice before reaching out to touch his sweater. It's thin and he has it pushed up to his elbows.

"Aren't you cold?" I ask.

He nods and says, "Why don't we go inside? How does that sound?"

"Mm-hmm . . ." says Sylvie.

Her lips are cherry red and she's running her fingers over them again and again.

"They're so soft," she says, turning her lips into a small smile. "Are yours soft too?" she asks.

She drifts toward me.

I wet my lips and touch them. They are soft.

"Have they always been like that?"

"Maybe," she responds.

Oh, shit, did I say that out loud?

"Shh."

She reaches out and touches my lips.

Oh, her finger feels soft too. The traction of her touch tugs on my lip. I reach out to touch hers.

Hers are more pillowy than mine. And wetter.

Without warning, Sylvie's finger goes deeper into my mouth, as I mindlessly open it for her. Her thumb presses down on my tongue, her other fingertips and fingernails barely, softly pressing on my jaw and cheekbone.

I don't think about what I'm doing as I mirror her movements with my own thumb on her tongue. I give a small gasp as I feel the hot wetness of it.

I catch her eyes, and she catches mine. I could fall in.

My inner thighs begin to go weak, a pulsing starting to run through my body. My heartbeat, but everywhere.

"Girls," says Sebastian, "it'll feel better inside."

It should have shattered the moment, but it doesn't. Instead, we just release each other and follow him like rose petals on a gentle wave.

We walk down the stairs and when the door opens, the golden glow of the house that was such a sweet relief when we first arrived is now even more inviting. I feel lucky, too, for the change in temperature.

Sylvie puts her hand in mine and we walk down the stairs together. Her hand feels so small and delicate. Our bodies are both so fragile—how do we just walk around every day and make it through alive?

"Because we're only so weak when we are allowed to be," says Sebastian.

He leads us to the living room again, where the lights have been dimmed substantially and an enormous candle burns on the coffee table. It smells like vanilla and tobacco.

I want to touch it.

Sebastian sits down on the couch. Miles comes over with a copper tray with a glass of red wine for each of us. We each take one. I take a sip and it tastes like touching silk.

Sylvie lies on her back and kicks one leg up on the back of the couch where she was sitting earlier—I thought she seemed casual then, but now she is positively spread-eagled.

"I have an idea," says Sebastian, standing up.

He goes over to the bookshelf and slides open a cabinet, exposing a beautiful record player.

Sylvie takes her shirt off, leaving only her bralette. Which is . . . way sexy, and not at all an everyday thing to wear under a T-shirt. Had she planned on someone seeing it?

I want to touch the shining straps.

I sit back down on the marble hearth as I had earlier, but it feels completely different. It is cold and flat and hot where the flames can reach. It is impossibly smooth and I can understand deeply how artists had thought and wanted to carve it into forms of the body.

I look at Sylvie again. I envy how bare her body is. Primal. Honest.

I take off my own shirt. I'm wearing a black bra.

The heat from the fire licks at my back.

"Oh, Jocelyn, it's snowing!" says Sylvie, stretching her head back behind her, exposing a long, swanlike neck.

I follow her long-lashed gaze and see that it is.

"Lucky to see the snow. I feel it doesn't snow that much here anymore. How do you like the wine?" Sebastian asks.

I take another sip. "It's fucking magic."

They both laugh and Sylvie writhes her way up to drink some. When she does, she says, "It's like flowers and . . ."

"Silk," I offer.

"Yes, silk . . ."

She takes another sip and sets the glass down.

"Both of you girls, get up."

We both look toward him and when he gestures with both hands to rise, we do.

"I want you to dance for me."

Sylvie smiles. I stare at him, trying to understand. I want to sink further into this feeling, not to exercise.

He lets the needle hit the record and then bounces around until he finds the right spot. It is a deep breath. Then an allegro beat I don't immediately recognize.

By the time the first lyrics hit, I recognize the song.

> *Man, she punched me like a dude*
> *Hold your mad hands, I cried*

It's "'Tis a Pity She Was a Whore" by David Bowie.

I can tell Sylvie doesn't recognize it, but she's a professional.

The song is up-tempo, more than 130 beats per minute, but any good dancer can keep up, if not excel.

When a moment ago I'd been lethargic, I now feel reanimated by the beat, which thrums deeper than I think possible. It feels like the music is coming from within me, especially once I'm moving, which I suddenly am.

"Have fun, girls—do not forget to have fun! For god's sake, you're on drugs! The song is tongue-in-cheek! Sylvie, let go. Look to Jocelyn, she's got it!"

I know the lyrics, so I can toy with those. I extend my hands toward Sebastian, I stretch my legs out long.

I look to Sylvie and give her a small nod. She nods back.

I go to her and lift her in the air.

"Release, Sylvie, *release*!"

She punches the air wildly in time, kicking with control until I set her down and she gracefully bows on the ground, and I spin in tight pirouettes, on my hardened, bare toes.

The movement feels good, the blood coursing through me amplifies the feelings I'm already experiencing. I feel euphoric. Ecstatic. Though I guess that is no surprise.

Sylvie spins around me and then in perfect time, matches my pirouettes.

We end at the same moment, Sylvie stretching her leg onto my shoulder as I do a *cambré* so deep I can see into the kitchen.

We let go and start laughing.

"One more," he says, changing the record.

We compose ourselves.

He puts on another one I know. James Brown.

I used to listen to that album all the time when I was a kid at Mimi's house, intrigued by the unusual repetition of words in "It's a Man's Man's Man's World," which is the very song he puts on.

The other song was fun, high tempo, energetic. But this is decidedly hotter.

The lazy, dragging three-quarter time. The strings.

Sylvie and I look at each other.

Sebastian comes over to us, speaking low now.

"Did you like when she had her finger in your mouth?"

"Aa—"

"Don't look at me, look at her. Look her in the eyes."

We obey.

My heart begins to thunder in my rib cage again, and I can see in Sylvie's eyes that it's happening to her too. A shade of darkness appears behind her pale irises.

We dance. It's sensual and charged with sexuality.

We move together, using the length and control of our limbs, the connection of our bodies to each other's, and the electricity coming from within.

Sebastian comments on the sidelines, seeming a hundred miles away.

"Touch her.

"Let her go.

"Do you want to feel the wetness of her tongue again?

"Is your heart beating harder than usual?"

When the song ends, we're forehead to forehead.

I don't know who moves first. All I know is that all of a sudden her tongue isn't on my thumb, it's in my mouth. The softness and plushness of her lips against my own feels completely different than with a guy. It feels like a soft-skinned body rolling around in the world's softest sheets.

My hand moves to her hair as my desire intensifies.

Her hand moves to my waist. Her other to my bra, where she reaches beneath the band and puts a thumb on my nipple, which is hard and alert. It sends a wave through me that ends between my legs, and without meaning to, I move closer to her. Our narrow hips are flat against each other.

It doesn't even seem strange that Sebastian is here. Somehow it feels right. Like our shaman is guiding us toward something we couldn't have known we wanted.

The feeling of her against me is so new and unusual. Her frame so similar to mine, I almost feel like I'm hallucinating the

whole thing, and it's all me, everywhere. An elaborate mastur-
bation.

But it isn't.

I can't remember afterward how we make our way to a bedroom, but we do.

It's a king-size bed, which I've never been in before. It feels
freakishly big, like it's a stage for exactly this.

Sebastian is in his joggers the whole time. At some point he
removed his sweater, but we had both missed it.

At one point I'm lying on the bed with my head in Sebastian's
lap. He's playing with my hair, and his fingertips on my scalp feel
as erotic as anything else.

"Do you like the way she feels?" he asks.

I nod.

Sylvie is kissing my jaw, then my neck, then my collarbone,
then my tits, my abdomen, my hip bones—and that's when I start
to writhe from the *want*.

She holds me down, and after what feels like a year of teasing
me, she puts her hot, wet mouth on me where I'm also hot and
wet. My body pulses deeply and I feel like she can probably taste it.

I *hope* she can.

I'm in a state of sensory inundation that I've never experienced
in my life. I've only had sex with two losers from my hometown,
and that was hard, sharp-angled, and had no build. With the first
one, I was fourteen. It was a first love sort of thing, but he was a
bad kisser. He was too wet, too hard, had no rhythm to it. He kept
his Metallica shirt on and his keys jangled on the futon next to us.
When he finished, not long after he started, I walked precariously
to the Jack-and-Jill bathroom he shared with his single father. I
was in the middle of using off-brand tissues from a beige box to
catch the results of the experience when his father knocked on the

door saying, "Hey, kiddo, don't forget to empty the dog shit bin in the backyard, okay?"

We slept together several times after that.

The next guy was the town bad boy, who I found out the difficult way was an absolute little bitch around his mother, and that he slept with a stuffed rabbit. If he had been a cool guy maybe I wouldn't have objected so much, but since he acted so *cool* all the time, it was not okay. And the sex was weird. Performative. He looked at his own abs the whole time and made these high-pitched noises I couldn't ignore.

It was nothing like this.

This is silk; this is falling endlessly into the soft thickness of the curtains I'd hide behind when I was young; it's candlelight and it's cashmere; it's dream and symbiosis; it's . . . symphonic.

The door to the balcony is open. I can hear the noisy streets, though they're quieter down here than in Midtown. Music and voices float up on the breeze that hits my bare skin. I feel like I imagine every bit of this, from the city to the sea. The voices outside, and the passion inside.

Sebastian doesn't touch either of us sexually while Sylvie and I explore each other's bodies. I taste every part of Sylvie and she tastes every part of me. We're entangled for ages, just feeling things, and feeling more, then cooling off, then heating up again.

Sebastian tells us what to do, sometimes.

"Touch her here.

"Put your palms on her thighs.

"Let your tits touch hers."

Then he asks questions.

"How do you feel?

"Do you like when she does that?

"If you want it harder, tell her. If you want more, ask for it."

Eventually it comes to a surprisingly natural conclusion. Sylvie and I take a shower and somehow we invite Sebastian in with us. He resists at first, and then says, "You girls are putting me through something tonight. I had no idea."

But then he takes his clothes off and joins us in his shower, where the water feels like rain.

I can't help but look at Sebastian's body as he washes his face and wets his hair. He looks like a model. On the cover of *Vogue Italia* or *Vogue España*. His body shows that he was an incredible dancer. Muscles that go so deep into the core that they practically replace the skeleton.

I want to see him dance too.

So many of the guys in the company are appealing. No one has anything but a beautiful build. Half of them are gay, a few are not appealing, and the others are too cocky to really become interested.

But this is a man. This is a real *man*.

"Can I ask you something?" asks Sylvie.

"Sure," he says.

"How old are you?"

He laughs. "I'm forty. Still feels strange to say. I've only had a few weeks to get used to it."

"And you have this house? Are your parents movie stars or something?"

She's kidding, but he shrugs. "Maybe."

He takes a few pumps of shampoo and has her turn around. He starts to wash her hair.

Envy, for the first time, sneaks into the scenario.

But it turns out I'm next, and he does the same for me, but it doesn't satisfy the envious part of me.

When we're clean, he hands us towels.

"Wait, are these warm too? Did they just come out of the dryer or something?" I ask.

"Heated rods," he says, tapping one and then handing a towel to Sylvie.

He wraps one around his waist, hiding his substantial appeal, and then hands us also two robes of plush, incredibly soft terry cloth.

He looks at us with our hair in towels and our bodies wrapped in the thick fabric.

"I have an idea," he says. He cocks his head at us. "How about the city's best Chinese?"

Sylvie and I both go, "Oh my god."

"That sounds *so good*," I say.

"Wow, I can't remember the last time I had Chinese food," Sylvie adds.

Half an hour later, we're stretched out on his bed eating General Tso's chicken, fried rice, dumplings, egg rolls, and watching *Breakfast at Tiffany's* on a huge screen that masqueraded as a painting.

The drugs have fully worn off and I'm finally getting drowsy but feel deeply content. I don't have the unpleasant sting of regret or fog of awkwardness I might have expected.

It's as if what we did was just a part of adult life I had simply never known.

Or maybe not adult life, maybe just chic life. Cosmopolitan life.

I eat until I'm too full to take another bite and set my plate aside on the rolling table he has pulled up beside the bed. I curl up with the plush pillows and watch Holly Golightly host her party, take the town, and then I fall asleep.

I wake up only once during the night, when the movie has ended and some black-and-white show has replaced it.

I feel something on the bed beside me and hear noises I can't quite understand at first. Breathing and whispering.

I try not to be noticed as I look.

Sylvie and Sebastian are having sex. Beside me. Practically on top of me.

I know that after everything that occurred that night, I should seriously not be alarmed or feel dirty about it. But there's something about the secretness of it, something about the fact that it's happening beside my sleeping body that makes it feel different.

I wonder then if they had both wished I hadn't been here the whole time.

I lie there awake, trying not to listen, trying not to breathe or be caught for a long time. The movie is an old Dracula one with bizarre imagery that's the last thing I'd want to watch right before bed and which completely displaces the bright colors of Holly's New York.

Tonight had been fun. Weird. Different. And now I just feel dirty. I know it will be the last time I *go there* with Sebastian. I wonder if Sylvie will feel the same in the morning.

Finally, finally, I fall back to sleep. But this time I don't feel quite as at peace as I did.

I feel guilty. I feel alone. And I want to yearn for home, but there is no home left to yearn for.

CHAPTER TWELVE

Sylvie

I smile coolly at the two men and put my hands on my hips. Sebastian's eyes scan my body. Looking for changes, good or bad, I feel sure.

"Well, I must say, I have missed watching you, Ms. Carter," says Sebastian.

Knowing he would be here did not prepare me for how it feels to see him again. I crave one of my vices, but remember the deal I made with myself.

This is quite a test from the universe.

"You are every bit as good as you once were. It's strange, because it's not what I've heard."

Sebastian's words sting, but there's no way I'm going to let him see that.

"Right, well, I suppose it depends on who you ask," I say.

"Come down here. I don't want to strain my neck to catch up with you. You must need a rest. Why don't we all go round the corner to Little Red Door—do you still like it there? Alex, what do you say?"

I *love* Little Red Door. They make some of my favorite cocktails in Paris, and I used to love the intimacy of the place.

"I would love to," says Alessandro. "I want to find out a little more about how you can dance like that but still remain on the basic."

I resent him for sounding so *on Sebastian's side*.

Sebastian scoffs. "If you want to know about that, I can certainly tell you." He pats him on the back and guides him toward the exit.

"I'll have to go to the hotel for nicer clothes."

Sebastian stops and turns around to me.

"Querida, you know a ballerina does not need to dress herself up. You are the decoration. Do not gild the lily, love."

He continues to leave.

I can't say no. Partly out of morbid curiosity and partly because I don't know how much power he still has. Just because he briefly cared to make me happy once before means nothing about what he'll do now. He wants to be placated. I'm good at placating him.

I have to go. This situation is too loaded to ignore. And for the first time in ages, I feel something. I'm not even sure if it's a good something or a bad something, but it's *something*. Is it because I stopped numbing myself, or is it just Sebastian? Or is it Alex?

I pull out my phone and send a text I never thought I would again.

Will you meet me? I need you.

The texting bubbles come up immediately and then disappear. I add another line:

I know. But Sebastian. And Alessandro. Whole thing. Little Red Door.

After a moment she responds.

You've got to be fucking kidding me.

I roll my eyes. Great. So that's a no.

I run to the wings and change quickly. I stuff my rehearsal clothes and pointe shoes in my bag, not feeling as if I have time to go to the dressing room. Thank goodness my warm-ups are semichic and black.

The streets are noisy and busy, even though it's a weeknight. There's a light drizzle, and my body feels like it's not structured around bone but around light, bending flower stems. I feel weird.

I can feel every beat of my heart. Every drop of rain. The unevenness of the streets beneath my slides.

I should never have sent that text. I will pay for that, I'm sure.

Little Red Door is packed, but there is a high top available in the very back. A red votive candle lights up the table. I wonder if Sebastian reserved the table somehow, though they definitely don't take reservations.

Judging by how quickly someone comes over to take our order, he is well known here. I suppose it makes sense now that he lives in Paris. Of course, he'd come back here, to this place, of all places.

And I'm sure the staff loves him. If nothing else, I can say that Sebastian is an excellent tipper and extremely charming.

"A corpse reviver for the reanimation of this girl's potential, and for you?"

Alessandro stares at Sebastian a beat too long and then says, "I'll have the same."

"Trois d'entre eux, alors, cher."

"Make it four," says a voice behind me.

Oh my god, she came. She actually came.

Jocelyn is an actual vision, perhaps seeming more beautiful and angelic due to my desperate gratitude.

Her hair is pulled back in a tight ponytail, her face glowing and a little damp from the rain. She's in her Burberry trench coat, and when she takes it off, she reveals herself to be in a black satin dress with extremely delicate straps. It's the perfect look on her.

"Way to make me look like I just got released from the hospital," I say quietly as she kisses me on the cheek, playing the French girl very well.

"Outdressing you is the cost of an emergency rescue."

"You look beautiful as ever, JoJo," says Sebastian.

"You look old," she says as easily as if she'd said *You look well*.

Sebastian is stunned for a split second, then bursts into laughter. "How have I lived without the two of you?"

Jocelyn—"JoJo"—and I share a look and say nothing.

The drinks arrive and Sebastian calls for a toast.

"To what?" asks Alessandro, who looks at me, giving me the ghost of a wink.

He's referencing the fact that I said I hate when people do that. This strangely foreign moment of recognition fills me with warmth.

"To my discoveries, JoJo and Sylvie."

I hold up my glass and clink it with theirs. I look at Sebastian and Jocelyn and think about how things used to be.

God, I have changed so much so fast.

I would never have believed it, but by midnight, I'm actually having a good time. I'm surprised because I've had only a little bit to drink and nothing harder to lean on. I haven't even craved a cigarette. I'm also surprised because if you'd asked me to come up with my nightmare dinner party, it would have involved everyone here. Jocelyn and Sebastian to trigger painful memories, and Alessandro, whom I wanted desperately to impress.

I'm currently cracking up, my hand in Jocelyn's, leaning on her so I don't fall out of my chair laughing. She's dying laughing, too, and it's somehow as if no time and no animosity have ever passed between us.

"Oh my god, we should go!" I say. "Not tonight, but before we leave."

"To a sex club?" Alessandro looks amused.

"Yes! They're so fun. Really."

"Don't tell me you've never been," says Jocelyn, leaning forward. She is still holding my hand, and now it's in her lap, clutched between her narrow fingers.

"I have not, and suddenly I feel like the prude at the table, and that, I have to say, is a new feeling for me." His gaze lands briefly on mine.

"It's a very good time with these two," says Sebastian. "Especially if you're the one taking them home."

My head whips in his direction and I feel Jocelyn stiffen beside me.

"I suppose you have this role now, in my place, no?" asks Sebastian, lighting a cigarette.

Alessandro looks between us all. Jocelyn and I stare at Sebastian, both of us visibly uncomfortable.

"No," says Alessandro.

"Oh"—he laughs—"my apologies. Well, if you get the chance, I say take it. If you want a little more unsolicited advice—" He leans forward on the table toward Alessandro, who does not move. "If you have to pick one, don't go with that one."

He points at me.

"She's a little hard to handle. Bit of a drug problem. Takes things personally. Used to be anorexic, but it doesn't look like she has that problem anymore."

He smiles at me. Jocelyn squeezes my hand.

The sudden downturn in the conversation hits me deeply. Pain is always worse when it follows joy.

I can't find anything to say, but Jocelyn speaks before I have to.

"Well, I don't think Sylvie has put any offers on the table, so Alessandro is probably not going to find out what bullshit that all was. Everything with you was always bullshit."

"Oh no? I heard about a little mishap recently in the quick-change booth in D.C. Was that . . . also bullshit?"

Jocelyn looks at me. I'm on my own.

I don't want to run away and I really don't want to stay anymore.

Alessandro moves toward me, his lips close to my ear. "What do you say we get out of here?"

"Yes," I say quickly.

He finishes the last of his gin, the large ice cube rattling as he sets down the glass. "We're going. It's getting late. It was nice to have a chance to get to know you a bit more, Jocelyn. Sebastian"— he holds out his hand—"an honor."

There's something cruel dripping from his words.

Sebastian doesn't notice, but Jocelyn is glaring at me in disbelief. It's only then that I realize I'm the one who called her here, and now I'm leaving her.

I'm leaving her alone with Sebastian.

"Jocelyn, do you want to leave with us?"

It's an incredible shame that these words do not come out of my mouth, but out of Alessandro's. And he sounds tense.

"That's a great idea," she says. She's pissed.

Somehow, the interaction doesn't read as strained to Sebastian, who still looks at ease and in control. Maybe he's incapable of losing control these days.

The three of us leave Sebastian, who is immediately embroiled in a conversation with girls who either know who he is or can just tell he's a man with power and money.

As soon as we're on the street, I breathe in the air, feeling as if I'd been underwater. It's dry outside now—the rain has stopped. Now it smells like warm wet stone and candles just blown out. All around us the streets are filled with people leading different lives than ours. The patios are glittering with clinking glasses; and the aromas of late-night butter and wine sauces waft through the air.

And when I open my eyes after only a moment of enjoying the Parisianness of it all, the relief of being away from Sebastian, I am slammed right back down to reality.

"You get how incredibly fucked this was, right?" says Jocelyn.

A few heads turn.

"We had a good time, didn't we? It was better than I thought it would be."

She shakes her head, unable to find the words to communicate with me. I can tell that's what she's feeling. I can tell because I know her. I can tell because I feel it, too, and I can't quite put my finger on why.

Jocelyn turns in a perfect circle and flies away from us. She's filled with rage, and it shows. Intensity always shows in her form, from her tiptoes to her eyelashes.

"This was—" starts Alessandro.

"Take me to your flat."

He looks surprised. "What?"

"You said you have a flat here, in Paris, right? Take me."

A car sloshes past us.

He nods. "Yeah, all right, let's go."

We take a taxi, which feels extremely retro under the circumstances. Between the rain of the night and the awkwardness we are leaving behind, I've never been so happy to be in the anonymity of an actual *taxi*. I'm just an anonymous young woman with an anonymous man.

Alessandro's hand finds my thigh. I put my hand on top of his and when he squeezes my leg, I squeeze his hand. My breath catches at his touch, and I feel a flutter in my stomach.

We don't talk about Sebastian. We sit in silence, but it's not tense—or, it is, but in a good way. His discomfort at the way things went at the end at Little Red Door seems to have turned into desire. If that's what always happens when he's upset, I'll take it.

I haven't wanted someone like this in a very long time.

For the last several years, my sex life has been completely utilitarian.

And for what purpose, really, I'm not sure, because it rarely resulted in anything much for me. It's really more of an ego thing than a body thing.

But this is different: this is an awakening of something inside me that I've been starting to believe was dead.

We arrive in front of an old building on a stony street with yellow streetlamps.

Alessandro pulls out cash, saying, *"Merci, monsieur. Gardez la monnaie. Passe une bonne nuit. J'espère que c'est chargé pour toi."*

"Oh, merci beaucoup, monsieur. Vous aussi passez une bonne nuit. Boire un verre pour moi, eh?"

The two of them laugh and I understand enough words to know that it's probably a very good tip and something about a drink.

We get out onto the street and he leads me to a scarlet door. There are brass numbers on the side of it: one seven six.

I look around us to see if I even know where we are. I don't.

It's another downtown of some kind, more restaurants where people are still having a good time.

Once inside, we climb a flight of steep stairs. It's dark at the top.

"You ready for this?" he asks.

My heart skips.

He presses a button that I think is an old light switch and then starts to run.

"Come on!"

I run behind him. "Why are we running?"

"The light is on a timer!"

We don't make it in time and the hallway goes pitch-black.

"Dammit," he says.

"Why would they *do* this?"

I cannot see him but reach for him and find his side. He takes my hand and squeezes it. "We have to be careful here. There's an obnoxious little table somewhere—ah, fuck! These old buildings with their antiquated electric."

From the sound, it's clear he's found it. "Oh, are you okay?"

He laughs, and I realize it's the first time I've heard him do it. It makes me laugh too.

"That fucking table."

"Aw," I say.

Suddenly he puts his hand on my waist and lifts me into the air. Instinctively I assist him though I don't know what he's doing.

He sets me on the table.

"If it's going to be here, it really ought to serve a good purpose."

I still can't see him. There's only the smallest sliver of moonlight coming in through a window at the end of the hall.

But I feel him.

He kisses me hard and his light stubble scratches at my skin in a way that makes me want more. He puts his hand on my throat and then kisses me there. His big hands wrap around my narrow shoulders.

With assertion, he throws open my legs and moves aside my underwear.

His mouth is on me in a moment and the intensity of the immediate feeling causes me to cry out.

"*Shh*, people are sleeping here."

I know it's true, but he says it like he's kidding.

"Oh my god," I whisper when his mouth returns to me.

Just as quickly, he releases me, and I'm alone momentarily in the dark.

"Alex?"

In my ear, he says, "Come on, what's taking you so long?"

I jump off the table and my legs are jelly. I let him lead me down the dark hallway.

Finally we arrive at a door, the one at the very end of the hallway, and he removes a key from his pocket and puts it into the lock with a thick, metallic grinding sound. The door opens and I can tell from the sound that it's a thick old door. Not the paper-thin bathroom doors that pass as front doors in the cheap new builds.

He hits a switch and a chandelier turns on in the dusty turquoise room before us.

"Wow," I say, stepping in. "This place is just . . . yours? Sitting here in Paris, unused?"

He shrugs. "My sisters and I share it. It was our grandmother's place. Most of the furniture here was hers. I never wanted to update it or anything. You know, some electric or plumbing issues of course I have had fixed. But for the most part it's just as it was left by her. She's the one who taught me French."

I gaze at the ceiling, which has ornately carved crown molding. The floor creaks a little as I step forward to look at a portrait on the wall. An old oil painting that looks worthy of a museum.

"Who is this?" I point without touching.

"That was her mother. She died in childbirth."

I make a face.

"I know, it's so nineteenth century, isn't it?" He reaches out his hand. "But follow me, because you haven't even seen the best part."

I follow him, and he opens a set of double doors. It's the bedroom. A large, plush-looking canopy bed.

"It's like time travel."

"Yes, only the sheets are washed with Tide by a cleaning woman who comes before I arrive."

I laugh. "So this is the best part? The bedroom? How cliché . . ." I say as he pulls back the heavy curtains on a set of French doors.

But then a gasp leaves my body. Like I've been punched in the gut. Before me lies a star-studded cloth of glimmering stars. Orange and white and gold and red. And standing amid them all is the shimmering Eiffel Tower.

"Oh—my . . ."

Alessandro laughs and opens the doors.

The air gusts in, blowing my hair back a little.

We step out onto the balcony. I wrap my hands around the ancient iron and look out.

And I'm suddenly reminded of a night five years ago that changed my life.

My heart starts to pound.

Sebastian. I cannot believe I was just with him. With him *and* Alessandro. It hadn't felt so dramatic during the moment, but now it feels too bizarre for words. A clashing of worlds. A return from the past.

Talk about time travel.

The little voice in my mind starts to whisper, *Are you ever going to talk about what happened? Are you ever going to do anything about it? Are you even going to* think *about it, or just keep pretending everything is fine?*

"Are you okay?" asks Alessandro.

I blink a few times and then look at him.

Here is this man before me; his station is above mine. If he wants to change my life for the better or the worse, he has the power to do it. And I am sucked in by him. By his allure, his ability to seem casual and nonchalant, like he barely cares about anything, when clearly, he cares deeply, unwaveringly, and passionately. I'm drawn in by Alessandro for so many of the same reasons that I was drawn in by Sebastian.

Am I an idiot?

Am I the girl who does not learn her lesson and she has to be beaten over the head with it?

"I'm fine," I say. "I'm sorry, it's nothing. I just . . ."

"Just what?"

I bite my lip and stare at him for a moment before looking out at the breathtaking view again and hate myself for being unable to enjoy what is happening in the now because I'm so hamstrung by the past.

I realize with a start that my emergency Xanax is not with me. It's in my hotel room. I hadn't thought I'd be gone this long or for the night.

The idea that a panic attack might take me over begins to creep through me, and I breathe in deeply.

I want the challenge. I want to become strong again like I used to be.

"Sebastian and I used to be together. Sort of. And it got . . . well, it got messy at the end. He sort of . . ."

Ruined me. The words David said come back to haunt me.

He takes my hand. "I know about that," he says. "I had forgotten about it. Just some tabloid shit to me, at the time. Never really thought about it. But I remembered it. Put it together." He grins a little. "Did some light googling."

"Ah. Dammit."

"It's okay. It's him. Not you."

The panic subsides a little. "I . . ." I'm not sure what to say.

"Why don't you take a moment," says Alessandro patiently. "I'll go get us some wine. Okay?"

I nod. I breathe.

He hesitates for a moment but then he leaves.

It has become one of my worst fears to have big feelings and nothing to do with them.

I cannot—will not—freak out, not here, not with Alessandro. For so many reasons. For one thing, what if he tells someone that I came over here and freaked out? That's exactly the kind of thing I can't have circulating about me. My reputation can't take it.

And for another thing, what if I do freak out, and as always, I go home, and the only way to feel better is to shut out the world until I'm asleep, only to wake up and do it again? What a waste of a night in this historic flat with this unbelievable view. How stupid am I if I just keep doing this? I'm coping instead of living. I'm surviving instead of breathing. I'm waiting for something, but what would it take for me to live again?

I make a choice, then, as I watch the lights twinkle before me.

Tonight, just tonight, I will try to do it the hard way. Not that anyone on the planet could really believe that drinking red wine with Alessandro Russo in his gorgeous, prewar apartment in Paris looking out at the City of Light is exactly the hard way.

But that's the funny thing about being broken; the good stuff sometimes has absolutely no relationship to the bad stuff.

Tonight I will pretend I'm happy and light and see if my heart takes the cue from my mind.

When he returns with the wine, I turn and smile. "Sorry, I'm good now. Just a bit of a long day."

"It's okay. You sure?"

"I'm sure. What's the wine?"

"Oh." He looks at it and sits down on the love seat and begins to open the bottle.

I watch his fingers wind expertly around the metal corkscrew.

"It's just a little Beaujolais. It's from a small vineyard of a family friend. My great-grandmother lived out the war years there. Not a bad way to pass the time, eh?"

"Not at all. Sometimes I wish life were that simple."

"What, simple like taking cover during a war by hiding on a large property out of the line of fire?"

"Oh . . . no, sorry—"

"I'm just kidding. Tell me what you mean. Here." He hands me my glass of wine.

We clink glasses and take a sip, enjoying the view and fresh air. It's delicious. "This is *very* good."

"It's special, isn't it?"

"Yes, definitely."

"Okay, now tell me what you mean."

"I mean . . . I know it's a gift to have a gift, you know? I know it's something a lot of people would kill for, but sometimes I wish I didn't even want this thing. It's so *hard* and it's, like, if you're not the best, then what's the point? It's not as if you can really get hap-piness from being in the middle," I say.

"It's not as if *you* can really get happiness from being in the middle."

"Right. Well. That's me."

"Me too."

"But you *are* the best. You're a household name. Everyone knows you, everyone will know you forever, whenever anyone . . . I don't know, *googles* the best dancers of all time, you'll come up."

"You could be the same. You're good enough."

"Maybe I was."

"Were you . . . better once? I don't understand."

"I don't know, I was at least very driven. I used to *breathe* ballet."

"What do you do now?"

"I don't know. The days slip by and I don't think anything happens at all. I rehearse, I perform, I take a break, I don't know."

"You're good, Sylvie. If you want to keep doing it, then be as good as it takes you to be happy. But you know that if it ever stops making you happy, you can just stop. You might have been a bal-lerina your whole life so far, but that doesn't mean that's who you need to be for the rest of your life. Not if you don't want to be."

My breathing quickens a little and I'm not quite able to tell why. I take another sip.

"How does it make you feel to think about leaving?"

"Relieved and then immediately panicked and out of control. I don't think it's possible for me to let go of it."

He nods. "I think you're better than good, Sylvie, and if you want to become the best, it's there for you. But you don't need to feel like that's your only way to matter."

I gnaw on my lip and decide whether or not to say what's really on my mind. I shake my head and decide not to, but then say it anyway.

"The thing is, I *had* it. I had it and then no one believed I had earned it and then I fucking lost it all because of—*shit*!"

I drop my wineglass, shards scattering everywhere on the balcony like a snowball thrown by a good arm, wine exploding across the concrete canvas.

"Oh my god, Alex, I'm so sorry. I'm so stupid and embarrassed—"

I drop to my knees and start to pick up the pieces.

"No, no, hey, stop, hey." He takes my shoulder.

I'm close to tears. The humiliation is too much. It's like I'm completely unsocialized. I used to be cool, I used to be composed, I used to have confidence. When did I become this boring drag of a girl talking about her feelings, shattering glass everywhere and spilling *special* wine?

"I'm sorry," I say, trying suddenly not to cry.

"It's okay. It doesn't matter—look."

And he releases his glass, breaking more glass and spilling more wine.

I gasp. "Alex!"

"It's okay. It doesn't matter. It's only a wineglass; it's only wine. Please. Don't sweat the small stuff. Don't cry over spilled wine. It's already done. It's okay. You need to breathe, please, it's okay!" He laughs. "Oh, Sylvie."

He pulls me into a hug and I start to cry, which only compounds my embarrassment.

But after a moment, when the crying really takes hold, I just accept his chest as a pillow and let him squeeze me. My fingers tighten around the fabric of his sweater, still a little damp from earlier, so my tears blend in.

After a few moments, I feel a little less heavy, the tears not in a knot in my throat anymore or a well behind my eyes. I breathe in and step away with a controlled breath outward.

"I'm sorry," I say.

"Don't say I'm sorry. You should rarely say I'm sorry. People often say I'm sorry when they should be simply saying *thank you*."

I smile and wipe at the inevitable makeup under my eyes. "Thank you."

"There you go. Watch your step. Just go inside and freshen up—the restroom is right over there. I'll take care of this."

"I—"

"You're welcome. Now get out of my way."

He winks and I leave the balcony, stepping carefully around the wine and glass.

The restroom is old and romantic with faded pinstriped wallpaper and a claw-foot tub. The mirror is a real mirror, not the cheap kind that warps everyone into fun house versions of themselves.

I look at myself and feel as though I don't even recognize the girl I'm looking at—but there's something about it that feels closer to *me* than I have looked in a long time. The unfamiliarity doesn't feel like a transformation so much as a revisitation after a long journey. I wash my face, deciding that no makeup is better than trying to salvage the bits that remain.

The soap smells like roses and the water feels good on my skin.

I brush out my hair and it is soft and buoyant after the humidity of the night. I breathe in deeply and feel somehow . . . better.

When, I wonder, was the last time I cried?

I open the bathroom door to hear that he has put on music and turned on a few more lights inside. I glance once more at the gorgeous view and then follow the noise to find Alessandro in the kitchen.

I look at the source of the music. Edith Piaf.

He's slicing a baguette and there is brie sitting out on its wax paper. There are raspberries in a paper basket. They're so fresh I can smell them.

"Are you hungry?" he asks.

I've barely eaten in so long. I haven't had an appetite in as long as I can remember, and I'm suddenly ravenous. "Please."

He hands me a mug.

"What's this?" I ask, peering in and then smelling it.

"It's your kiddie cup of wine. Less likely to break this one."

He grins mischievously and I roll my eyes, smiling. "Honestly it's probably for the best. Do you want help?"

"Okay, yes. Why don't you rinse the raspberries. They're from the farmers market, so they should be okay, but you know. Nature."

I take them over to the porcelain sink and turn on the faucet.

"So, when do you have enough time to do things like this? Stock your refrigerator with fresh farmers market groceries?"

"Well, if you look," he says, opening the door to the fridge, "there is almost nothing else in there. Some champagne, some butter and eggs, more cheese. Not much. But you must survive somehow. And in Paris, to me, this is the ideal stocking to have in one's own kitchen. All the Parisians I know, they go out and get their food fresh for dinner that night. The rest is just little snacks. And wine, of course—wine is always on hand."

I take a guess at a cabinet and find a bowl for the raspberries.

"I like that idea. I never cook. Can't do it at all. I've tried, but I'm a disaster."

"Well, when did you have the time? Don't beat yourself up about it. Ah, but see, what a beautiful job you've done on the raspberries! This is excellent. See, you're nearly a chef!"

I laugh as he throws a tea towel over his shoulder and then pops a berry in his mouth.

I take one, too, and it's the most delicious raspberry I've ever had.

"It's good, right?"

"Amazing."

He looks at me for a moment and then steps toward me. Gently, he takes my chin in his hand and looks down at me. I feel vulnerable and nervous as he looks into my eyes—no one has looked that closely. Not in a long time.

But I let him.

"You are beautiful, Sylvie Carter. You really are."

My heart skips. "I—"

And then his lips are on mine. He kisses me softly at first, our hands finding each other's bodies so we can pull each other closer. He tastes good, he smells good. He *feels* good. He *is* good.

The kiss feels different. It's gentle in a way I've never had. There's something behind it. Real feelings. Not obsession or a need to please. Not even sex. It's a magnetism that comes from the heart, not just the body.

As his hands touch me, I feel like I want to record every moment with my body, never forgetting how this feels.

We begin to kiss with more urgency, his breath deepening and my heartbeat quickening. He presses me against the wall, and my desire for him increases just as his does for me.

He lifts me off the ground with expert, practiced grace, and in turn, I wrap my legs around him.

He pulls me away from the wall and walks me, still wrapped around him, into the bedroom. He never stops kissing me, even when my hair falls in his face, he just moves it out of the way, curling it behind my ear and taking me where he wants me.

Once in the bedroom, he lays me down on the bed and I pull his shirt off. He lets me, and this time I get to relish the view of his strong, lean torso that the Internet would kill for.

He bends over me, my hands on his waist and his back as he kisses me, now pressing his lips everywhere he can reach.

"Fuck, Sylvie, I've wanted you like this since I saw you that first day. You're so intoxicating to me."

A moan comes out as he kisses me beneath my breasts on my rib cage. He peels off my top and unhooks my bra and throws both across the room. The bra lands on a statue of a saint, and I laugh. He looks and laughs, too, before kissing me hard and biting my lip.

It sends an eager shudder through me and I push him off to climb on top of him. It has been a long time since I've taken control over anything, especially a man. In all the hookups I've had over the last several years, I've practically been a passive participant. I'm the one bent over or on her back. I'm the one against the wall or saying, *yes, okay* and allowing it to happen.

It's not like me anymore to want desperately to make someone *else* feel good, even before I make myself feel good. But that's what I do.

I unbutton and unzip his pants, which are made of some soft, thick material that I can't stop touching.

He's incredibly hard and I feel flattered that I'm the one he wants that badly.

When I feel him, he reacts strongly, grabbing my upper arm, which his fingers wrap completely around.

"Sylvie . . ."

I love the feel of my name in his mouth.

In return I bend down and put him in my mouth.

He lets out a moan that makes me want him more, and I bet he can feel it, as I press my hands down on his hard, sculpted legs.

After a few moments, he pulls me up, my ear to his mouth. He says, "I need to be inside you. Now. Will you let me?"

I nod. "Yes, please, god, yes . . ."

He whips off my underwear and then pulls me back on top of him. It makes me gasp when he first enters me. I feel him everywhere and somehow he hits every spot of me at once.

It's a blur of grabbing and scratching and breathing. We move as if choreographed, but with such an organic, natural flow that it seems so *right*. It's so clear to me that we're feeling the exact same way. Everything between us feels like a language being spoken fluently and with the relief that people must feel when they've been away from their native country for too long.

And that is exactly how I used to feel when I danced.

CHAPTER THIRTEEN

Jocelyn

H urry up!"

"I'm doing it—give me a second."

Julian wrestles with his hooks as I readjust myself on the dressing room counter.

"Julian, we've got about five more— Oh god." I suck in a breath and plant a hand on the mirror in front of me. He pushes his hips into mine and I remember again why I'm having this fling. He's got no personality but he's an amazing dancer with a huge dick.

I look in the mirror at my own reflection instead of his, which is fine, because he's too busy looking down at himself to notice.

He grips my ribs and I grab at his hand, grinding back into him so he can go deeper.

He reaches around for my clit and finds it with remarkable accuracy.

The music from the stage is filtered through the speakers and the door. I know Sylvie is out there right now dancing her solo, which means everyone is watching the stage, even from the wings. They always watch when she's dancing.

He thrusts into me and I moan a little louder than I mean to.

We're dancing *Don Quixote*, and it might be my imagination, but ever since we got to Spain, every one of us has been a little hotter than usual. In part, it's because we're in Barcelona, which is beautiful and romantic. We drink Cava and wander the streets where the locals dance to flamenco music; and we join in, the music raw and echoing through the acoustics of the streets. Our hotel is beautiful but not removed from the culture of the city, which is sometimes the case. I've been waking up in the night to the sounds of couples arguing, flirting, musicians playing, teenagers laughing and speaking in loud, expressive Spanish. *Don Quixote* is also just plain *fun*. It's hard work, all of it is, but when it's fun, too, it's a little easier to let loose and feel free.

I don't even mind the interrupted nights of sleep or the amount of money I'm spending on bubbly wine, because with every moment spent in this world I grow further from the one I came from. And that's all I've wanted since I was old enough to understand my life.

Applause surges outside.

Julian pulls me in harder, going deeper and faster. He grabs my tits, pulling them out of my costume, which isn't easy. I start to get close but am suddenly interrupted when he pulls out and finishes outside me . . . and all over my costume.

"What the *fuck* is wrong with you?"

He isn't even finished yet when I spit the question at him.

Blood rushes to my cheeks as I realize I have no idea what to do next. I can't even reach the stain, I only saw it happen in the mirror.

He looks mortified, to his credit, as he puts himself back

together, before then saying, "I'm so sorry, Jocelyn—I have to go, you *know* I have to go, I'm so sorry."

He flees from the room, leaving my scarlet costume to match my hot, flushing skin.

Sylvie comes in almost as soon as he leaves, and immediately knows something is off.

"Jocelyn? What's up?"

She's catching her breath from the stage, and I'm catching mine too.

I move out of the sight of the mirror and back away. "Nothing, everything's fine."

"What just happened? He didn't . . ."

"No—what? No, no, oh my god." I sigh. "No, he just—"

I bite my lip and take a deep breath. "He just . . . he just fucking came all over my costume and I'm going to murder him, and I can't reach it and now I'm going to go out there with a big wet, white stain and Diana is going to kill me for looking messy and then fire the shit out of me when she realizes what it is."

I'm speaking fast, but Sylvie is running to her bag. At first, I think she heard her phone vibrating or something and is just trying to get away from what I told her.

"Turn around."

"What?"

In her hand she's holding a washcloth and her Nalgene bottle.

"No—oh my god, you can't."

"I'll wash my hands in isopropyl alcohol for the rest of the night once the show is over, but in the meantime, turn around."

I do so, incredibly reluctantly. She takes me by the hips, still holding her tools and forces me into position. And here I am again, bent over in front of the mirror while someone goes at it on my ass.

She scrubs and scrubs, then pulls out a blow-dryer and holds the fabric taut to dry it.

"What's happening in here?" asks one of the other girls, walking in and heading straight for the hair spray to fix one tiny strand of hair that's out of place.

That's how meticulous you have to be.

"Some idiot left a bottle of CeraVe on the chair and it opened all over her costume when she sat down to fix her ribbons."

I know the girl isn't going to ask for proof, but immediately worry that she will. But Sylvie has a small bottle handy already and picks it up with a roll of her eyes.

Satisfied, the girl cringes. "Oh my god, that's awful." She looks at the wet spot, patting her hair as it dries. "You really better get it out or it's going to look like she got jizz all over herself."

Sylvie laughs. "Seriously."

I smile tightly.

A moment later, we're alone again and Sylvie looks at me in the mirror. We both burst into laughter.

When she finishes, my costume looks good as new and it's time for me to rush out to the stage.

I make it just in time to glare at Julian, who's coming into the wings, and then make it into my position.

All in all, the night is okay. I feel like I dance well in front of an enthusiastic audience—even when they're quiet you can tell how engaged they are. I have sex endorphins and performing endorphins coursing through me. I have a friend—which is the only thing I was sure I *wouldn't* find upon joining a company.

There's nothing I could imagine that seems like it could go wrong.

Ha. Famous last words.

That night, when we leave the Gran Teatre del Liceu, I think I know the night I'll have. I think that Sylvie and I, as we leave arm in arm, will get to the Bar Bodega Montse, and order a few glasses of muscatel, eat some paella, discuss how I will *never* fuck Julian again, and possibly even find a few hot Spaniards to flirt with.

But instead, I hear *"Jocelyn Rose!"*

Despite how little I was expecting it, there is no mistaking that singsong voice or the use of my middle name.

My mother is in Barcelona.

My loud, brassy, fake-tanned cow of a mother is in Barcelona.

"What . . . the . . . fuck?"

"Is that your mom?" asks Sylvie.

"Tell me you don't see a resemblance."

I release Sylvie's arm and walk toward Brandy Banks. In a movie, she might be played by Jennifer Coolidge, but then it wouldn't quite work because Jennifer Coolidge is beloved and my mother is—I believe I mentioned—a horrible bovine monster.

"Surprise!" she says when I'm within ten feet of her. I stay at a healthy six-foot distance.

"What are you doing here? How did you . . ."

Afford it? Keep track of a passport long enough to make it to a different country? Navigate the arrangements of everything well enough that you could make it to my performance—and without suitcases, no less?

"Sweetheart," says a man coming up behind her. He's older and looks rich—my mother raised me to spot that with dependable success. "How's my little Brandywine?"

She giggles—*giggles*—and leans into him. "Georgie, this is my daughter, Jocelyn Rose."

My spine tingles with the irritation of being called by my first and middle name. She always does that. She clearly thinks having two feminine names makes me sound . . . something. Something better. And by extension, makes her sound better.

"Jocelyn Rose, so nice to meet you. It's about time. George Longworth, a pleasure. And you're Sylvie Carter, aren't you?" He holds a hand out to each of us respectfully.

"George Longworth?" asks Sylvie. She smiles. "Oh, wow, it really is a pleasure, I didn't know you'd be in Barcelona."

Who is this man? Why does Sylvie know him? Why does his name sound so familiar?

"Well, I wasn't going to be, but I met this lovely creature a few weeks ago at the bar at the Top of the Standard—and when it turned out that she has a daughter in the company, I was blown away. I mean *what* are the odds that I struck up a conversation with her and she's the mother of one of our new ingenues?" He laughs and winks at me.

"Head of the board," Sylvie whispers to me covertly as my mother and George Longworth do a few pecks on the lips.

"Fuck."

What are the odds? Well, they're pretty good. If I know my mother, and I hate that I do, she did enough research to find out exactly who she wanted to get in good with, who was single, and where they like to eat and drink.

That she could do this, that she would do this, does not surprise me. That it seems to have worked? That blows my mind.

"Anyway, when Brandy told me she hadn't had a chance to go *see* her daughter dance, well, I just had to get her over here. She wanted to keep it a surprise. I hope you're not too excited, there!"

He puts a hand out and then laughs hard. Brandy does too.

Sylvie smiles awkwardly. I raise my eyebrows. "That's amazing. What a whirlwind romance you two are having."

I can't believe it. In a matter of five minutes, everything has changed. My mother is not only here but is here and putting me in a position where I have to suck up to her and her new boyfriend, because he's someone who—if he wanted to—could make or break my career.

I remember his name now. Matt Martin had told us about him in the frenzy of the first day when I was ushered through the building at breakneck speed and told all the things to do and all the things to avoid.

Getting on George Longworth's bad side was one of them.

My mother has drawn a line in the sand between us, using a hot-pink acrylic nail, and now I must toe it. And I might be one of the country's best ballerinas—I might be—but even I don't know if I can do it.

"Hey," says Julian, coming up beside me. "You guys coming to Montse?"

"Ooh, mind if we tag along? I've got to piss like a racehorse and I'm so hungry I could *eat* a racehorse!"

Julian's eyes go wide, I feel my soul leave my body, and Sylvie—who has at some point grabbed my wrist—tightens her grip.

George gives a shocked spike of laughter and Brandy's tinkling, fake girlish laugh plumes around it. "You're a real pistol, I tell ya. I could go for a bite myself, and I'd love a chance to get to know the two newest and brightest."

Julian looks at me and goes white as a ghost. The misplaced cum earlier was one thing, but this time he's really done it. He just had to mention everyone's destination in front of *her*?

"See ya there, Julian."

He looks sorrier and more confused than I knew he could look. "Okay, see you soon . . ."

And he vanishes with all the other dancers flocking down the narrow corridor of Carrer de Sant Pau.

And then I have no choice but to go along too.

Sylvie and I lead the way, keeping a much brisker pace than Brandy and George can do. Brandy, I'm sure, is defending her slower pace by talking about her ankle, which she calls an old cheerleading injury but which I know to be an old sprain from my ninth birthday, which was spent in a bar called Peeping Tom's. She had climbed up onto the bar and fell *behind* the bar, breaking several bottles and a few shards of my developing dignity.

That was back when she didn't dream as big, aiming only for the hotshots like the general manager at the local bar.

If George Longworth is any indication, she has clearly stopped believing that even the sky constitutes a limit.

"I take it you still don't really get along with your mom," says Sylvie.

"Did you ever see *Heartbreakers*?"

"No."

"Of course not. Well, it's a mom and daughter con-artist team. Basically that's my mom's dream. I just got out in time."

"Yikes."

"You have no idea. It's amazing how an absolute idiot can also be that smart. Or, not smart, maybe, but . . . conniving. Because you see, what she did here is not just start dating someone rich. No, she started dating someone who can ruin my *life*. She found a way to control me, just when I finally couldn't be touched by her anymore."

"How can she control you?"

"Because! If I do what I want, which is to tell her to fuck off, then he's going to think I'm a total bitch. I have to keep her happy now, which if there's *one* thing she loves more than anything else—it's when people need to suck up to her. I have to make sure she's happy. And even worse, I can't control *her* at all, so if she's embarrassing or if she does something weird . . ." I glance back at her, where I see her pulling at the corners of her eyes. I turn back again, hoping to god that wasn't some fucked-up racist joke she learned from her long-dead, fucked-up racist father. "If she gets weird or makes *him* unhappy, then I am at risk. Again. Because I don't know that guy. What if he's cutthroat? What if he wants to end my career? He can just do it! Matteo said not to mess with him, and we don't know what he meant by that."

"Couldn't she ostensibly also . . . make your career by dating him? Because that has to be her goal, right?"

I shrug aggressively. "I have no idea what she wants. I suppose that after my being in the company for all of a year, she's shocked I'm not already successful. What she wants is: she wants to be rich. She wants *me* to get rich and she wants me to owe her. She wants me to be her road to a *classy life*," I mock her, even though Sylvie doesn't know her well enough to recognize that as one of her constant slogans.

"It's kind of weird," says Sylvie. "I mean . . . now what if you get a principal role or something? Will it just be because of that?"

I turn in shock to look at her. Is she trying to be an asshole? It almost seems like she's taking my sudden and greatest fear and making it come true. Brandy hasn't been back in my life for more than ten minutes and she's already cast doubt on my career.

"I'm kidding," she says. "Obviously. Jocelyn, your success will always be your own—you're amazing. This will blow over."

No, you're *amazing,* I think. For *Sylvie,* any success would be so obviously her own. For me? Maybe not as much. I am good. I am maybe even great. But lately I've begun to wonder if I have the piece that Sylvie does that really makes her special.

After all, lately she is getting chance after chance to dance principal and soloist roles and being groomed with so much attention that it seems clear that everyone in the company expects her to be the Next Big Thing.

And now I'm feeling even less confident. Now that the limping, loud, crass reminder of my past has flown in to torment me. Brandy.

"I don't think it'll just *blow over*, Sylvie; that seems a little naive, if I'm honest."

Can you *truly* be special if you come from a shitty neighborhood and a shitty house and a terrible mother? Maybe, but can you do it without being the sweet, doe-eyed prodigy always depicted in the rags-to-riches tales?

Because I don't know if you can. Sylvie could do it. I don't know if I could. And worse than that, I don't want to feel like this—it's so unlike me to think I'm not special. That's a particular ego death I'm not sure I can handle.

I realize that I'm still looking at Sylvie like I hate her. Which I don't. I just need a place to put my anger.

"Sorry," I say. "Maybe we should just go somewhere else." We'd been standing across the street, not wanting to go in with Brandy and George and waiting until they'd gone inside already.

"Um . . ." Sylvie gazes into the restaurant and I follow. Sebastian. We can just barely see his back, but we know him so well by now that it's unmistakably him. And I know Sylvie enough to know that she *really* does not want to go somewhere else. Not if Sebastian is in there.

Once inside, we make our way to Sebastian. And I hear her before I see her.

My mother's voice, rising above the din. She's in the middle of telling a story that involves a lot of gesticulating. She's talking to Sebastian.

Then she pulls back to raise her hands above her head like she's holding a beach ball.

"Oh, and there she is now!" She beckons me over.

"Oh god," says Sylvie.

"Oh god."

Chapter Fourteen

PARIS
NOW

Sylvie

"*Un thé à la menthe, s'il vous plait.*"

I give my order to the teenage girl behind the counter at Little Café, pleased with myself for being able to communicate just a little. Though if she comes back to me with any further questions in French, I'm probably not going to understand them, and my worldly ruse will be uncovered.

For the first time in a long while, I remember how those early days of traveling with the company had felt. How exciting they had been. Every stolen moment with the city had felt like sipping starlight. Every turn down an unfamiliar narrow street felt like a new beginning. Every morning felt like a chance.

The girl doesn't say anything more in French, instead in English asking me if I'd like anything else and then giving me my total when I shake my head. My eyes linger on the flaky, buttery croissants as I pay.

I lean on the counter and watch everyone around me. Outside, people are smoking and laughing. Some of them are having champagne. It's funny to imagine that they might be looking at an empty, leisurely day. One devoid of harsh impacts to a sharply structured and toned body. One devoid of being screamed at by someone who is allowed to cruelly and aggressively shout that your pinky is a millimeter out of place.

Or, as Diana freely does in front of as many other people as she can, announce that you look *constipated*.

It makes me cringe. I can't believe she says things like that to me without any guilt whatsoever.

My tea is ready and I thank the girl and walk out of the café and onto the cobblestoned street. Rue de la Verrerie. This area looks just like the Paris I always imagined when I was little. Windows thrown open to the city streets below, pigeons living well on pastry crumbs, and the chic bourgeoisie speaking fast and loud or intimately and with the undertone of sex that seems to be the foundation of the French language.

A surge runs through me as I remember the night before. Well, to say I *remember* it is not quite right. It's more like a song thrumming in the back of my mind constantly, and when I tune into it, I begin to sing along. Any moment where I think of anything else is almost an act of meditation; a denial that the scent, the touch, the slick wetness, the heat of skin with the blood rushing beneath it . . . that those aren't the senses eclipsing everything that surrounds me.

And how is it possible that, in a city like this, one that I and a million others have dreamed of, I should be so distracted from its beauty? So distracted by last night that I hardly notice any of the world around me unless I *remind* myself to.

I pass a shop selling macarons, ones I'm sure have that perfect crisp, delicate crunch on the outside and light, cloudy cream on the inside. I'm sure they dissolve in the mouth, making anyone lucky to eat one before having a sip of Veuve or a swish of Sancerre. And yet for once, I don't crave them. Instead, my core-deep yearning is for something far sweeter, far more lingering. I'm pretty used to ignoring my desire for delicious foods that would put an unnecessary ounce on my waistline, but if I were to feel as I did with Alessandro last night, I believe I'd be forever cured of any ache for indulgences like that.

It's like graduating from cigarettes to heroin. Or boxed wine to champagne.

Only hopefully not as likely to be my undoing.

I mosey down the streets, looking in the shop windows, dipping into a few and smiling and shaking my head at the shopkeepers who ask—always in English, how do they know?—if I need anything. My fingertips run over the different fabrics, I smell the candles and perfumes, tilt my head to read the spines of books.

And there it is again, not a memory coming to mind, but like a pulsing heartbeat, a palpitation of *remembering*. His hands on me, my hands on him, the way his muscles moved beneath my fingertips, the way he seemed to read my mind.

I pass the grand old Hôtel de Ville, which is actually city hall, and then turn the corner to walk the bridge over the Seine. There are lovers everywhere, I notice. Every time I see a couple, I take a sip of my tea. The mint and the heat run through me, filling my chest and throat with a blooming hot and cool that insulates me and braces me from the chilly breezes that whip through the narrower corridor and rustle the trees that might have stood for a century or more.

I look up at one of the rustling trees and take in the way its branches sway. It's like dancing. The music from *Sleeping Beauty* swirls in my mind, particularly the fairy songs. I think of myself dancing right now, how light and free I could feel. I am soft and full of natural movement, my face is relaxed, my muscles strong but loose, my gestures and phrasing *easy*. Ancient tension has fallen away.

I imagine Diana, and the look on her face if she sees me move the way I could right now. She wouldn't say I was fucking *constipated*, that's for sure. She'd say, if she could admit it, that I moved like the Parisian spring breeze itself.

What if I could stay like this? What if I could feel this way all the time? What if I could breathe this deeply and feel so at ease? And if I did it all with Alessandro at my side.

It's crazy how someone can fall so fast into another person that they begin to already imagine a life spent by their side. It would scare off anyone who knew, but don't we all do it? At least those who can still *fall* like this? Which, incidentally, I didn't think I still could. It's amazing how quickly my heart and body remembered how to succumb so completely to desire. When so recently I believed myself to have moaned my last gasping *please* to someone I needed desperately.

It feels like being saved.

With a start, I realize that I haven't had any Xanax in almost forty-eight hours.

Is that part of it too? Or am I just able to cope right now because I actually felt something good for once?

I don't know, and I don't even want to think about it. I don't mind whatever it is. Like accepting that the power drug that helped save your life was actually a placebo.

Sure, but if it worked, then it worked, right? Anything to be whole again.

I was willing to take anything. Ever since I got to the NAB, that's been the way I looked at life—give everything a chance.

Not that it really worked out that well.

No, I don't want to think about that.

Just raspberries and wine from a family vineyard. Soft sheets and sparkling lights.

My eyes shut of their own volition as I catch my breath and think of our bodies against each other once again. There it is.

I can't even think of my own body without thinking of his.

Yes, Sylvie, yes! This is good, this is very good, keep it up, let's go!"

Diana's roar is not angry today, it's hungry. The success is feeding her approval, and the approval is fueling my success.

For days now, I have been dancing like I used to. The blurry haze around everything has lifted, and I can hit every position with strength and power in a way I had feared I no longer could.

Everyone has noticed. When I step onstage, the other girls watch me—and this time not just to see what happens when Diana or Jocelyn and I head off against each other.

No, they watch me because of my dancing. Though I remain focused, I can see their looks of approval and surprise.

Jocelyn and I have even been somewhat friendly. Or at least, compared to how we have been.

Everything is starting to feel a bit more like it used to. When Sebastian pops in without notice to visit and observe, I manage to completely ignore him.

When we finish today's rehearsal, Diana approaches me. Her eyes are narrow and her mouth is a hard line.

"What did you do?"

"What?" I ask, taking deep breaths to steady and lower my heart rate.

"You either found better drugs, fell in love, or did some sort of exorcism. Which is it?"

I laugh. "It's . . . none of that. I just remembered who I am. I remembered I'm good."

I glance behind her and my eyes land on Alessandro. She sees it on my face and looks behind her, then snaps back to me.

"You've got to be kidding me, you stupid girl. Do you learn nothing? Nothing?"

She slaps me on the side of the head. Not too hard but definitely hard enough to make her point.

"Hey!"

"Don't *hey* me, girl. What are you thinking?" She shakes her head and then tsks hard.

A sick acid starts churning in my stomach. "It's not . . ."

What isn't it? I don't even know what to tell her.

"Do something for me?" she asks.

"Yes, what is it?"

She comes uncharacteristically close.

"One hour, meet me at that café over there—what's it called?— the only one right there with any decent espresso . . . Little Café, which is mysteriously in English like half the places here now."

"I know it."

"Okay, one hour—we need to talk. Now, go. What are you waiting for, go."

She walks away from me and I stare at the floor, biting my tongue. Am I about to lose everything? Right when I decided I could not lose it?

No, no, no.

Jocelyn is nearby, I see when I turn. "Don't give me shit," I say.

But she looks dumbstruck and simply shakes her head, holding her hands up in surrender.

The fact that she has nothing to say is worse than if she were scathing.

Diana is already at the café when I arrive, which I was trying to avoid by getting there ten minutes early, but I should have known she would beat me to any punch.

"Hello," I say formally, as I sit across from her.

"Hello, Sylvie."

She is smoking a cigarette and drinking a glass of red wine. I feel a surge of pride as I realize I still don't want a cigarette.

The server comes over and asks what I would like. "Just tea, please."

He nods and leaves.

Diana gives me a look of distrust, as if it's a show for her.

"I just want tea," I say.

She is silent for a moment, then she ashes her cigarette and leans toward me.

"I don't know when you're going to get it through your head, Sylvie, but you have to care a bit more about what you are doing here. None of this running around making mistakes with men who will leave you. You have to remember you are with the NAB: this is not some silly little job. This is big. This is it. This is what you trained your whole life for."

"I'm— I mean, wow. Everyone else *runs around*—"

"Maybe they do, but they still deliver quality." She breaks the word *quality* into three sharp, staccato syllables. "Everyone else shows up every day as if it is their *first* day with us. They show up to dance as if their lives depend on it. Because they do. And if they don't behave like that, they are gone. You are the only one left who doesn't bring her all every day."

I grind my teeth. "I do well. I'm good at what I do."

"Sure, in fact, you're so good that even when you're doing a terrible job, a tenth of what you're capable of, you're still better than half of the corps. But is that good enough for you? Is that what you want?"

I hesitate and then shake my head.

The server returns with my tea.

"Listen, it is not my job to tell you what to do with your life. The only reason I am telling you anything at all, the reason I correct you so much, is not because I hate you, which is probably what your self-obsessed little mind thinks. It is because I care about this company, and unfortunately I care about you. I have this creature in my pasture here who could make everything better for all of us. You have that power and you choose to live up to the least of your potential. The middle? Is that where I thought Sylvie Carter would be? Hmm? It is a real question."

She narrows her eyes at me, tightens her scarf to her neck, and inhales the cigarette. She is so fucking French.

"No, it is not. I guess."

"No, it is not. I thought I had a star. And now, I have one, and what did you do? You slept with him. After everything that happened in the past, I cannot believe you would be so foolish."

"It's not like that."

"Was it like that when it began with Sebastian?"

I pause. "No."

"No, it seemed all well and good just like this probably, somehow, does to you."

"Everyone sleeps with each other and fools around. I don't see why you're so focused on me and what—"

"Because everyone else does it without it breaking them into a million little pieces. That's what happened to you, and I don't want to see that. Do I care about you? Yes, actually, I do. I don't like to see a young girl with so much potential flush it down the drain for man after man, especially when it takes away from the rest of us. You are better than this and smarter than this. I know you had that little list when you started—"

"God."

"I know it's a sore subject, dear, but you have to face the reality here. You had a list of rules when you began. How many of those do you stand by? What happened to the girl who trained so hard and so beautifully for so long? Is she still with us or did she die five years ago?"

"I don't know."

She breathes in deeply and then takes a final drag of the cigarette before putting it out on the ashtray provided on every table.

"Listen, Sylvie. I hate to tell you this, but the board and Robert are about this close to letting you go. You're getting older and you're occupying a space that could be taken by someone who really wants to be here."

"Oh my god," I say, breathless. It's like a stab through the sternum. "What? What, since when? With no warning? Just—"

"This is your warning, love. And all the criticism, those were your warnings too. Drink your tea."

I obey her, having nothing else to say or do.

It runs through me, a little too hot, but I welcome it.

"I hate telling you this, I really do. This is not where I saw your career going, it really is not."

"What do I—do? What do I do?"

"The best chance you have is to start showing that you care. Stop showing up with bags under your eyes and minibar charges on your hotel room bill. Work a little harder. Read back through those rules one more time and find the girl you were. She was good. Lately you've been dancing well. But it's not even close to your potential. It's not even close to what it needs to be for you to stay. I'm hard on you because I care, Sylvie. I believe in you. I've wanted to *shake* you for the last three years, I want you to snap out of it. For you, not for me. I can find other amazing dancers. But you're special, and I wish you'd remember that."

I feel stunned and empty. I had been so proud of my dancing lately. For her to say it isn't even close . . . I feel completely hopeless. I can't even believe how quickly I feel as bad as I do.

"Well, thank you, I guess." My eyelashes flutter.

"You're welcome. I hope you can fix it in time. I really do."

She stands up. She throws some money down on the table, pats me on the back, and then leaves.

I'm practically catatonic. My blood is pounding in my ears and my skin feels ice-cold. I feel suddenly incapable of the fight. Finding out I'm on the chopping block is too much. It's too far to climb.

I snap out of it and finish the rest of her wine. As soon as I do, I slam the glass down and speed out of the restaurant.

If you know where to look, in any city, you can find a place to lose yourself. In any lost place, you can find someone who will give you drugs.

If you look hard enough and know who to ask, you can even find yourself a wonderful, intoxicating, only slightly terrifying sex club.

I need to lose myself. I need to feel everything and nothing.

I call Alicia, rolling a pill between my fingers in my jacket pocket. Molly, scored from a guy who looked like he was trying to channel Sid Vicious.

"Hello?"

"Hey. I found a sex club. Want to go?"

"Oh my god, I was *literally* just talking about doing that again to David the other day. It ended with his nurse-guy, by the way."

"That's too bad." I'm distracted, looking at shop fronts, trying to find a place to buy a dress rather than go back to the hotel.

I find a place pretty easily and walk in.

"And I'm literally in the middle of composing a text to Bill because I just can't. I can't be with someone named Bill."

I cover the mic, pointing the salesgirl to the dress on the mannequin. *"Taille trente-deux, s'il vous plait."*

She nods and walks off to get it.

"I think that's for the best. Bill sounds like a drag. Anyway, so, sounds like everyone is down to go to the club."

"You're cool if . . ."

"Huh? Oh, David?" I think about how he fully abandoned me the other day because things got *messy*. "Whatever."

"Cool. Okay, send the location."

Half an hour later, I'm in a slinky slip dress with a new La Perla bra and thong and have used all the samples at MAC to put my face back together. The Molly is in my bra.

I think of Alessandro and how much I wish I could just be ensconced in him again.

I don't want to admit it, but Diana is right. I can't get everything from some man. What if he . . . What if it happens again?

My mind is in montage mode. Images of my night with him, but they're starting to mingle with memories from the past.

Sebastian telling me he liked the nude leotards on me. That I looked good in white too. The way I'd started to wear those colors. He used to tell me what he liked all the time, and I never took it as a compliment alone, I took it as a clue. How to win his heart.

The dress I picked just now is one I know he'd like. It's like my own taste has sincerely changed so deeply that I relearned what I liked, all for him.

And it still has hold of me.

The club is very close to the Palais Garnier. A nondescript building, no sign on the door, down a nondescript street. The door to the club doesn't even have an address on it—you just have to use context clues.

Once you arrive, there's a doorbell and a camera above. They look at you through the camera before they buzz you in. Then, once you're in, there's another chamber where you wait for them to buzz you through that.

Alicia looks pretty hot in a leather dress I could never pull off and would never try to, and David has pulled out all the stops, in his best tailored suit. He smells like hot man musk. He doesn't mention our tension and neither do I.

We're given a card for the bar tab because no wallets or bags are allowed in. When we close out, we're told to collect the card again.

From the entrance we turn a corner and go down an elegant spiral staircase lit with candles, no light bulbs. There are bowls of different kinds of mints, which the first time I saw them seemed strange, but now I get it.

"Trick or treat?" says David, walking down the steps and popping one in his mouth.

Downstairs is a large space that feels cozy and intimate and grand all at once. Despite the building surely being an industrial structure, the ceiling and walls are draped in heavy velvet and other fabrics that make the whole thing feel like some sort of dark, twisted night circus.

Everyone is sexy, gorgeous, and looks like they have secrets that run deeper than a place like this. Every woman is in heels, but most are in sky-high ones, many with the telltale red bottoms, like I am. It just seems right to wear Louboutin to a den of depravity.

Everywhere you look in the main room, there is *confidence*.

This is why I wanted to come here. Right here.

My eyes are alive with the sight of it all. I can feel the fire behind my alert stare burning so brightly that I almost wonder if it's lighting up the room.

We sidle up to the bar, where a bartender sets fire to the oils of an orange peel. He then uses a pair of metal tongs to pull a brandied cherry out of a jar, its oxblood juices dripping. He puts it into a cocktail and hands it to a man who takes it and turns away with his tall, svelte female partner. I can't place her, but I'm pretty sure she's a Victoria's Secret model.

We all order a death in the afternoon. After we clink our glasses, I surreptitiously slip the pill onto my tongue and swallow it back with my drink. I don't know why I'm hiding it. It's not as if either of them would judge me. I think I'm just ashamed to have backslid, and something about hiding it from them feels like hiding it from myself.

We give the bartender our drink cards.

The thing about a sex club is that no matter what you want out of it, you can find it. You don't have to touch anyone or be touched. In fact, unless you ask to engage in some way, you can also be completely ignored. It's like being a ghost if that's what you want.

And then of course, if you want to feel utterly, primally human, you can do that too.

No one has sex in the main bar area. Here is basically the foreplay of the place. It smells like matches from the bar; yeast from the champagne bottles; and good French perfume. The tables are glass and the chairs are soft, but not meant to be sat in for long.

All around us, couples or threesomes or more, of all combinations of sex and age, leave to find one of the rooms that are designed with sex in mind.

"Do you guys want to do a shot too?" I ask, my eyes landing on someone who, for a moment, I think is Alessandro, but I realize is not.

"Uh . . ." hesitates Alicia.

"Fuck it," says David.

"Three absinthes," I say to the bartender. "Blanc, please."

"I don't think absinthe is exactly a *shot* thing," says Alicia.

"Come on," I say.

He louches the absinthe, and we watch as it clouds.

When he hands them to us, I pound mine, only to turn and see David and Alicia staring at me. "What? I said shots!"

Alicia cringes, and David shrugs and pounds his too.

She takes half and shakes her head. "I'm sorry, I just can't do more than that right now. We have a show tomorrow, and I don't want to feel like shit."

I roll my eyes.

We begin to float around.

There are small rooms off the beaten track. A couple leaves the doorway as we approach, and we take their spot.

Inside the small room, which can't be more than eight by eight feet, there are a few divans. On one, there is a man lying on his back. He has a strong, capable-looking body and tattoos. Again, I am reminded of Alessandro. A woman with skin the color of caramel and hair an unusual shade of red is straddling his face, grinding on his mouth, and letting out a gasp or moan every so often. At the man's lap, there is another girl, this one with short, platinum-blond hair and icy-looking skin. She is sucking his cock and playing with her clit.

"That's a lot of multitasking," says David.

"Determination," says Alicia with a shake of the head.

Neither of them know about the past with me, Jocelyn, and Sebastian. All they know is the horror of me getting arbitrarily eviscerated by the press after, and then my peers. I feel like their heads would spin around like the *Exorcist* girl if I told them. Not because it's naughty or unusual even—sex is everywhere in ballet. But because it's me and Jocelyn. Everyone knows we used to be best friends, but no one knows how deeply close we were.

No one but Sebastian.

There are other people in the room in sexual tangles, including one couple—two men engaging in *extremely* tender anal sex, which I didn't really even know was possible.

In the next room, there's a mostly female orgy going on, and we lose David to a man who approaches him and invites him to the lounge for another glass of champagne.

"I could never do it," says Alicia, gesturing at the female orgy. "I'd get performance anxiety."

"You perform in front of people all the time! Legs spread, even."

"I know, but it's not the same!"

I look at her and think about how weird it would be for us to hook up. Like kissing my sister. Being with Jocelyn wasn't weird. And in fact, she feels much more like my sister than Alicia. The way we fight and the way we fucked.

"I'm going to go find someone to make out with," says Alicia.

She doesn't check to see if it's cool with me, even though it is. She goes off and disappears.

I go to the bar and get another drink.

I hesitate and then order one more absinthe and pound it.

Absinthe is strong. The louche dilutes it a little, but it doesn't change the fact that it's anywhere from ninety to one hundred and seventy proof—I know, I looked it up once. I don't know about the bottle I'm drinking, so I ask to see it.

The bottle has a big eye on the label and is called La Fée. The fairy.

I think of *Moulin Rouge!*, which I watched for the first time in my own naked, postsex tangle with Jocelyn and Sebastian. We were here, in Paris, and after watching, we got drunk on absinthe and wandered the streets, singing the songs and dancing, laughing, kissing, sharing a cigarette. We walked to the real Moulin Rouge, where a show was about to begin. Without thinking about it, Sebastian handed over his card and asked for three VIP tickets to the 11:00 p.m. show.

We had champagne and ate macarons and watched as, for once, we were danced *for*. The show was a spectacle of feathers and glitter and diamonds, and it was so weird to see the movie and then *be there*.

That night, Jocelyn said, quite seriously, that there was a part of her that wished she was on that stage instead of on ours.

I sort of miss those days.

The drugs are definitely hitting.

It gets hazy not long after that.

My mind is a flash of pitch-black scenes cut between moments of happiness and those of abject misery. Diana's face, her roaring voice, the idea that I might be told to leave the company. Alessandro's face close to mine. The thrill of his touch. His warm breath on my skin. Jocelyn's angry, beautiful face as I left her alone with Sebastian. Sebastian . . .

Things I don't dare to think cross my mind, like how I still remember what it feels like to want Sebastian. And Jocelyn.

The relief combined with terror of losing ballet streaks through me.

My body, which I'm twisting and stretching and moving through this crowd of strangers, aches for something I know I can't have.

I wander through the club in a haze. I'm not even sure what's reality at this point. I feel as if I'm drifting through my own imagination.

It looks like there is a leather mattress in the middle of the cave. The cave is even more intimate than the rest of the place, even though it's bigger. The lights are an undulated red-pink, and there are straps and handcuffs on the walls.

A girl is hanging from one of the walls, holding a leather whip and wiggling it, inviting us, someone to engage with her.

A tall, strapping guy walks up to her and takes the whip.

Where a moment before, she looked so alpha, she is now beta to him.

She turns and he begins to whip her once, twice, and then three times. The woman moans in ecstasy as he then puts his fingers inside of her.

I am hungry for more, I want to be whipped or be the one whipping, I'm not sure which.

Another man comes up and touches him from behind. He continues to engage with the hanging girl.

I find myself moving forward to the front of the watching crowd, to get a better view. I'm drifting in such a way that I don't even feel like I'm in reality. Maybe I'm not. Maybe it's all fantasy.

From behind me a man starts to kiss my neck sensually. I tilt my head back into him, into the subtly tingling pleasure of it. I move my hand down to his hard cock pressed behind me. Then I hear my name called softly and turn to see Alicia.

I think she is laughing. "We're gonna go. Are you good?"

I feel myself nodding, though I feel like I'm in a different scene altogether. She laughs and whispers, "Okay, bye, babe!"

The man has moved on and I turn back to the woman still hanging from the wall. I'm drawn to her confidence and before I know it, I'm in front of her.

"Mm, une jolie," she says. She has harsh black liner and piercing grey eyes, plump lips and a nose ring. She looks like she could tear my head off. No wonder she likes to be whipped.

I start to take the whip from the man when he hands it to me, as he falls into lust with the man behind him.

The hanging girl says, "Unh, unh, unh! Naughty. Dress!"

She is like a playful *fée* herself, completely nude but for nipple piercings and a clitoral piercing. I can't help but look at all of her.

I take off my dress.

One of the men takes it and I thank him.

My bare skin gets a chill, even though it's warm in here.

She lets me take the whip. Expertly, she winds her hands around the leather bondage on her wrists like an acrobat, and turns herself around, stretching her legs out and presenting her ass for me.

A thrill runs through me.

I whip her on the ass and she lets out a cry of ecstasy. I do it again, and again, and her smooth ass turns pink; I can see it even in the dim light of the cave.

I don't quite have the conviction I should have, hitting her. I feel funny doing it. Not confident enough.

She turns around again and spreads her legs, nodding at the whip. I raise an eyebrow, asking if I'm understanding it right.

The two men move to me and begin to worship me from my ankles up to my thighs, but going no further. I shut my eyes and feel it for a moment.

"You want?"

One of the men gestures to another set of shackles.

I'm hazy, yet my mind and body are feeling everything with heightened intensity. I know exactly what I want.

"Yes," I say.

He helps hoist me up. My legs are spread, I am hanging, completely at the whim of a stranger.

He circles me and says, "Do you have a safe word?"

I think, quickly, and I land on "Juliet."

"Juliet." He nods.

He grabs my ass, rubs it gently, and then I know it's coming. The smart of the whip.

My breathing catches when he reels it back again. He flips it around, to the other side, where there is a gentler leather end. He smacks my pussy with it and I call out.

"Again?" he asks.

I nod.

The pleasure and pain together feel like what I need, somehow.

It's unfamiliar and strange and those facts turn me on even more. I am soon dripping.

The other man has begun pleasuring the woman next to me, and she looks to me and smiles, then reaches her hand out for me to take.

I do.

"Je vais jouir! Je vais jouir! Je vais jouir!" she screams out.

She doesn't just cum. She squirts all over the man touching her.

She lays there, moaning lightly.

The man looks at me and asks if I want the same.

I say yes.

He unshackles me and lays me back on the leather mattress. His head moves down my body from my tits to my stomach to between my legs. Stopping there to tease my clit with his tongue. My hips arch in pleasure.

In front of me, the woman plays with my tits, licks my lips, and tells me to feel it.

I get the feeling she's a regular here.

Within moments I am calling out, yes, yes, more, until finally I cum. It's a release like I've never felt.

When I am finished, I unwind myself, legs shaking, and grab my dress off the floor. The woman winks at me and turns away.

I drift through a blur of bodies feeling as if I'm floating on a cloud of human desire. I feel my own body as if it were a stranger's.

Eventually the drugs start to wear off and I feel tired. I start to feel stressed, but I can't tell why. There is a feeling of dread in my stomach. I can't remember if that was really me, or was I watching the whole time? I don't know what's real. I manage to stumble into a cab and back to the hotel just after 2:00 a.m.

In my room, I start to panic. I don't know what was real and what wasn't. I feel hollowed out, liberated in a way, but flushed with too much booze.

I'm full-blown spiraling and I can't even really tell why.

I get into the shower, dress on, and let the water run over me, hoping the feeling will stop. It doesn't, and now I'm dizzy too. I should have water and food.

I can hardly see. I'm hot and freezing all at once and I can already tell I won't remember a lot of tonight. I'm glad that I won't. I look at the bottle of Xanax on the bathroom counter and want to throw it off the hotel balcony. I am better than this. Or at least I was.

I still am, right?

I put the bottle back down and decide not to risk my life; I'll be asleep soon anyway.

I get out of the bathtub and peel off my drenched dress, walking nude out of the bathroom and over to my bed. I sit with splayed legs for a second before looking at the zipped compartment in my suitcase. I can't believe I even still hide my old diary. Everyone knows what's in it. I can't even believe I've *kept* it. It's humiliating to revisit.

All these pages admitting to wishing I was a famous ballerina, looking forward to it. Believing in myself *and* the world around me so deeply, like life was going to be fair. Happy, even. I'm not a bitter old jaded hag now or anything, but I'm sure not that naive girl anymore.

I unzip the pocket and pull it out. What *ever* possessed me to buy a pink diary?

On the first page, there are the rules.

Oh, the rules.

I read them carefully, though my eyes are seeing double. Maybe it's less reading and more viscerally, instantly remembering each and every one.

THE RULES:

1. Be good. Be very good. Beyond reproach.
2. Do not reward yourself—dancing with the NAB *is* the reward, not dessert.
3. Sleep.

4. Drink rarely, and only a delicate glass here and there. Do no drugs.

5. Do not have sex with *anyone*. Not unless it is *truly* meaningless—which is very unlikely—just avoid it altogether. (Sidebar: when they call you a prude, tell them you're not but that you just don't want the drama—it's true and it's respectable.)

6. Put no shit talk in writing. Ever.

7. Do not let friendships get ugly. Better to have no friends than to get involved and risk the drama.

8. Befriend the staff without being a brownnoser. Just be above all the pettiness—they'll eat that shit up.

9. Dance as Juliet by the time you are twenty-one.

I laugh and shut the book. Jesus. I've broken every single one.

CHAPTER FIFTEEN

Jocelyn

Everyone else screams with delight to learn that we've been grounded. No flights will be leaving for at least an extra day because of a massive storm in the Atlantic, and that means that we have an unexpected change in plans—an unpredicted break.

Instead of the days off for travel and jet lag, and the lower-key rehearsals that usually kick us off in a new city, we will jump on a plane, land, and go straight into the thick of it. But nobody is thinking about how hard it will be once we land in Vienna. Everyone is thinking about the fact that we've been given an unexpected reprieve. A chance to really *be* in this city, where we usually move so fast that a drink grabbed here or there hardly constitutes any kind of memory and doesn't count as a vacation.

Everyone else looks excited about the news. I'm tense as a coiled spring and can feel my mother's presence in the theater, thirty rows back, where she sits with George Longworth, who can, it turns out, get her into any rehearsal she wants to go to.

They say money can't buy you happiness. Well, sometimes it can buy you abject misery.

Or at least me.

I look to Sylvie, expecting her to feel my gaze and turn my way, but instead, I see that she's already locked in a tight link with Sebastian's eyes.

I don't know how people aren't figuring out that something is going on between them. He looks down at her with a wink in his grin, and she looks up at him, chin tucked, eyelashes up toward him. He looks like a hungry predator, and she is his coquettish pursuit.

Flames of envy rage through me.

In the last several months, I've borne witness to this sort of thing a lot.

For months, Sebastian and Sylvie and I have been in this bizarre world together. Something more than *appropriate*; but I'm sure if Sebastian had to describe it to someone, it would sound completely innocent.

Sebastian has spent endless extra time coaching us. We've spent late nights dancing the same things over and over. He shouts at Sylvie for her to engage more with her originality, to let her uniqueness shine through. He begs me to tighten my technique. Then, he takes us to speakeasies that require passwords for entry and serve drinks made with egg and vinegars and have intricate garnishes. He takes us to his place, where sometimes we simply stay up talking and watching ballets or old movies. They sit too close on the couch.

If he says something about her is good, that thing becomes huge for her—she will change to enlarge that *thing*, whatever it is.

I can't help but feel the same, in a way. But I try, at least, to hide it. To act as though the world does not revolve around Sebastian. And Sylvie.

Look to each other, he will say, practically pressing our faces together like a kid with two Barbies.

But he and Sylvie have something else going on. And we all pretend they don't.

I will return from the kitchen with another bottle of wine, feeling like they have just broken apart. Sometimes she will "forget something" after leaving, and then go back, leaving me to go home alone.

They're hiding a romance from me, and I can't bring myself to ask about it. Because if I do, it will only confirm that I'm left out. And worse, it will show that I feel that way. That I care.

Sometimes it hurts my feelings so much that I will feel truly depressed. I will get home from the rehearsals and the times we have together and just . . . start crying. Because, the thing is, I love being part of it. I love the movies and the cocktails and the extra rehearsals. I love feeling special. Seen by someone who looks at so few.

If I mention it or, worse, call it out, I fear I will get cut out completely. And then any chance to succeed through Sebastian will evaporate. I have this awful feeling I would lose my friend, my chance at advancement, and my only real social life all in one fell swoop.

Sometimes I just want to curl up in a ball and be transported back to when I was four years old and had an entire lifetime ahead of me and could make different choices.

Of course, me missing my childhood is like someone missing their old group of friends and then remembering that those friends were fellow inmates at a maximum-security prison.

On the stage, Diana finishes speaking.

"And that's about that from me. Sebastian?"

Finally, he stops looking at Sylvie and she rubs her face to cover her smile.

"Yes, uh, so the schedule when we arrive in Vienna will be extremely intense and very high pressure, as we still have to perform our scheduled shows. Unless of course, this storm, these storms, continue to get worse; in which case we will reconvene and discuss when we must. In the meantime, please be careful, and of course, enjoy beautiful Barcelona."

Everyone cheers. Diana rolls her eyes. Sebastian claps and laughs before nudging Diana and saying something that looks like *Oh, lighten up.* Matt looks extremely stressed, and I laugh to myself. It's all going to fall on him—every changed plane ticket, hotel reservation, and contact with the other theater.

We all walk back to our hotel, a slew of skinny little ballerinas given the gift of a normal day or two, floating down the streets of a foreign city.

The energy that afternoon is electric. The skies are that weird orange-grey that can only really exist around a big storm. Thunder cracks and the wind blows.

The streets are usually always empty in the afternoon in Spain; only the tourists trek them, seeking shade by the buildings. Before we travel to a new city, I read all about it, wanting to know how to fit in, how to feel like one of the ones *in the know.* I learned that one from a Rick Steves podcast. Apparently all the locals go inside in the afternoon, usually because it's too hot, and they have a siesta. Then they have a walk at around five or six, the whole town out in the streets, still hours before they have dinner. But today the windows are thrown open; there is energy and camaraderie in the city.

What is it about bad weather that brings people together?

"What should we do?" I ask Sylvie.

"Well . . . actually, Sebastian invited me to dinner. It must be something just to do with me or I'm sure he would have invited you."

Usually, she would look guilty, but instead she looks like she is badly hiding glee. I feel hurt, left out, but try like always to pretend I'm fine.

"Okay—what's going on," I ask. "What's got you so particularly cheerful?"

She hesitates and my stomach sinks as I realize there actually is something behind it.

"What is it?" I ask again.

She looks around and then pulls me aside into a candy shop.

The smell of fudge fills my lungs and I breathe it in, loving the scent as much as I'm desperately seeking oxygen.

Then, here, by the lollipops, she says it.

"I'm going to be Juliet."

My gut goes rancid. "What? How? We only got soloist promotions a few weeks ago."

How is it so definitely her, not me?

"I don't know. Sebastian told me they had a staff meeting and my name was brought up and he pushed it. He just told me, it's a sure thing."

Her delight is as sickeningly sweet as the cotton candy that whirls in the machine behind us. "But you can't just go straight to— How is he— Why?"

She looks a little insulted. "Well, I mean, I think it's because I'd be good. Why, don't you think that . . . do you think—"

"I'm not saying you wouldn't be good," I say. "I'm saying that it seems like he's, like . . . pulling strings or something."

She raises an eyebrow. "I'm not getting this just because of our little . . . thing."

"Not just because of it, no."

She looks hurt and is starting to look angry. She picks up a bar of chocolate and sets it down.

A pang of empathy and guilt washes through me.

"I thought we always knew that was kind of one of the benefits we were hoping for with him. Not that we'd get unfairly pushed forward, but that . . . you know, he's doing this with us because we're special, and eventually he might feel ready to point that out to . . . you know, the others."

I go on, "Look, I'm sorry, I didn't mean that. Of course you deserve it. I'm sure that the only benefit of your relationship with him that you're getting is that he's telling you and he shouldn't be telling you. I'm sure that's it. I'm sorry. I didn't mean to imply otherwise. You're amazing and you should be Juliet. You're a lot better than any of those other bitches."

She is like a comforted kid: all it took was a few lies. She smiles at me and says, "You're not just saying that?"

"No. I'm not just saying that."

Sylvie sighs. "Okay, good."

"Why wouldn't you tell me sooner that this was happening?" I ask.

"I'm telling you now."

She picks up the chocolate bar and heads to the counter.

"Just this?" asks the cashier, who can clearly tell we're American, which I hate.

"Yes, thanks. Gracias." She smiles self-consciously.

She has the air of a girl who has nothing in the world to worry about because everything is going her way. And from her perspective, I guess it is. Why wouldn't everything go her way? She's the one with a penthouse in Manhattan and a family home in Nantucket and a pair of golden fucking retrievers.

My mother passes by the door outside and I step out of her sight line. I hear her saying something about dinner.

My life, on the other hand, might need revisiting.

CHAPTER SIXTEEN

PARIS
NOW

Sylvie

It feels like I've only been asleep for a few minutes when there is a knock on my hotel door.

I look around. I'm alone, thank god.

I go to the door and peer through the peephole, clutching a blanket around me.

It's Alicia.

"Open up, it's me." After a pause, "Alicia."

I unlock the door, impressed by my ability to be as fucked up as I was and still manage to get back and lock up so well.

Oh, and look at that, I put on the DO NOT DISTURB sign.

"Dear god, you look fucking terrible," says Alicia, inspecting my face, my neck, and then pushing her way in.

I don't even have the energy for a witty comeback, so I simply allow her in. Still embarrassed from last night.

I see my reflection in the mirror and have to admit—it is shocking.

I let the blanket fall and step into the bathroom to retie my bun and wash my face. I scrub with soap until all the black, streaked mascara has stopped staining the water and the white porcelain.

It does little to help, as it seems that the black, grey, and blue hues beneath my eyes are coming from within and not without.

"Are you doing okay?" she asks, sitting on my bed and looking in my direction. There's something about her that looks vulturine. "You seem sort of . . ."

"I'm fine."

I remember Diana's words yesterday.

"But like, it seems like something is going on. You can tell me. You can totally trust me."

"I know I can," I lie. I hadn't even been listening to her.

"Because really I just want the best for you. I know everyone else is a little weird about you, but if something else is going on, really, you can tell me."

I snap. "Alicia, I know, you said that already. If I need you, I'll tell you."

She reels back, like I've smacked her.

"Fine. I was just trying to help. Good luck with all that today." She gestures at me. "Didn't Diana give you a warning yesterday?"

I hadn't told her that. Had I? Wait.

"How did . . ."

She rolls her eyes. "Just get yourself together—have a coffee or something."

Alicia leaves, and I experience a crushing feeling of dread.

It then occurs to me that Alicia, who I know to be an extreme gossip who revels in the drama of others, might only be friends with me *because* I'm a mess.

It makes more sense the more I think about it.

She isn't a real friend, who'd come to check up on me. She just wanted to see if I was alive. She would love to be the one to discover that I had OD'd or slit my wrists.

I pause my getting ready and throw open the window to smoke a fast, desperate cigarette while looking out at the beautiful city.

The rehearsal day does not go great. I'm off. I'm rocky. I can tell Alicia has told people about the night before.

Alessandro is busy. Jocelyn avoids eye contact.

I feel like a complete outsider again.

I slog through the dark, surreal day, amazed that I can even remotely keep it together. At one point I break out in a cold sweat and use every muscle in my body not to shake like a freezing cartoon character.

It's all a blur and I feel mad at everyone, like I deserve better from them.

It's not until I return to my hotel room that I burst into tears and slide down the door dramatically and cry until my stomach aches. I'm beyond thankful I'm not cast in the show tonight.

And then I can't help myself. I open the mini bar and take out a small bottle.

I stare at it. I must stop this pattern.

Instead of opening the alcohol, I take almost an hour to get ready for bed, doing a long, thorough ritual. I listen to a podcast on old movies and sit on the bathroom counter with my feet in the sink and pluck my eyebrows, extract a few oily blackheads that surely took hold from the nights of unremoved makeup. I whiten my teeth. I exfoliate my whole body and face, shave my legs and my underarms. I slather on a thick overnight moisturizer everywhere.

I even do a hair mask, one I had saved in case I had a date or something, but which I realize would be put to better use tonight. When I need to simply give myself some love.

I slide into a soft pajama set made of worn-in linen and which makes me look like I belong on a seventies album cover.

It's when I brush my hair down into my face and clamp it with two fingers, thinking maybe I should get bangs—that's when I realize I really am hitting rock bottom.

No one spiraling should consider a haircut of any kind, but particularly not bangs—not when they spend half their life sweating.

I go to bed to the lullaby of the Turner Classic Movies channel, which is showing *It Happened One Night*.

The TV glows and I have forgotten to worry about my life. I fall into a sleep I feel will be truly restful, but instead, I wake up within two hours and spend hours trying to fall back to sleep.

I toss and turn in bed, my attempt to be good and go to sleep early thwarted completely by insomnia and a racing mind.

I look at the clock. Two.

It's only eight in New York.

I grab my phone from its spot on the charger and go to the top contact on my list of Favorites.

Anna.

It rings a few times and I sigh, realizing it's most likely going to voice mail. She's probably busy. I am about to hang up, unable to think of a decent message to leave, when she answers.

"Right? Just one sec— Hello? Sylvie?"

"Yeah," I say.

"Sorry about that—we have some people over." Her voice becomes distant as if she's moved the phone away from her face. "I'll be back—there's another bottle of muscadet in the fridge. No, no, in the bar fridge."

I hear the cheerful sounds of a dinner party fade away. I make the guess that she's moving onto the balcony off her bedroom, which is where she usually talks on the phone, no matter the time of day.

"Sylvie? You okay?"

I nod, which she can't hear, so I say, "Yeah, I'm sorry to interrupt—nothing's wrong. I shouldn't have called."

"Oh my god, you're so fine—don't worry about it. I see these assholes all the time."

I know it's not necessarily true, but she's nice like that. She'll always make time, and there's an almost psychic ability that she has to always know when she really should.

I suddenly have a deep craving for Anna's house. She lives a life of rooftop bars and backyard barbecues, trips to the grocery store for ingredients for a complicated dinner she's cooking with her boyfriend. She has a dog and just paid off her car. She is working on a capsule wardrobe and has girlfriends over to watch Bravo. She has favorite cheeses and complains sometimes that she is *bored*, when what she means is that she's got a few hours to kill before her next plan or a day without responsibilities.

Her life is completely foreign to me.

"So what's going on?"

"I don't even know. I'm lost. I feel like I can't—I don't know—can't *outrun my past*." I laugh at the drama of it. "I'm doing everything wrong."

"So, Sebastian, or what?"

Sebastian is never a very good topic for us.

"He's here, actually. In Paris. He got a job as a ballet master here."

"They gave him another job? How did anyone employ that man?"

"I don't know. He's charming. He's good at what he does. He comes from money. I'm sure between all that, he was able to buy some favor."

I get up and go to the window to smoke a cigarette.

"I think I fucked up."

"What happened?"

It's not a curious *Oh no, what is it?*

It's the urgent *What happened?* that might follow getting a call from a police station.

I tell her what happened. I tell her about Alex. I tell her what Diana said. I tell her what I did last night. Not in detail, but enough to tell her that the gossip running around the company is real, and I'm trying not to be humiliated.

I had been *trying* to feel free. We ballerinas *did* things, like go to sex clubs, all the time. But somehow, attached to my own past and isolation, I know everyone looks at it differently.

I tell her that we're gearing up to do *Romeo and Juliet* again and sitting on the sidelines is killing me. I'm on the basic, but I'm so, so far down the list. I'll never get chosen. And even if I do . . . could I do it anymore, or have I lost the innocent Sylvie who so deeply connected with that character?

I talk again about Alex. About my feelings. About how he is.

After my story, I light another cigarette, and then breathe in deeply and wait for some sort of measured response. Maybe something that makes me yearn for a more repaired closeness between us, like, *Well, just be careful, but if you think he's a nice guy . . .*

Instead, I get a sharp, "What *the fuck* is wrong with you?"

I feel slapped. "What— I'm just telling you what happened— you don't need to bite my head off. God, that's not why I called you."

"No, you know exactly how fucked up this is. Jesus, Sylvie,

you're just going to make the same fucking mistake again with this Alessandro guy. How do you not see the similarity?"

"Anna, no. I know! I thought the same thing. But this is not what happened with Sebastian, I'm not a fucking teenager and he's not . . . you know, my superior."

"But he is, isn't he? Can he hurt your career if he wants to?"

"God."

"And you know you're hitting rock bottom, as you say it, but I can tell you're smoking. So it doesn't sound like you're stopping."

Rage surges in me. The inevitability of the frustration of going to someone for advice when you've stopped feeling like they understand you.

"You don't understand."

"You don't need to have a full-blown crack addiction to recognize that you should maybe take a break from all the vices. It sounds to *me* like you're all kinds of messed up right now—stop adding that to the mix. You don't even know what you took last night." Her voice falters. "I cannot imagine doing something like that."

"Of course you wouldn't, because you're out there playing *grown-up* because that's what you think you ought to do."

"Oh, don't begin to act like your choices are better than mine."

"I'm in *Paris*, at least. All you've done is move over the bridge to Jersey."

I'm in awe at my own words, but I'm also shaking with anger and cannot stop.

"When was the last time I did *anything* for myself?" I ask. "You wouldn't know because you only text me now about our relatives having weddings you know I won't be able to go to and shit like that. I wanted to hook up with Alex, so I *did it*. You have never understood how much pressure I'm under. I didn't call you so you could tell me how stupid I am and how I'm making mistakes all over the place."

I hear her set down a wineglass. She waits a moment, and then says, "I think that's exactly why you called."

"What is that supposed to mean?"

"I think you called because you're about to make the same mistake again. After what happened with Sebastian, you're lucky you even got a chance to keep dancing, especially with a company like that. You're going to risk it all by sleeping with the top jackass and you're not going to just keep getting chances. You know that, right?"

I can't come up with a response to most of it, so instead, I say, "Don't try to act like you understand my world."

"I don't have to understand your world to see the pattern here. You're about to do *Romeo and Juliet* again. You're making the same mistakes."

A silence plumes between us.

"I—"

"I don't understand your world. You know what, I don't. I don't understand it and I don't understand you. But what I do understand is that you were so angry at yourself last time that you changed. Deeply. Something's missing now. For me, this isn't about your career. Fine, if you want to blow up what you worked your entire life for, then go for it. But I don't want to see you keep sabotaging yourself because it's fucked up and you're my sister, and I . . ."

It's where she should say *I love you*, but I can tell she's too angry.

She's silent for long enough that it might seem like we got disconnected, but I know she's still there.

"I have to go," she says eventually. "I have people over and you can't just call and interrupt my life just to say you insist on making mistakes and don't actually want advice. That's . . . it's so stupid I don't even have the words. Goodbye, Sylvie. Good night and good luck."

She hangs up on me, and I stare at my phone in disbelief. I'm angry, but I can't tell exactly why.

There are two voices inside me. One of them is the truth teller. The one who sees things how they are and tells me, whether I like it or not, what I cannot admit to myself. The other is the liar. The one who acts on fear and anxiety. The one that tells me to *stay scared* because *I will fail* and who tells me not to take a risk because I'll fall.

They speak the same language but seem to have an almost imperceptibly different dialect. It makes it hard to tell which is speaking.

Right now, I'm not sure which voice is telling me that Anna is right. That I called her because I know I'm wrong, I'm making a mistake, and I'm a fucking idiot.

What happened before nearly ruined my life. Actually, it did ruin my life—I just found a new one.

I look at myself in the mirror.

I'm still young. I'm still lucky. I'm still a ballerina. I'm still traveling the world. But there's a hollowness to me now that I'd be in deep denial not to see.

Something has to change.

CHAPTER SEVENTEEN

VIENNA

FOUR YEARS AGO

Jocelyn

For a decade straight, Vienna was picked as the most livable city in the world. After visiting for the first time, I could completely understand why.

It's not just the most beautiful city I've ever seen, but it's also filled with the most beautiful *people*. Is this what happiness does to people? Makes them that much more attractive?

It's already our last night in the city, and I wish it wasn't, but I'm at least grateful that at the end of our intense run, we have a free night, followed by a late flight the next day. It means we have a little extra time and that I can window-shop from the street for all the apartments I'd like to have. After getting the extra time in Barcelona and then an actual good flight out of there, we're having unusual luck. A little taste of freedom.

Tonight, Sebastian has invited me *and* Sylvie to a gallery opening.

I'm relieved to be invited, and surprised when Sylvie texts me that she can't get ready with me like we usually do on nights out.

Things have been unusually tense between us lately, and I can't put my finger on why exactly. She's going to be training alone with Sebastian to be Juliet, which I'm "welcome to join," but have not been explicitly invited. In fact, I get strong, silent vibes telling me *not* to.

The cast for *Romeo and Juliet* went up and Sylvie's name was on the list of casting with the principals.

I'm not the kind of girl who has a million friends. I tend to have one and really spend time with them. Almost like a romantic relationship, but not, because while I have no trouble sleeping with a girl, I have no interest in loving one in that way.

I'm putting in a particularly concerted effort tonight, and I'm not exactly sure why. Sebastian texted Sylvie and me and told us to bring out our best looks, that this is a night to be photographed. But that isn't quite why I'm trying so hard. There's something I want. I just don't know what.

I've done a full bronze smoky eye, even contoured my nose a little, and my cheeks. I've filled in my brows, done a primer *and* finishing powder. I outline my lips with a pencil that looks like my own lip color but a little darker and a little better. I dress them in an unsmudgeable lipstick of the same color but one shade paler.

My hair is wavy, wild, and sexy. It has volume and texture and just a little bit of shine.

I'm in a bandage-style black dress I got at House of CB in London but have never had a chance to wear, despite toting it to every city. It's long, to mid-calf, and makes me look even longer and leaner than I am. It has a sweetheart neckline and impossibly thin straps. It's the kind of tight that's actually more comfortable than being naked. I spent five hundred pounds on it, which I couldn't afford then and can only barely afford now.

I'm wearing it with a pair of shoes even more out of my price range, but I couldn't pass them up. They're black Jimmy Choos, with ribbon ankle ties and embellished heels that would be too much with any other dress.

Even I, who sometimes suffer from an inferiority complex and am often hard on myself, could look at myself tonight and say . . . *damn*.

I've really brought it.

We're supposed to meet in the lobby at eight thirty, and I find Sylvie in the lobby bar with Sebastian. They're a few sips into their champagne, and it makes me wonder if I had perhaps been on a separate text and told a different time than the *real* time.

I recognize the feeling suddenly in the dynamic. I feel left out.

No one likes feeling left out of a threesome, but is it anything but inevitable?

That's it. That's why I'm dressed to the nines. Because I'm sick of feeling passed over, and I'm sick of feeling like second best. And maybe tonight, I want to be seen as beautiful. Maybe tonight, I want to seem like I'm every bit as worthy of attention. Maybe not of being Juliet, but of being loved more than—or at least as much as—anyone else.

Sylvie's eyebrows rise when she sees me and says, "Wow, you look amazing!"

Sebastian, however, stands and says, "Another spritzer," to the bartender and merely reaches out a hand to beckon me toward him. He gives me a quick, dry kiss on the cheek and says, "How are you?"

It's all very polite and not quite what I'd been expecting when I made myself into what I believed was my very best version of me.

But that's the thing about the ballet world. Every day, you can do something that most human beings can hardly dream of, and every day you can be told it is not good enough. Every day you can be told that there is someone better. And somehow, there always is.

They finish their drinks over the next twenty minutes as I have mine, the spritzer he'd ordered without asking me. I can't be mad though: it *was* what I wanted.

Then we leave for the gallery. It's raining in Vienna; it seems that the whole world is drenched in bad weather. We take the small umbrellas handed to us by the doormen and get straight into a cab they'd called for us. We're only going a couple of blocks, but Sebastian wanted to protect our shoes from the dampness and our ankles from the danger of slipping. We sit cramped together in the back, and I've decided to *not* get in my head about things between us, and instead to enjoy the night.

It isn't so hard. After all, there's a reason Sylvie is my best friend, and a reason I've spent the last year in a strange entanglement with Sebastian and let him do things to me that I would ordinarily not let anyone do.

The gallery is called Belvedere 21, and it's about two and a half kilometers from Wiener Staatsballett, where we've been performing.

It's sleek and sophisticated, and I don't like it. It's cold and feels like school.

What I do like is how everyone here is drifting around in diamonds and couture. How they survey the pieces with actual consideration, that maybe one might come home with them.

I hate to admit it, but I have inherited a deep, deep desire for wealth from my mother. The only difference is that I want to earn it. She wants to earn it, too, but she thinks earning it means lying on your back and fucking every rich man who will touch you until something sticks.

A waiter walks over with champagne and holds out the tray for us. I take one with a smile and a clumsy *danke schön*—which is one of those German expressions that's so overused by English-only-speaking Americans that it almost sounded obnoxiously inauthentic.

Quite immediately, Sebastian is pulled into a warm greeting by a chic-looking woman of the Diana type.

"Oh, I'm so glad you could make it!" says the woman. She looks to Sylvie and me. "Now, who are these enchanting creatures?"

"This wonderful gazelle is Jocelyn Banks," he says, pushing me forward slightly.

"Hello, nice to meet you," I say, stopping just short of, for some reason, trying to curtsy.

"Jocelyn, this is Marisol Bauer, the curator here and one of my favorite women on the planet."

"Oh, *stop*," she says, then shakes my hand. "How wonderful to meet you. You are a ballerina?"

"Yes," I say. "I've been with the North American Ballet for about a year now."

"Lovely," she says, and moves on to be introduced to Sylvie.

"And this"—Sebastian claps a hand over her shoulder—"is our rising star, Sylvie Carter."

She shakes Marisol's hand. "Nice to meet you. This is a beautiful gallery. I'm so excited to see the show."

She sounds like a fucking Disney princess all of a sudden.

"Keep an eye on her—she's going to be so big that she'll be a household name. I'm telling you; she's got *it*."

Marisol actually gives me a sympathetic smile before nodding at Sylvie. "Well, the best of luck to you. I'm sure you will do beautiful things."

We keep moving, floating through and meeting strangers with the same introductions. Each time I hear that Sylvie has *it*, it hurts more.

Pretty soon, we've been trotted around like horses for long enough and I break away to stare at some art. Eventually I've peered into the void of each and every abstract painting; and once again in my life, decide I don't understand it. But not that I don't like it. Especially these, there's something about them that I do like.

After the last painting, I look around, listening to the calm jazz piano and dusty, lilting snare, which sounds like the rain outside. I try to be the sort of statuesque, glamorous woman who can merely listen to what I think sounds purely like background music. I'm too bored immediately.

I finish my second glass of champagne and decide to get the fuck out of this delightful place.

But what a waste of a good outfit.

I walk out of the gallery, completely unnoticed by anyone, and turn right. I stop at a place that looks so wonderful it truly takes my breath away. It's just a little bookshop and café, and what I want right now is local food and wine and honestly, just my own company. I'm sort of sick of everyone else.

The restaurant is cozy and sweet on the outside, with a wooden sign that bears the name Liesel's.

Inside is a collection of travel books. It smells like sawdust and old books, despite the fact that the place looks old and the books look new.

But it also smells like food. I keep looking and realize there's an entire restaurant in the back. Small, cramped in the best way.

I walk over to someone and ask in rocky Viennese German if it's possible to get a table for one. When not surrounded by people I think might judge me for the effort, I feel confident enough.

Once seated, I look helplessly at the menu.

"American?" comes a voice from the table nearby.

I know right away that he's talking to me, but I pretend not to hear.

"Excuse me—you're American, right?"

I turn to see a thin man with dark hair and confidence that seems somehow at odds with his appearance. He isn't bad looking, not at all. He just doesn't look like the kind of guy who would be beaming with confidence.

He has extremely nice teeth.

"Yes, I am."

"Me too. Or I was. I moved here a few years ago. I just wanted to let you know that if you need any help with the menu, I'm happy to help."

"Thanks," I say.

The girl who sat me at the table comes back and asks if I know what I want. I point to an item and say, with an obvious question mark, "One of . . . these?"

She looks at me. "Are you sure?" She then glances at the other American.

She then laughs kindly, if dismissively.

He smiles at her. "Just a moment." He looks to me as she walks away. "Do you want me to help you find something good?"

"I guess. Why not?"

He scoots his chair over. "What are you in the mood for? Are you hungry?"

I wait for the *You look like you need it* that often follows men talking about food with me.

"I'm starving."

"How adventurous are you?"

I look at his face, searching for a creepy vibe. I don't find one. He looks back at me, appearing aware of the obvious innuendo, but not grasping for the low-hanging fruit.

"Very," I say.

"Good. Would you like to share a meal with a stranger?"

"I suppose you mean you?"

"No, I've got a friend who's looking for a date tonight."

I arch an eyebrow. "You're funny, huh?"

"Hilarious."

With the soft, muted trombone and candlelit vibe of the place, the unfamiliarity, the repartee between us sort of *feels* like being in an old movie.

He kind of has Gene Kelly energy. Charming and somehow masculine despite the silliness of his general . . . everything.

"Cheers." He holds up his glass of wine.

"Cheers."

We clink glasses and they ring out in the small, cave-like room. I take a sip. "Oh wow, that is good."

"So, what brings you to Vienna?"

"I'm a ballerina. I dance with the NAB, the North American Ballet."

"Holy smokes, no kidding."

I laugh. *"Holy smokes?"*

Something about him makes me feel comfortable poking fun at him right away.

"What?" he asks, amused. "Never heard a guy say *holy smokes* before?"

The server comes back.

"Bist du bereit?"

"Do you mind if I order?" he asks me.

So polite. "No, of course not. Just—no eggplant. I hate eggplant."

He stares at me a beat too long, smiling. Then orders confidently in German. The server nods and walks off.

"Wow, you really speak the language."

He shrugs. "They're right about immersion. I told her to bring us her favorite, the most adventurous thing on the menu, and the crowd favorite. Just so you know. Don't want you to feel left out."

Huh. I realize in that moment that I've been feeling left out for a long time. Then this strange expatriate goes and says something like this.

I take a sip, then remember to be polite too. "And what do you do?"

"I'm an artist. A painter, actually. In fact, I'm playing hooky right now. I've got a show just down the block. I'm supposed to be there, but I hate those things. Everyone walking around, looking at my work. It's not even the judgment that bothers me—I don't mind if someone hates my work. It's really the bullshitting that gets to me, you know? I work mostly in abstract, so it's all, you know"—he waves his hand—"kind of nonsense. And then you get these women in shoulder pads saying it's about my tortured youth or something like that."

"At Belvedere 21."

He tilts his head at me. "Yes, that's right. Don't tell me you're just coming from there, seeking an obsession with my mother in my choice of blues."

"I'm not wearing shoulder pads, am I?"

"None whatsoever."

"But I did just come from there."

"Mm. Well, what did you think?"

I open my mouth and something about him—I can't lie. I feel myself blush and start to smile.

"Ah, I see." He leans back, hand still on the table, one arm over the back of his chair.

"I'm sorry! It's— I'm not saying they're . . . I just don't get abstract art."

He smiles and leans back in. "Can I be honest with you too?"

"Please!"

"I hate the ballet."

I snort into my wineglass. "Really?"

"It's the same thing as you. I get that people like it. I get that it's beautiful. I get that it's hard. But for me, my personal enjoyment of it—I just don't get it."

We both laugh and I hold up my glass. "We're a match made in heaven."

We eat and drink for the next hour. Everything they bring us is incredible. Even when told, I don't know what most things are. I don't care, I love everything.

It's the best dinner I can remember having in . . . well, it sounds dramatic, but maybe ever. Eventually, the food is gone, the wine is running dry, and there is a line of people waiting for a table.

"Are you going to go back to the show?" I ask.

"Well, it ends at eleven. I suppose I should make something of an appearance. Would you mind possibly getting dragged back there with me?"

"To leave because you don't like the art and return arm in arm with the artist. Quite a twist."

"I'll take that as a yes."

He pulls out cash and throws it on the table.

"How much is my half?" I ask.

"Please," he says. "I'm loaded." He winks.

On the way out, he gives the woman who works there a friendly embrace and kisses her on top of the head, saying some very fluent goodbye. All the employees watch him go, saying their own goodbyes. Clearly, he's a regular and very well liked.

Outside it's raining again, and I crouch under an awning. I left my umbrella in the cab.

He takes off his jacket and hands it to me. "Here, you can use it as a tent," he says.

"Oh, I can't, it's *your* show!"

"My show? I'm three hours late to my show. Being a little soggy is hardly the worst they'll think of me."

We jog quickly to the gallery, which is—to both of our surprise—even more packed than before.

Inside, he's greeted with warm enthusiasm by everyone, but somehow doesn't lose touch with me. I feel like a clingy hanger-on, but he brings me along for the ride, neither possessing nor dismissing me. To someone, he introduces me as a beautiful Louisianian he was hoping to make an expat.

After that he turns to me and says, "I need to talk to you."

My chest seizes, as it always does when I think I'm in trouble. "What is it?"

He pulls me over to the piece that is hues of buttery yellow and powder blue. "I don't know your name."

"And I don't know yours."

We look at each other in awe, and then both say, "I'm—"

He says, "You go first."

"I'm Jocelyn Banks."

"Lovely to meet you, Jocelyn, and I'm Jordan Walsh-Morales.

Or, as it says on the paintings, J. Walsh-Morales. Or, really, as it says on the paintings, J. Wa-Moreh . . ."

I look at the signature and get the joke. "Nice to meet you, Jordan."

"Nice to meet you, Jocelyn."

"There you are!" says Sylvie, coming over with Sebastian. She leans in toward me. "Warning, your mother is here."

"What?"

"Jocelyn Rose!"

"Oh god, no. How is she here?"

"We missed you. Where were you?" Sebastian does a double take and realizes who else is in our little corner. "Oh, J. Walsh-Morales, nice to meet you. Sebastian. Jocelyn, I hope you were on your best behavior—this is the artist of all these wonderful pieces."

I seethe. I'm not his fucking child. Between him and the presence of my mother, I feel as though I've been floating high above the planet for hours and am suddenly plummeting back to earth, ears popping all the way.

"And what she's doing here is I invited her," he says, leaning toward me. "I like to make you feel things, little one. When I let you be free, you get complacent."

I pull away from him.

"Jocelyn Rose, my darling daughter!" She comes over with George. Her eyes widen at the sight of Jordan. "Oh, my goodness, you're the artist! Wow, you're such a celebrity! And you're so *handsome*, oh my goodness. I expected some brooding type, but you've got such a nice face. Watch out, George, I might have a new man in my crosshairs!"

She looks approvingly at me.

I want to puke.

Jordan looks a little stunned by all the weird energy and I

don't blame him. I feel suddenly responsible for all of it, as if I've invited them to be as irritating and hovering as they are. Or at least as if they're some terrible, fun house reflection of me and what I surround myself with.

"We were just talking about getting a piece or two," says George. "George Longworth."

"Nice to meet you, George," says Jordan. "And you . . ."

"Oh, I'm Brandy Banks!" says my mother, holding out a hand and pushing back her fur stole, which I know to be real, and which I know to be exactly not chic because no one likes real fur anymore. Everything about her outfit is like a nine-year-old saw a movie of glamorous people and threw it together from things she could find in her grandmother's closet. "So nice to meet you. I like the one upstairs that looks like a carousel."

"Yes, we were looking at that one too," says Sebastian. "It's amazing how you managed to capture so much in that image. It seemed to me to be so clearly representational of the transition from child to young man. The invasion of darkness in what should be so lovely. It's so expressive, really. Without saying anything too obviously, you say things with such clarity. It's really magical."

"Well, thank you so much. If you'll excuse me, I have a few other people I need to talk to." I deflate, until he adds, "Jocelyn, could I convince you to join me?"

I reinflate with pride at being invited to go along with him.

As soon as we are away, he says, "That Sebastian guy. Quite the shoulder pads on him, huh?"

I cover my laugh and let this strange, pleasant stranger guide me through a world I've never been a part of.

Not long after that, we leave. He takes me out to the streets of Vienna, where I remember again that I've lost my umbrella. He offers me his jacket again, but the rain is warm, and I tell him I don't care.

I stop at a shop window and see the mascara under my eyes, and instead of being embarrassed I laugh. I turn to him, and he places his thumbs under my eyes and wipes away the pigment before putting his hand behind my neck and another on my waist and pulling me close and kissing me.

It's an instant choreography. Like we've been kissing each other for years and we know just what to do. There's no misstep— not too much or too little. His hands on me feel right, feel good, feel safe, feel comfortable.

Feel nothing like the experiences with Sylvie and Sebastian, which suddenly seem so back-alley.

"Will you take me to your apartment?" I ask.

He smiles. "Are you sure? I'm content to walk around this city with you all night. Just holding hands if that's what you want."

"I want more of you. Maybe if we had forever it would be different. But I leave tomorrow. And I can't wander forever."

His apartment is nearby.

Everything about this feels so new, so different.

Most of the romantic tumbles I've had lately were frantic and primal. Racing to get laces undone before being slammed against a wall or flipped over onto my stomach and then yanked up onto all fours.

The guys have mostly been dancers, some random guys from hotel bars here and there. It isn't always sex, but it is always emotionless.

Then of course, there is the stuff with Sylvie and Sebastian. That felt more like art than sex.

But this is nothing like any of that.

He opens the door to his apartment, and it smells familiar and feels alive. It feels lived in. It smells like coffee and paint, but also open windows and fresh laundry. He shuts the door behind me, and the silence of the room doesn't feel stale or cold, it feels electric and palpable.

Jordan lifts my chin and looks me in the eyes before kissing me. It's soft and gentle. I feel my heart turn to liquid as he puts his arms around me, pulling me closer. He holds me tightly, his body seeming stronger and bigger than I initially noticed, when it's not pressed against my small frame. He's too tall and broad to be a dancer, but he's strong and firm. I want to know what from. I want to know everything.

I want to ask about every item in his home and find out just how it has come to earn a place here. I want to know what he would be doing if he were alone right now.

I want him to stay entangled with me forever.

With every single touch, I feel myself sink deeper into the soothing of his embrace. His fingers work the delicate straps of my dress. The stubble on his cheeks against my smooth skin, the taste on his tongue of the red wine he'd chosen at the gallery, the scent of wood and smoke mixed in with his own natural scent.

I let the dress fall to the floor when he unzips it completely. I unbutton his shirt, his hands in my hair as I try to concentrate on freeing each button from its hole. Once his shirt is off, I let my own body fall against his. The heat of his skin lights a fire in me. My entire skeleton feels like it has lost its strength. I spent a life-time keeping myself tight and rigid, but here I am, shifting from solid bone to cascading sand at Jordan's feet.

He pulls me into the bedroom, where I lie on my back, only in a thong and thigh-high stockings. I hadn't worn them thinking they'd be sexy for anyone but me. But now here is this stranger who feels like so much more than that, peeling them carefully off my lightly shaking legs.

He kisses my anklebone, my shin, my knee, his fingers grazing the inside of my thighs, then kissing my stomach, cupping my breasts and kissing my nipples. Then with just the right amount of urgency and control, he bites the sensitive part of my neck that I'm always urging lovers to find.

I let out a gasp and he moans as the need for each other increases.

I grasp at his back as his arm goes beneath the arch in my hips. He pulls my lips to his and kisses me deeper than before. Our tongues move perfectly together.

I reach for his waistband, opening his pants with trembling fingers, and grasp for his hardness. I'm desperate for it. His breathing changes as I begin to touch him.

He touches me back and I have never felt so instantly close to climaxing. I don't even have time to pull his pants off or do anything but move my thong out of the way. I pull him into me, and we connect like we're made for each other.

I think of nothing else but what is happening right now, right here, for the first time in my life.

CHAPTER EIGHTEEN

DELTA FLIGHT 817
FOUR YEARS AGO

Sylvie

On the plane from Vienna to New York, I try to sleep, but can't. The score of *Romeo and Juliet* is racing through my head on a loop.

When the flight attendant comes around with drink offerings, Jocelyn and I get a bottle of white wine. It will be swill, it almost always is on these flights, but it's free and unlimited. Or at least we'll never hit the limit.

We pour it into our little plastic cups and start a game of rummy.

Once the wine kicks in and everyone else is sleeping around us, Jocelyn gestures for me to lean closer.

"I think you should break it off with Sebastian."

"Shh!" I say.

"No one is listening."

"They're gossip hungry—they're always listening." I lower my voice. "Why are you saying this? Is this something to do with this Jordan guy?"

She hasn't been able to stop talking about him, and it's weird. It makes me feel rejected. Moved on from. I've always had this weird feeling she might just quit ballet forever and stay in one of these cities and I'd be without her. This time, it feels like that had almost happened. So, I have to hate Jordan.

"Because." She searches my eyes for something. "Have you really not heard?"

"Heard what?" When she doesn't say anything, I arch an eyebrow. "Spit it out."

"I—"

"This is about me being cast as Juliet, isn't it?" I cross my arms, petulant, childlike. "I really thought our friendship was more sacred than this jealousy bullshit."

I don't even believe what I'm saying. I'm just afraid to hear whatever it is she has to tell me.

"Well, yeah, in a way it has to do with you being cast as Juliet. Don't you think it's shady? Wouldn't you rather be cast because you're good, not because you're fucking the guy who can make your dreams come true?"

"Shh!" I shake my head. "God, you're really not listening."

"I'm not listening? Sylvie, do you even like him? Or have you really become so blinded by your ambition that you'll just fuck some—"

"Lower your fucking voice." I grip her arm.

I feel as though I'm in a burning building and I smelled smoke a long time ago but stayed on the thirteenth floor, pretending I didn't, and now the flames are starting to lick my flesh.

And then I decide to make everything worse. "I'm really surprised you went for that guy. I mean, it's whatever, it's just a fling, but he's such a . . . dork. Right? Like not very cool or sexy or anything. I mean it's cool that he's so rich and does such great art, but in person, he was just sort of . . . goofy, right?"

Her cheeks grow red. "I didn't think he was goofy. And what's wrong with that anyway?"

"Really? Not at all? I mean he's sort of like a sidekick in a movie or something."

"Why are you saying that? You know I liked him, so you're just, what, shitting all over his personality to embarrass me or something?"

I try to look scandalized. "What? No! It's not like you're going to see him again anyway, right? He lives in Vienna and there are a thousand other guys out there. I don't know, maybe I was just trying to help you get over it or something."

"Who asked you to do that?"

"Or maybe not! Maybe I just thought he was weird! I'm sorry, I don't know—you're not giving me any way to win right now!"

She sets down her cards. "I liked him."

"Okay!"

My temper, the one I'm always tamping down these days—except for over the last few days—is rising.

She rolls her eyes. "You're always doing that. And I mean even the way you acted with Sebastian, right in the beginning—it was always just you trying to win, trying to be the best, be the most loved. It's fucking obnoxious."

And then, suddenly I'm powerless over the words coming out of my mouth. "Excuse me? Okay, yeah, maybe he and I have connected a little more than you and I have—or I mean more than you and he have. And that's undeniably true, right? Which makes sense, I mean you're not even into him. Not like that. Are you?"

"It doesn't matter," she says, evading the question. "But it's just all so fucked up. I mean, if you're getting the role of Juliet, then, I mean, come on. He's just giving you the role. Probably because you're sleeping with him."

"I knew you weren't done with that little jab."

"It's not a little jab, it's the truth. Come on, you've only been in the company a year and you got *Juliet*? There are so many other dancers who are more qualified for that."

"But it's not about qualifications; it's about technique and talent and just who's *right* for it."

"And you think you're right for it? You're ready for that?"

"I'm a thousand percent more right for it and readier for it than you are."

"What the fuck?"

"Well, you're really not even in the running for something like that, are you? You're not a Juliet!"

"So, what am I right as?"

"Right now?" I slouch in my seat, rubbing my temple. "I don't know, right now I see you as only ever a soloist, so maybe one of Romeo's harlots."

Jocelyn's eyes widen at me in shock.

"A whore," I add deliberately.

"That's great."

"Well, come on. After *Jordan*, I don't know where you draw the line. Who knows, maybe you're like your mom. You both don't fit in this world."

She reels back like she's been slapped, but then seethes. "So, shall we revisit your list of rules you set for yourself? To see where you draw the line?"

"Oh, fuck you."

She pulls them up on her phone with too-fast ease.

"Let's see here. *Be good. Be very good. Beyond reproach.* Well, you are good, but not beyond reproach. *Do not reward yourself.* I remember you buying a chocolate bar the other day and—"

"Oh my god, I had no idea I was being seriously watched all the time."

"*Drink rarely, don't do drugs.* Whoops." She shoves the bottle toward me. "*Don't have sex with anyone, write down no shit talk*—well, I could find some of that for you."

"Yeah, the next one is don't let friendships get ugly. Looks like I failed that one too. But that one might be because I picked the wrong ones."

"Oh, this is great, this is great . . . *befriend the staff without being a brownnoser.* Well, holy shit, I mean you definitely got close to the staff. Although you have been pretty close to kissing his ass, quite literally."

I swat at her phone. "What the fuck is your problem?"

"I don't need my phone to know the last one, though, do I? *Dance as Juliet by the time you are twenty-one.* Well, looks like that's one you'll see through. It only took breaking all your other rules and it's also ridiculous, I mean those rules are—what are you, thirteen?"

She hates her mother for being mean. But whether she likes it or not, Jocelyn has clearly inherited her talent.

"You're such an asshole. Sebastian said you were a flake and I never believed it."

"I'm a flake? I'm a *flake*?" Jocelyn looks aghast. "Well, maybe I am, but now you're going to succeed because of a man. I hope that feels good."

"Oh, shut up. Like Jocelyn Banks is ever going to have the ring of a household name. No, you're just here to make the best look amazing. You're good, but you didn't spend a lifetime doing this, and I did. It shows. I worked my ass off to get here and I deserve to play Juliet and you're freaking out because you don't know if you have what it takes to be here, but you also don't have anywhere else to go. Unless of course your mother's scheme works, in which case you can always move in with them. Or better yet, follow in her footsteps and become a gold digger." I feign dawning comprehension. "Oh my god, is that what you were doing with that artist? That makes so much more sense. Like mother, like daughter."

There's sudden turbulence on the plane and it wakes everyone up. Most people stay calm, but when it continues for more than a few seconds, it starts to get on the nerves of some people, including, unfortunately, me.

I have an intense fear of flying. I usually never make it through without grabbing Jocelyn's hand and squeezing until our knuckles are white.

But I'm prouder than I am afraid.

"You really don't know anything about Sebastian, do you?" asks Jocelyn, tone now biting.

"Of course I do."

When the plane seems to drop several feet, lifting each of us out of our seats, an involuntary sound emerges from my throat. I do not reach for her for comfort.

"So you know that he's with Victoria Haley?"

The ballerina-turned-actress's face swims into my mind. Her movie posters and tabloid pictures. I don't read any of that stuff and I rarely see movies, but you can't stand in line at the grocery store or check Instagram without seeing something to do with her.

"That's just a bullshit rumor," I say, though I haven't heard this particular rumor and it's more that I'm wishing it out of existence.

The plane rocks and shakes and my heart pounds. There are gouges in my legs from my fingernails.

"I don't think it's a rumor, Sylvie. They just walked a red carpet together. Why do you think he wanted to keep you such a secret? Obviously sleeping with you would be bad for his career and a thousand times worse for yours if it got out, but I don't think he's that cautious. He could find a way to spin that. No, I think you're a shameful secret. You're something he's hiding away because he's—"

"I know all about Victoria," I lie. "It's just PR. It's just for funding and to get his name in the papers, and for her to keep her name as a ballet dancer."

She doesn't believe me. She knows me too well. "If that's true," she says slowly, "then you are both shameless ladder climbers. Fuck it. You deserve each other."

The plane drops again suddenly, dramatically enough that other people are starting to sit up in their seats with worried looks on their faces.

I'm not sure what's making me feel worse. Because angry or not, part of me believes what Jocelyn is saying. Part of me trusts her more than Sebastian. But if I trust her more, my whole life will crumble.

Because I do know Sebastian. If I tell him I've heard the rumors that he's with some movie star, he'll tell me the truth. He'll say it's not a rumor, and then the life I have with him will be shelved out of sight. As if it never happened. I can feel it in my bones. I'll lose Juliet. He'll start treating me like everyone else. At his core, he's cold. He won't look at me fondly and think of the way we once were—it'll start to feel as though it was all a dream.

Without him, what do I have left? Besides Jocelyn, I never talk to the other dancers anymore. I've been so confident that I had Sebastian on my side that I've now totally alienated Diana. She used to like me, but now I've rolled my eyes at her. Ignored her. Behaved as though I didn't need her. Because I didn't.

Without Sebastian, it's all over.

As the plane lurches once again, I reach frantically into my bag and retrieve my emergency Xanax. I haven't taken any since I was maybe fifteen, but I always have it on hand.

I break one in half and put it under my tongue.

"What is that?" asks Jocelyn.

"Just Xanax. It's not a big deal, just . . . just leave me the fuck alone, Jocelyn."

Returning home, I feel terrible.

I'm so jet-lagged from Vienna, and am desperately, furiously sad. I can't even really say what's hurting me so much. It isn't just fighting with Jocelyn—although that feels more like an ending than just a fight.

I lie on my bed and feel my heart begin to race. I bolt up. Fuck.

Heart palpitations. Just what I need right now. I take another half a Xanax and collapse on my unfamiliar bed and fall asleep feeling the most alone I can ever remember feeling. I grab my phone and put on the music that will soothe me: Prokofiev's *Romeo and Juliet*, like I did when I was younger and freaking out.

For the next two days, I sleep and go to the gym and Pilates and eat greens and lean fish. I'm trying to get myself back to normal. Lately I've been slacking. I get the feeling that the change in routine is making me better in a way, shaking up my obsession with perfection—but it isn't me. I have to get back on track.

I try to think of Sebastian. Try to remind myself that something with him is beginning. That the Victoria Haley stuff is all bullshit—even though I'm too afraid to google it.

I send him texts.

Not going to buy groceries—dinner?

No response.

Hey, would you meet me to rehearse? I'm hitting a couple of rough spots.

No response.

I know anything more would be way too much, so I leave it but suddenly feel rejected by him on top of everything else.

When I wake up the morning of a rehearsal day, it's to a frenzy of texts and notifications on my phone. So many after such silence that I wonder if my phone had merely been disconnected—something weird between Europe and the United States?—and is just getting the service back. I find myself hoping it's true—not just for word back from Sebastian but for word from Jocelyn.

Nothing from either of them. Instead, a text from Anna, in addition to a million missed calls from her.

Are you okay?? What the fuck is all this news about you and Sebastian?

My heart plummets.

I google myself.

So many articles come up.

The first one on The Cut is called: BALLET FINALLY GETS INTERESTING—AND I CAN'T TELL IF IT'S HOT OR GROSS.

Then the rest.

BuzzFeed: TEN THINGS YOU NEED TO KNOW ABOUT THE SEBASTIAN ALVAREZ/SYLVIE CARTER AFFAIR (AND A FEW THINGS YOU WISH YOU NEVER HEARD).

Page Six: A LOVE TRIANGLE—AND AN INVESTIGATION IN THE WORKS?

Variety: SEX, DRUGS, AND PIROUETTES.

I click on the article in *New York* mag.

My eyes race over the article, picking up snippets of information.

Sebastian Alvarez, son of seventies icon Lilia Montenegro, is accused of having an affair with a teenage ballerina, but denies the allegations. In an effort to clear his name, he announces his relationship with Victoria Haley, who trained with the Royal Ballet and more recently starred in a psychological thriller that took her from being a dancer who can act to an A-list headliner.

Vomit appears in my throat, and I cough and run to the bathroom, throwing my phone down.

I puke up green bile for five full minutes before recovering enough and going to get my phone and torture myself more.

I get in the shower, holding my phone out of reach, letting the water run over me as I try to calm my overbeating heart.

Sebastian has gone public with a relationship with Victoria Haley, even saying that, quote, "We just stopped by Cartier the other day, actually. Let's just say, I know Vick's ring size."

This is devastating enough. But it doesn't stop there.

Sebastian has posted screenshots of conversations with me, all of which make me look desperate and cloying, and all of which keep him innocent.

It isn't just the missing responses from him, although those are there too (he usually calls me). It's the content. I have been so open and desperate for him I hadn't even considered that it might be a risk. I look back through my own texts to see if he has deleted anything to make himself look better. But no. He just never said a word in text that made it appear as though he had anything but a platonic relationship with me—from his side.

How could I have missed it?

How?

Everything from him is about ballet, rehearsal, or simply looks as though he ignored my flirtatious texts—when, in reality, he would always call me. That's where he did his dirty talk, his flirtation.

One of the screenshots shows my diary—when I openly sent him my diary rules. What a naive fool. He'd called me sweet when I showed them to him. Now I realize he was just making fun of me.

Someone has zoomed in and made an article just about those.

There's a line in one of the articles that implies that I've got a drug problem. That I can't get through the day without abusing a prescription.

I shake my head in awe, reading it. What the *hell*?

How did this get out? How did this begin?

It's impossible to know exactly how it had leaked, but I have a guess.

If it wasn't Jocelyn going straight to the press, then it was her refusal to be quiet on the plane.

Someone must have overheard us on the plane.

When I walk into the theater later—no one speaks to me. I expected people to be talking about me. Looking at me. But instead everyone averts their gazes, which is so much worse.

Like falling and having it be okay enough that your friends can laugh—versus getting so injured that it's not funny at all.

Sex is no big deal in a world like this one. But sex to put yourself ahead of everyone else? That's social suicide. Everyone hates that. Everyone works too hard to have an opportunity stolen from them by something cheap and sneaky.

I do not get cast to dance as Juliet.

Over the next several weeks, I lose every friend I thought I had, and I refuse to speak to Jocelyn, even the one time she makes an attempt. My name is moved back on the basic. I go from learning every soloist part to being swiftly removed as Juliet and taken off the soloist casting.

I go from being an up-and-coming star, the one to watch, to being an outcast.

And somehow, Sebastian comes out largely unscathed.

I will never know what kind of connections he had to use to take care of what happened. He's fired from the NAB right away, but somehow manages to get even the NAB to say that it has nothing to do with the scandal, and all to do with the fact that he'd been tapped to choreograph a sexy, dark remake of *The Red Shoes*. Whoever does his PR is a genius, because all they do is start an Instagram and post Polaroid photos of behind the scenes on the first few days of shooting, and there's a huge following. People can't stop being excited about it.

He's on *Watch What Happens Live*.

When Andy Cohen asks about the scandal, Sebastian says, "Well, you know, the funny thing about that whole story is just how overblown it is. Of course, this girl is young, she's nineteen. I'm in my forties. I know how it looks, but the ballet world is different. In order for this strange storytelling to exist, there's a connection that happens between everyone who has to work together onstage. It's more than simply teacher–student, costar–costar, or anything like that. It's more like a constant metamorphosis, and it's done in unison with those around you. And I can't say that this is the first time I've had a girl who developed feelings for me—I'm not trying to brag, you understand, only to explain how common this is. It's like in therapy when there is that—what's it called?—transference. It's like that. They grow and they feel something they never felt before, and so often they think it's love. Sylvie Carter is a really beautiful, talented, and wonderful young girl. Is she"—he makes a cringey face—"the type of girl you would risk your career for? Not so much."

The crowd laughs.

"Wow," says Andy. "Harsh!"

"It's not that she's not great, I'm not saying that. I'm not saying that." He plays to the crowd, lowering his hands as if they're the jerks who need to be reined in. "It's just that it makes me a little sad for this girl that she considers what we had to be anything close to an affair. I mean you heard those rules she wrote down, right? This girl came into this world with an *agenda*. A plan."

"See, that terrifies me," says Andy. "If I met a girl and she had a list of nine things she wanted to do and they were that strict, I'd think that was like nine red flags."

The audience laughs again.

"I hate to agree with you, I really do. But the point is, you see how this sort of rigid world affects some girls. Some of them can't take it. They have to obsess over every minor detail until they think they've secured themselves some sort of safety. And to be honest with you?"

The audience waits with bated breath.

"It makes me a little uncomfortable to be considered a part of her obsessive little plan to become . . . what . . . the world's best ballerina?" He cringes again, looking sad, moving his head side to side, like he's trying to find a way she might be. "I just can't see that for her. And in fact, I bet she sees it, too, and that's why she's so desperate to try to plan what she can. Because it's never going to happen for her. I've been doing this a long time and she just doesn't have that *it* factor."

A little bit of the truth and a whole lot more lying has just undone a lifetime of work.

CHAPTER NINETEEN

NEW YORK CITY
NOW

Sylvie

We're back in New York City, and I'm sitting on the edge of my bed, in my apartment, waiting.

I know I won't be Juliet this time. It's not like before, where the pain of hoping and wanting was eclipsing everything else. That had been hell in the truest sense—a person's hell can really be grown from the detritus of someone's destroyed, obliterated heaven.

I won't be Juliet, but I can find a way to be me again. And it starts with breaking the patterns that have held me captive.

I bite the tip of my tongue, waiting for Alessandro to answer. I tensely tap the floor with the side of my crossed foot. He has to answer. If he doesn't, I won't have the guts to go through with it later.

"Little swan," he says. His voice is cool, sexy, and not expecting anything bad to come from me. Why would it? I have only given to him.

"Hey," I say curtly. My voice is harsher than I meant, and

certainly more than I thought I'd be able to muster. "Do you have a second?"

He hesitates. No one ever says anything good after asking that question.

"Er—yeah, sure. Just give me a moment."

His end of the line goes silent. I gnaw into my lip and carve gouges into my knee with my fingernails.

When he returns, he asks, "What's wrong?"

"Nothing. I just want to talk about the other night." I shut my eyes and think of myself on the stage, dancing as Juliet. I quiet the part of my mind that insists I'm overreacting to my own patterns.

But I must overreact, I think to myself.

"The other night . . . it was good, right?"

"Yes. It was. It's not that it wasn't. It's just that I c—" I stop myself from saying *can't*, which is an arguable term. "I don't want to do that again. It was . . . it was special, and I don't want you to feel weird or anything about it. But it's not something I can do right now."

"Is this because you have feelings? Because it wasn't just sex? Or the opposite, and you felt nothing and that's why you're running away?"

He sounds cool, calm, and collected, but I can hear the insult in his voice. It's the same tone he had when he talked about the costume for *Swan Lake*. Something is not going his way and it doesn't fit him well.

"It doesn't matter, I really— To be honest, I've gotten too far off track with my own life and my career. I'm not dancing as well as I should be and I spent my life doing this, you know, and for the last few years—" I stop myself from going too deep. "I haven't been at my best. Having something with you is going to interfere with that, no matter what, good or bad, and I've embarrassed myself enough."

"I don't understand, Sylvie. Are you telling me you're afraid I'll hurt you or are you telling me that you have no interest? Or are you telling me that tired old line about a relationship not fitting into your life right now, when I never even asked for it?"

The rejection stings. "I didn't say I wanted a relationship."

"Neither did I. You're calling to tell me you don't want to sleep together again—is that what I need to be clear on?"

I pause. "Yes."

He pauses too. "Is this something you're doing in order to be complicated?"

"Excuse me?"

I feel and sound offended, but there's a weird part of me that feels like the answer is *yes*.

But I imagine going for it. I imagine us trying to be together. I imagine for just one moment the embarrassment and pain that will happen if he's the one who calls *me* and asks if I *have a second to talk*.

Between that and everything I know I need to address with my career, I resolve further.

"I'm not trying to be complicated. I am trying to be clear. I didn't call expecting it to make much of a difference to you at all, necessarily. I just want to tell you not to bother putting your energy toward me and not to be surprised when I don't put mine toward you. It's just not what it's going to be. It's fine if you didn't expect a reprise anyway. I'm just letting you know where I am." Then for added effect, "It's not that big of a deal."

He is silent for a moment. "Okay."

"Okay."

"See you in an hour."

My heart lurches with sudden hope. "What?"

"Rehearsal, Sylvie. I'll see you at rehearsal. Goodbye. Thank you for being so clear."

He hangs up.

Of course he meant rehearsal. I obviously know that. I look at my phone screen and feel like an idiot.

He so clearly doesn't care. Why did I bother calling? Who would even assume he'd *want* to hook up again? Just because we have, doesn't mean we would. The mystery is gone—we had sex and it's over.

But couldn't it be possible that he spoke the way he did because he likes me? And I just told him it would never happen again?

Maybe.

I shake my head. This is exactly what I don't have time for. Exactly what I shouldn't be filling my mind with. I'm still sore, I'm still tired, I'm still riddled with hangover guilt. And I'm terrified that when I see Diana, I'll be fired.

The fact that I haven't been fired yet is somewhat shocking. My fear is that what's taking so long is that letting me go is more than just a singular decision. It must go through other people. The dissolution of my contract might take a few days. So maybe it was seen, the decision has been made, and I am just a sitting duck.

A sitting swan. Waiting to die.

I pull out my phone and send two texts.

One to my sister.

Hey. I am sorry for how I acted the other night. I think you were right. Maybe I was a little right too—what I did shouldn't be that big a deal, but you were more right because it is anyway. I told Alessandro it's over and I'm going to do what I love again. It's been too long, and you're right. Love you. <3

The other one to Diana. We are free to text her, but no one ever does.

Diana, I deeply apologize for my behavior. Not just lately,

but in the last couple of years. I let someone get the best of me and then I found the worst of me. So did you. I want you to know that I am fully committed to—

Halfway through writing it, I burst into tears.

I breathe through it and keep writing.

I am fully committed to this company, and I am going to do everything I can to show that. This text is meaningless, and I know that—only action matters. But I want to tell you anyway, just so that it's been said. I am sorry I ever made you doubt me.

Neither answer right away.

Finally, my sister responds.

Thank you for apologizing . . . It's okay. I just want you to remember that I don't need you to keep giving ballet your all (of course I don't). If you quit tomorrow, that's great. If you give it your all, that's great. I just don't want you to be in between, because that's when you become unhappy, and I don't want that. <3 Talk soon.

Diana answers too. With merely . . .

Hmm.

I keep waiting for something else, but nothing else comes. My mind reels and I do everything I can to look good, strong, solid that day at rehearsal. I order a juice for detoxing. I eat two eggs and nothing else. I drink water. I have an electrolyte pill. I apply a liquid foundation and subtle blush to look healthy. I am ready to pretend that I am ready for anything.

D iana is not in her usual mood. Instead, halfway through the day at the company meeting, she's laughing with Robert before gently quieting the stage full of sweating, panting dancers just come from other rehearsals.

"Everybody, everybody, thank you. So." She claps her hands. "We have a very exciting new addition to our little company here today. As everyone knows, having the pleasure of Alessandro dancing with us has been invigorating. To have someone come around who truly is one of the world's living legends has been an honor for us all. And now I would like to do something a little unusual, I want to announce our Juliet. Of course, usually we would have started today's rehearsal with everyone knowing who our star performer would be, but this took a little showmanship. Because none of you, especially some of you, are really going to see this one coming."

My stomach tightens, the kale and ginger from this morning's juice seeming to whirl around inside me, preparing me for . . . what? Do I think it's me?

"This one is a little rough around the edges. A strange pick for Juliet. Not because she's not an incredible technical performer, not because she doesn't have the right look or shape or anything like that. But because she's a tough cookie." She smiles. "She's not just good, she's brilliant. It took some time to bring out her best, and it took Sebastian to bring it out of her."

To my gut-curdling dismay, Sebastian walks out onto the stage.

Everyone applauds, which makes no sense to me at all.

I look to Jocelyn, who looks to me right away.

Our shared ghost.

He looks at us both. His eyes linger on mine, though maybe it's just my perception.

And once again I wonder if it's me. Am I Juliet?

Is it one of the rest of them?

Or . . . is it Jocelyn?

I'll be furious if it's Jocelyn. But then, Diana said the person isn't quite right for Juliet, and I'm far more right than Jocelyn is. Even though she's a principal, I'm still more right for it. Or maybe I just want to be.

Could I dance as Juliet? Would they give me that chance?

Diana knows it's what I want. She knows I was once groomed for it. She must know that I can do it.

If I'm being given that shot, then I'm being tested. I know that for sure. But *oh*, to be given that chance. Again . . . and to not screw it up.

"With no further ado, let me present our Juliet."

Everyone looks around as Diana leads us into an applause.

Diana looks me dead in the eyes. I'm staring at her long enough to be the last to see that Victoria Haley has just graced the stage.

Victoria fucking Haley. The one who used to wear a Cartier ring, bought for her by Sebastian Alvarez.

She comes out with all the confidence in the world. Tan skin, dark eyes with kohl liner smudged just so. Puffy lips. Voluminous hair tossed to the side and falling to her narrow waist. She's in a sports bra and leggings; her abs have a permanent line down the middle even when she breathes in to laugh and say, "So lovely to be here."

She has an accent that isn't immediately easy to pick out, but everyone on the stage knows because everyone on the stage knows Victoria Haley. Victoria Haley, who spent her childhood in Villaviciosa and then moved to London when she was *discovered* as a dance prodigy. Her mother married a man in Parliament, Roger Edwin Haley, and Victoria went from Spanish poverty to English wealth and being a ballerina at the National Ballet of England. She spent her summers visiting Spain and the English and French countrysides. That is, until she was *asked* to be in a psychological thriller where she played a ballerina turned actress who stole an incumbent president's heart. Despite the schlocky plot, the movie was obsessed over and became an instant cult classic. And then, of course, she was cast in the dark reboot of *The Red Shoes*.

Which Sebastian choreographed. Which happened right after their engagement. Their relationship, instead of being like my own with him, was regarded generally as being hot and scandalous instead of shameful and flawed.

And when they broke up, they had the nerve to remain friends and, again, avoid being the center of a scandal.

"It's so nice to see all of you. I've been so excited about this for so long, and it's been hard to keep under wraps. I wanted to tell everyone. But of course I couldn't. I'm not as comfortable on the stage as all of you are these days—I've gotten so out of the habit. So I'm going to rely heavily on you all for your advice and wisdom." She lays a hand over her heart.

It's clearly intended to *appear* to be coming from a good place. But it doesn't play that way. Because she doesn't seem like someone not used to the stage. She's standing in front of us all, hands now on hips, her chest and navel extended out toward us, her chin held high, that bored look on her face and a small smirk playing on her lips. She doesn't seem uncomfortable at all; in fact, she seems as if she's been on the stage her entire life and she's been told she's a special little angel the whole time.

Alicia pats me and whispers, "This is so cool. Oh my god, I can't believe it's Victoria Haley."

I think back to when Alessandro arrived. Alicia behaved the same way, but then, I had cared so much more about his arrival and been so much less resentful that her enthusiasm hadn't irritated me.

I don't respond to her at all.

"I'm so excited to be working with Sebastian again on the real *stage*," says Victoria, looping an arm around him. He puts his own over her shoulders. "He's a genius."

"It's easy to look like a genius when you're working with someone like Victoria," he says. He sounds lazy and confident, and I want to kill him.

"And just to acknowledge the elephant in the room, yes, we were together, but we also admire the shit out of each other professionally." She looks up at him with an infuriatingly adorable nose crinkle.

He does it back, and laughs.

"So!" Diana claps her hands together. "These are going to be very different *Romeo and Juliet* performances. These ticket sales are going to surge. The audience for this is going to be completely diverse. We always have a discerning audience, but this time, it's going to be only the highest echelon who can get tickets for such an experience. We're considering adding an extra few performances, so stay tuned and be prepared for that. Okay, as exciting as this is, we need to get down to business, so everyone get to your rehearsals and get working, as we need to really bring something out of this run of performances. We have Alessandro Russo and Victoria Haley. This company is about to be seen in a new light by major mainstream media. Got it? Let's go."

There is an intense excitement on the stage. A high energy, a dog-whistle-high key between all the dancers who can't believe they're about to dance a show that will get so much attention. All of the principals are annoyed by the usurping of the role, but even their wry, *let's see how this fucking goes* attitude is making it a more charged atmosphere.

Everyone's freedom, clout, and influence just increased exponentially by the casual appearance of Victoria Haley. As if Alessandro hadn't been enough.

It's not that we care about celebrity necessarily, though it's nice, and it helps, and it's interesting. And sometimes, people are famous for particularly cool reasons that we truly care about.

It's all that, for better or for worse, and our specificity and our value as artists are more appreciated, more seen.

But that's not how I see it at all.

All I can feel is that Victoria is leading the life I am supposed to be leading. The life I thought I'd have all those years ago. Why did Sebastian pick her? Why?

Because she was already a prima ballerina?

Everyone from the stage goes where they belong, including me. I stay in the background, where everyone now expects me to be.

I feel embarrassed for having thought, even momentarily, that I was up for the part, but at the same time I feel infuriated by the fact that someone—some celebrity—can come in and eclipse us all. There's no reason to think she will dance this any better than any of us will, but she will definitely help to boost the company, and that's what they care about.

That afternoon, I dance harder than I can ever remember dancing. I push myself further. I sweat. My heart pounds as I dance the role of a harlot. It's a vulgar, rough part and it's a way to bleed out my anger.

When we're finally free to go, I'm the first out and to the dressing room, first one to leave.

I storm through the other dancers and walk all the way home without stopping, and when I get there, I collapse at the end of my bed, feeling the weariness of years weigh suddenly heavily on top of me.

I thought I was coping. I thought I was fine. But all I was doing was surviving.

I can't do it anymore. I can't just survive. I can't have *coping* be all I do.

It's not about deciding not to drink as much or not drink at all. It's not about deciding not to take a Xanax every night or whatever else I can find. It's not about not getting caught up with some guy who might distract me from what I really need to be doing. It's not about risking falling in love or getting hurt.

It's about the fact that I cannot, I will not, just keep living life in order to merely survive, cope, and scrape by. I don't know when I stopped living to be alive. To thrive. To be my best. To be happy.

I look around my apartment. A pile of pointe shoes in the corner, a practice tutu on the chair at the dining room table. A thin layer of dust has settled on everything. The walls are empty; paintings and frames sit on the floor leaning against the wall where I've been intending to put them up for an embarrassing amount of time. I moved to this apartment a while ago, hoping a change of scenery would help me feel at home when I was alone. But it never did.

Whenever I'm alone, I flee.

I call my sister.

She doesn't answer on the first ring, not the second, not the third. I think it's about to go to voice mail.

"Hello?" she says.

"I'm sorry I only call you when something is wrong lately."

"What's wrong?"

I sigh and put my face in my spare hand. "I just got home to my apartment in New York. They cast Victoria Haley in *Romeo and Juliet*. I had just decided to get my shit together and really perform and then they bring in someone else. I—I didn't really expect it to be me, that would have been . . . but the fact that it's not even someone else who *earned* it just makes me feel hopeless, Anna, I feel hopeless."

"Well . . ." she says hesitantly. "It's okay if getting your shit together takes a second. And it wasn't going to happen in time for—I mean isn't *Romeo and Juliet* next week?"

"Yes."

"Okay, so that's pretty reasonable, then, right?"

"I don't want to be made to feel better. I don't want logic."

"Okay. Got it."

I sigh and tears fill my eyes. "I just, I've worked so hard. And yeah, I fucked up a few years ago, but it's so unfair that I got punished forever like I did. And Sebastian shows up today *with* Victoria—"

"Wait, what?"

"Well, I told you he was in Paris, too, right?"

"Yes, but you only said he was there. I didn't know he was going to be around."

I tell her what happened in Paris, leading up to the Alessandro hookup that I already told her about. By the end I am crying and trying not to.

"Is there someone you can talk to?" she says. "Not like a therapist or something—you already told me you won't do that, for whatever reason."

"My last one hit on me."

"Right. Well, that's reasonable. Doesn't mean therapy isn't a great idea, but anyway that's not what I meant. Is there someone there you can talk to who gets it? Who is in this same world as you and who will understand your frustration?"

I consider David and Alicia.

"I'm not saying I don't want to listen," she adds hastily.

"No, I know."

We get off the phone, her reminding me she loves me, me assuring her I'm fine. And I call Alicia, who is with David around the corner at her apartment. They tell me to come over.

I walk in and they are blasting nineties throwbacks.

They scream and come over to me, hugging me. "There she is!" says Alicia. "We haven't actually *hung* in forever. Do you want one of these?"

She holds up one of those terrible malt beverages that's gotten a recent rebrand into being something cool.

"Do you have any gin or anything?"

"Sure, but I don't have any tonic or soda, I don't think . . ." She looks in her fridge. It's just a little fuller than mine.

"No, just on some ice is fine."

An old Christina Aguilera song starts up.

"Oh my god, I love this song," says David. "How are you, sweetie?" he asks, giving me a hug and kissing me on the cheek.

"I'm good."

"How *wild* is it that Victoria Haley is Juliet?" he asks.

"I am seriously still so blown away," says Alicia, getting ice from the fridge icemaker. That ice always tastes weird.

"Doesn't it bother you that they didn't cast someone from within the company?" I ask. "It seems like such an obvious cash grab."

"Maybe it is. We all know the arts need to take the money when they get the chance, so I don't really care. Also it's fucking cool. And, *god*, she's hot," says David. "And it makes us all look better, so I think it's great. I want to be her friend. No, scratch that, I *will* be her friend."

I have no doubt.

Alicia gives me my gin and we sit around the sectional sofa.

For the next two hours, I try very hard to have a good time.

But with a somewhat brazen shock, I realize that I don't want to be with them. The nineties music is one thing. The low-budget drinks are another thing; that's fine, I don't need them to spend a fortune, it's not that. The sycophantic behavior about Victoria is one thing.

The fact that this whole season we haven't really connected is another thing. The fact that I don't feel like I can be honest about how heartbroken I am without feeling like they'll talk shit about me when I leave—that is the worst thing.

And the more I think, as they chat inanely before me, I know that it's more than even any of *that*. It's the fact that when I'm with them, I have to float along, pretending. I am not really with them, not really in it, not really in the moment. I spend the whole time aware that I am "socializing," trying to be interested in what they say and trying to be interesting too. I learn nothing when I talk to them—I simply socialize until the quota is filled.

At around nine thirty, they light up a joint and ask if I want any. They know I always turn it down. It makes me panic. By ten fifteen, they're repeating themselves and zoning out. Not like cartoon high people, not like I have a problem with them getting high, but being on the outside just puts them on another level. It's then that I realize, with full clarity, that we are *always* on separate planes.

I'm not even contending that I'm on a better one. Merely that I don't get what they like. I don't like what they do.

"Okay, I'm gonna head out," I say a little while later.

"No!" says David. "Oh, come on, I was just about to make you guys watch this amazing new Lady Gaga album release performance. It's seriously wild."

"No, I'm good. I'm sorry. Tired."

I spend five full minutes disentangling from them, and then

finally burst out onto the street and take in the deep breath familiar only to those who know what it is like to feel emotionally claustrophobic.

I imagine going home to that empty, cold apartment.

I can't do it.

Instead, I go to a completely different address. Somewhere I should not go. Somewhere I will likely be turned away or regret trying to go.

I don't call ahead or text to say I'm coming. I just walk straight there, cutting expertly through the streets to get to my destination.

When I arrive at the building, I type in the code. It still works.

I go up two stories and get to the door.

I knock the common *it's someone you know* knock. The door opens, and I say our code word.

"Red."

CHAPTER TWENTY

Jocelyn

Candles burn in every corner of my apartment, and I have the windows open. The breeze gusts in, making some of the flames flicker every now and again, casting whipping shadows on the books on all the shelves. Books are the one thing I was able, allowed, and could afford to collect growing up, so my apartment is overrun with them. Favorite childhood books like *The Phantom Tollbooth*, favorite classics like *Rebecca*, contemporary obsessions like *Gone Girl* and *Big Little Lies*. Some have been read so many times that they're taped back together or falling apart and need to be repaired.

My sectional sofa is made of plush cotton and has cozy faux fur blankets thrown over the back. The coffee table has Scrabble on the shelf beneath it and a box, which I made in art class in high school, that I use for the remotes. There is also a copy of *Strangers on a Train* that I'd started before leaving and forgotten to pack.

My pantry is stocked with sauces and canned items; my freezer filled with homemade broths and my grandmother's Bolognese, which I'm saving for the right moment, since it's one of my favorite meals of all time.

Tonight, I made a steak with chimichurri and ate it watching reruns of *Grey's Anatomy*. I had opened a bottle of petite sirah I picked up from the wine shop on the corner.

Now I'm cleaning up and have on David Bowie's *Let's Dance* album. I'm in my coral-colored satin palazzo pants and the matching top. My hair is up in a scrunchie, and I have on a thick coat of moisturizer, still trying to undo the effect of all the flights.

In short, it's the perfect solo night. Exactly the kind of night I need in order to recover from everything. Yeah, I didn't start cooking until eight thirty, and most of the dancers probably got home and ate an energy bar or had a smoothie or, at most, ordered takeout. But I need the reset. I need the return to *home*.

I'm happy to be alone, happy to be with all my candles, my books, and my string lights. My apartment might be a little young, not super sophisticated, but I don't care because I never got the chance to decorate just for me when I was younger, and I can do anything I want now.

At first, I'm not sure if I really heard anything, but then I stop and listen again.

There's a knock on my door.

I open it up hesitantly, wishing I had a peephole.

"Red."

It's Sylvie. It's Sylvie, and she's invoking our code word. The code word that means *I need you*.

We developed the code word years ago, saying that no matter how mad we got at each other, no matter what happened, if we said that word, we would be there for each other. We pricked our fingers and pressed them together like boys in a tree house in a Stephen King novel. And when we said *no matter what*, and *no matter when*, we hadn't envisioned exactly *what* and how much time would pass that would make it unimaginable to one or both of us that we'd be standing in front of each other now like this, with everything that's passed between us.

I can't think of anything to say, so I just stand aside and let her in.

"Your apartment is still so cozy," she says.

"Thanks. Wine?"

"Yeah. Thanks . . ." She looks around while I get her a wineglass. "My apartment feels like a showroom in a store where I don't want to buy anything."

I hand her the wine and nod.

I look out the window to the fire escape, where we used to drink and talk all night. I notice she's looking too.

"Wanna go out there?" I ask.

"Sure. Can I borrow something to wear? I'm sick of this."

She's in tight jeans and a skinny-strapped tank top. It's cute, but she looks like she's going to dinner in SoHo, not having a late-night drink on a fire escape.

"Go ahead."

I grab a candle and my oversized cashmere sweatshirt and crawl out the window. I sit in what used to be my usual spot when we'd sit out here together. She climbs out a few minutes later in my old high school boyfriend's sweatshirt and a pair of leggings and fluffy socks.

We're silent for a moment, and then I ask, "What's this about, Sylvie?"

She chews on her bottom lip. "Do you ever wonder if you still want to be in this world?"

Her question shocks me. Coming from her, it's unexpected; but more than that, I've been thinking it for days. I've been longing for some life I don't have. I want to be home and buy produce and use it before it goes bad. I want time to watch shows and read books. I envy groups of diverse friends I see in the windows of restaurants. But I'm not going to quit. I can't quit ballet. What else would I do?

"Sometimes," I say, settling in the middle for an answer. "It's exhausting. And after today, them bringing in Victoria Haley, I mean, it's kind of like, what are we really shooting for if they'll just bring in some celebrity to eclipse all of us?"

"That's how I feel. I feel like I've trained my entire life for something, and it got stolen from me. Sebastian," she says as explanation.

"I know."

"And then I never fought to get it back. I've just been floating by. And now I don't even know if I can still get it back or if it's too far gone."

"It's not too far gone for you. You're really gifted."

"So are you. You've made it. You're a principal."

"Not in the same way as you."

She shrugs and looks into her wineglass.

"Why did you leave me alone to deal with everything back then?"

Oh, shit. "Sylvie, I didn't. You wouldn't talk to me!"

"Did you say it so loud on the plane so someone would hear? Did you tell someone to listen? Did you just sell the story yourself?"

I expect to have to defend myself, but she bursts into tears and shakes her head.

I move toward her and hug her. Her body feels familiar and foreign.

"I know who it was now," I say.

She looks at me.

I take in a deep breath. "My mom."

Sylvie squints, a few more tears falling from her eyes. "Your mom?"

"I talked to her recently. At the time, I asked if it was her, and she told me she had no idea what I was talking about. I asked her yesterday and she told me she had done it. Thought I knew. Thought she told me before. Was, of course, completely unrepentant. She said that *of course* she told the press. She thought it was what I wanted. Why else would I have had the conversation right behind her and talked so loud?"

Sylvie's face is blank. I go on.

"I didn't, though. I didn't even know she was there. I was in a haze from the whole Jordan thing. That took me forever to get over, which was so weird—I mean, we only spent one night together." I shake my head, feeling stupid. "And then I lost you at the same time. I wasn't paying attention on the plane. I didn't believe her back then, but I felt powerless against her. When she told me yesterday . . . I felt like a complete idiot. I hadn't meant for her to know, but it's *my* mom. It was because she was trying to manipulate everything for *me*. It's a complete mess. I feel—I've felt—horrible. For years."

She sits up straight and glares at the street below us.

She furrows her brow. "Well, then you could have defended me when it came out. At least. That's why I thought you'd done it. Because you just *let* our friendship end."

"I didn't know what to say. You were getting dragged. And you'd been such a dick right when it happened, I wasn't exactly feeling like defending you."

"You could have said I wasn't crazy and that he was an asshole. Anyone could have said that."

"I could have said that."

I look at this girl who used to be my friend, who has turned into something of an enemy over the last few years. I can see why she came here tonight. She's hollowed out. Beneath her eyes, she has dark shadows. She's thinner than ever. She doesn't look like she has any hope left at all.

"Is it okay if I stay here tonight?" she asks.

"Yes."

She digs in her pocket and pulls out a pack of cigarettes and a pink lighter. "Want one, for old times' sake?" she asks.

I've never had a problem with getting addicted, so we used to have them together occasionally. But then I noticed her smoking by herself. Not just for fun. "Sure," I say.

I remember the girl who thought having a hot chocolate was naughty behavior. I'm mad at myself, in a way, for encouraging her to let go and drink a bit, but I'm furious at Sebastian for preying on an innocent girl and getting her fucked up all the time.

She lights mine for me, and I take in the first inhale of tobacco I've had in years. It feels good washing through me, but I can tell that if I have a second one I'll feel sick.

After a little while of silence, I say, "Sebastian looks terrible."

"He does, doesn't he?"

We catch eyes and start laughing. It isn't true. We just wish it were.

"Did you see Victoria dance at all today?" she asks.

"Yeah. As of today, I'm dancing Lady Capulet."

Her eyebrows shoot up. "Really?"

"Yes. They removed that newish girl today, I can't remember her name. Lauren or something. She wasn't doing what they wanted, so they asked me."

It's sort of a slap in the face to play Lady Capulet if you're a principal.

"I'm going to get back to the dancer I was. I hope it's not too late."

A pang of empathy rings through me. "It's not."

"Let's change the subject," she says.

I think I see tears in her eyes.

That night, we get in my bed together, listening to an Agnes Obel album we used to listen to all the time.

It starts when I feel her shaking on the other side of the bed. I reach over and scoot closer to hug her from behind. She puts her hands around my wrist and arm.

It isn't long before she seems to stop crying. But the natural, organic detaching from each other doesn't come. Instead, after a few moments, I feel her grip my arm tighter.

My heart skips a beat, and my eyelids flutter open.

I can't tell if what I think is happening *is*, so I try to be subtle. Try to return the energy if I'm correctly reading it, but not overstep, if I'm imagining it.

I open my palm on her chest, my thumb on her collarbone. She presses into my hand and she, or I—I can't even tell—pulls my hand down to her bra.

The unspoken nature of it means that even as it's happening, it's as if we don't want to move too quickly or speak, like we might scare it away.

I feel her heartbeat quicken beneath my hand and I breathe in sharply with a surge of desire that moves through me. I breathe in the smell of her hair, which is like flowers and herbs but also cigarette smoke. In the moment, it's intoxicating.

What is happening? We have barely spoken in the last few years, and now suddenly we're back here? We have never done anything without Sebastian around. It has always felt performative, even though I liked it with her. But it has always been part of a dynamic with him. Not like this.

It feels new and scary and *naughty* but also familiar and comfortable and like revisiting a warm memory.

Sylvie moves her hair out of the way, so my face is on her neck. I kiss her there. It's so soft; I hadn't remembered how soft and different it is to touch a girl like this. She lets out a small moan and then turns over and puts her lips on mine.

She kisses me and pulls me closer, and I kiss her back, both of our tongues soft, wet, and warm. Both of us are gentle but eager.

Beneath my heavy comforter, in my soft linen sheets, we strip down to nothing piece by piece and our bodies connect over and over in different ways. She lies on top of me, her hip bones jutting into mine, her nipples mirroring mine, our stomachs flat against each other's. She kisses my neck, I kiss hers. I put a hand on her ass, which is muscular but soft too. I spread it apart as she grinds down onto my thigh, her wetness reaching my own.

I grip her, trying not to leave fingernail marks in her back, running my fingers up and down her spine and feeling her tight body that feels so similar to my own but also foreign and exciting.

We once joked that we liked hooking up because we love ourselves so much.

But again . . . it has never been like this.

Never alone. Never just because we wanted it.

I can tell when she's getting close, the muscles contracting around my fingers over and over and over until . . .

Afterwards she collapses into me, heart pounding and breath shaking. But she reaches down to me, and starts touching me again, then moving down with her mouth. It only takes a few minutes for her to make me come too. I can smell her on my fingers, mixing with my own scent, and it feels so illicit.

When I finish, we entangle every limb, say nothing, and fall asleep almost instantly.

CHAPTER TWENTY-ONE

Sylvie

I can't believe how *not* weird it was to have that little rendezvous with Jocelyn. In fact, I feel like through doing it, I got back some power I had lost. I hadn't realized how much it was bothering me that we had stopped getting along. Had hated each other. I always thought that without her, I had eliminated a stress. By not engaging with her, I had believed that I was avoiding something hard. But I think by doing so, I'd actually put myself through something worse.

If we had talked sooner, had it out, been angry, it wouldn't have been bad. It would have been horrible. But I was beginning to think it was even harder to lose someone I so deeply cared about. Every day without her had been stressful with her absence. Painful just because it was unfinished, broken between us.

And I hadn't realized how brittle the wall we'd built actually *was*. Just as quickly as we'd fallen into friend-love with each other, we had fallen apart, and when we tried to repair the relationship, we had figured it out so quickly.

And if we can just avoid hating each other, then we might just get to keep each other forever.

When I went to her apartment, it was out of desperation. It was because I needed to be around someone who knew me. Being around Alicia and David that night had felt like being around someone else's friends when your actual friend gets up to go to the bathroom. You can make conversation, but you sort of just wish it was you and your friend.

I wasn't sure if Jocelyn was going to slam the door in my face. I wouldn't have blamed her. And if the situation were reversed, I might have let her in or I might have slammed the door. I'm glad she didn't.

I'm really glad she didn't.

It feels like the first time I've been *myself* in a long time. We went through the Sebastian thing together, even if the mark it made on my life at the end was different from the mark it made on hers. She knew me. I knew her.

And so I decide to try and give her a gift.

I text Matt, the company coordinator, who has always, despite everything, seemed to like me. He's always stressed, and no one likes him, so I think he understood when no one liked me. I, for one, have also always liked him.

He was the first person I met when I started with the company.

I text him and ask if he might be able to help me find somebody. The artist Jordan Walsh-Morales.

He finds him quickly, and before I know it, I'm on the phone with him after sharing almost no words with him in the past.

"A surprise to hear from you," he says, when the *hellos* are over.

"I'm sure it is. Listen. I know this is kind of an insane

question. You're probably married with two kids and a beach house by now or something, but just in case you're not—"

"I'm not. I'm single. Is this about Jocelyn?"

"Yes. I think she might still think about you sometimes. I mean, I actually know she does. And if there's any chance that you do too . . . I mean I don't know, I'm probably totally overstepping, I don't know why you two never kept in touch or what happened."

"It was just life. It was something really special when we met," he says. "I've created an embarrassing number of paintings about it. About her. Not that she'd like them. She hates abstract art."

"She just doesn't get it. That's what she says."

He laughs. Just from the laugh, I can sense a charm in him I hadn't seen before.

"That's right. I still think about her too. Nothing happened. I think we both wanted things to be different, or at least I hoped that was the case, but her life—your life—is demanding. The world is big. Missed calls and forgotten texts made it hard to keep the magic alive. But I never thought it was gone."

"Could I possibly persuade you to come to New York? I don't know where you are in the world. Or what your life really looks like, or if you'd even want to, though it sounds like you might. But I mean I'll pay for your ticket or hotel or whatever I have to do."

He laughs again, and I like him more. "I'm in LA right now. I hate this city. I've been looking for an excuse to avoid every meeting this week. When should I come?"

The tickets for *Romeo and Juliet* have sold out faster than any performance in NAB history. The PR manager for the company, who we never hear from, has said that given the lull in specialty headlines lately, she thinks we're going to capture tons of attention.

There are multiple injuries in the company. Diana is taking no prisoners this time, and neither is Sebastian. Sebastian is psychologically trying to destroy everyone on the stage at all turns. He's not even supposed to be doing it, he's supposed to be there for Victoria, and yet he's talking to everyone.

"This show could make or break your career," I overhear him saying to Alessandro. Alessandro hardly is there to be intimidated, but I can tell it's getting under his skin.

"It needs to be different. *Why* are you dancing like you don't know the world is watching?"

"You look like a cow being milked—try to act with emotion, not perform like a victim."

"Is there anyone on this stage who wants to remain employed?"

"I feel like every hour I look at you, you've gained a pound around the waist."

"Maybe it's just that I left the United States for a while, but I tell you, this is some of the sorriest performing I can remember seeing."

"You are not here to stand out."

Those are just a few of the things I hear him say. Jocelyn and I are the only ones completely unaffected by his railing or his torment. While half the dancers, especially the young ones, run off-stage to the bathroom to hide tears after a rehearsal with him, we are immune. I've heard it all before. Jocelyn has heard most of it before. He cannot harm us, though he tries.

To me, he says:

"You're washed up and you never even succeeded. Is that what you envisioned when you were four years old in that studio? That the end of the line was two decades of trying as hard as you could and finding that you were not good enough?

"You've gotten soft in the last few years, Carter.

"I cannot remember what I saw in your dancing. Perhaps I was just younger and stupider then, like you were."

Diana is cutting off the pianist the second a knuckle or hair is out of place and making us start again.

Nothing is good enough. It's hell.

Alicia twists her ankle in rehearsal. David loses his temper rehearsing Mercutio. Mike, the stage manager, walks in on two dancers using the principal's dressing rooms to fuck (and the mean rumor is that he didn't shut the door *right* away). Apparently it was a real spread-eagle porno-type situation. They were filming it, and now everyone is pretty sure they have an OnlyFans or something and that they've been doing this for ages.

Pretty good idea.

Rumors spread through the company like wildfire when Mike lets slip that he's looking for another job because the company is out of funds.

The girl he overshared to apparently tearfully told this to one of the other girls, who told Alicia, who told me and about twelve other people.

People start putting things together. We haven't been given as many shoes lately. The flights have been longer, with worse connections. And the powers that be have been angrier than ever.

Apparently, the pure chaos that's going on now is what happens when a company is in debt. The stakes are too high. Reason goes out the window and everyone is afraid of losing everything.

It brings into starker comparison just how much I do not want to; I just cannot lose ballet.

And then, on the day of the last *Romeo and Juliet* performance, something wild happens.

During the morning spacing rehearsal, Alessandro lifts Victoria like always, and then when she goes into the *arabesque penchée en pointe*, she somehow teeters over and falls face-first onto the floor.

I'm there, I see it happen, and I still can't figure out how she lost control. It's like she deliberately threw herself out of Alex's grasp. But when she collapses, it's with a scream. When she looks up, blood is streaming down from her nostrils.

"You fucking *idiot*! You fucking moron, *idiota*!"

Alessandro looks bewildered, and I understand why. He didn't drop her, she fell on her own, it had nothing to do with him. I, and everyone around, stand and watch, to see what is going to happen.

"Is it broken?" says David beside me.

I shake my head, squinting. "It doesn't look like it, but I can't tell."

"I mean it is bleeding a lot."

"You don't think she's going to not dance tonight, do you?"

"For a bloody nose? She should. Do you think she's that vain? Not unless it's broken."

We exchange a look.

She leaves, pinching the bridge of her nose. Sebastian comes in behind me as she's leaving.

"What the fuck happened?"

"She fell over and I think her nose is broken."

"She *fell over*— What the fuck do you mean, she *fell over*? She's a prima ballerina, she doesn't *fall over*."

I shrug. "She did."

"Fucking junkie," he says, pushing past us and following her.

"Is he talking about Victoria?" asks David.

I squint at him. "As opposed to what?"

He holds up his hands in innocence. "I'm just asking. I don't know what you get into these days."

"What does—"

I glance over at Diana and Robert, who have just come in. I can just barely hear her.

"Don't *know* what, Robert. Alicia is injured, Christine danced last night, and Jocelyn is already dancing Lady Capulet."

And that's when I realize what's happening. They're coming up with a backup plan in the unlikely event that Victoria will not dance with a broken nose.

Diana and Robert look around, realizing we're all listening, then leave, Diana pushing through the doors and out into the hall.

I get up the guts and follow them. At first they don't see me.

"I can't imagine it's so bad that any doctor wouldn't let her. No. I'm only worried about her choosing not to. No, I don't think she will. Of course not, it's one performance. This is the night, this is *the* night, everyone who bought tickets tonight is with press or paid ten times inflated prices. If she can't dance, I don't know. I don't know what to do. Robert, I do not know. We are unusually underequipped at the moment."

When she notices me, she glares and does a shooing motion, but I don't go.

"I can do it."

There is a sound behind me, and I look to see Alex coming into the hall as well. I feel simultaneously more self-conscious and bolstered by his appearance.

"You can do what?" She looks genuinely clueless for a second and then her eyebrows disappear into her hairline. "Dance as Juliet?"

"I can do it. You know I know the part, I was supposed to do it before, and I didn't. I've been training my whole life for this, you know that. I never stopped learning Juliet."

"There are other dancers who have been—"

"This is a disaster," says Robert, sounding as if he might faint. "I need to start calling other companies for a replacement."

Alessandro is standing beside me. He gives me a look of encouragement.

"Think about it," I say, trying again, my heart pounding. I breathe fast, looking between Robert and Diana but holding my gaze on Diana. Robert hardly knows me, as he works with the principals and directs Diana to lead the soloists. It's down to Diana. It's her call. "You just said it: everyone who bought tickets tonight is really, really expecting to see Victoria Haley. They're going to be livid when it's not her. Furious. Enough to tear this place apart. But if it's me, they've got a story. They've been writing about me for years because of the Sebastian scandal. They want to hate me. And if they do, then they write about it like a shit show. But I'm good. You know I'm good. Especially as Juliet. If you can't have a star, you need news. Better or worse, I'm news. And no one here is better equipped to handle the barrage of hate that anyone who dances in Victoria's place is going to get."

"She can do this," says Alex.

I look at him and a small smile graces my lips without warning.

Diana breathes in deeply and shuts her eyes. She looks to Robert. *"Qu'est-ce que tu penses?"*

"Je n'ai aucune idée. Nous n'avons personne, nous n'avons rien, ce spectacle va entrer dans l'histoire comme un putain de désastre!"

"No, it won't," says Alex, smoothly understanding every word. "It will be great. It will be special. Different. They want special and different."

Robert and Diana communicate silently now, both asking the other to accept the bet. Diana breathes in deeply again.

"God dammit." Her accent is thick. A sign she is tired. "I can't believe we don't have an alternate waiting in the wings. Sylvie, you've been on thin ice; there were conversations about ending your contract, a decision merely has not been made yet."

"I know. But you don't want to fire me because I'm bad. You want to fire me because I'm a fucking mess. In this case, I'm good, and I'm a mess. It's kind of perfect for what you need tonight. I know the role backward and forward. Everyone is going to see the performance as it's meant to be tonight, but it's going to be danced by me and not by the one they want. I can do it."

She stares at me for a long while and then releases my gaze. "Stay here. Don't go back in there. Stay here."

Robert and she leave together.

She clicks down the hall and away from me. I sit down on the cold wooden floor and wait. It's the longest wait of my life. Alex stands beside me, not saying a word, but also not leaving.

When Diana reappears, she says, "I heard you told Sebastian to *fuck off* last night. Is that true?"

Dammit. I cannot win.

"It's a real shame if that's what prevents you from saying yes to my proposal. Because I have to stand by it. Sebastian is a monster."

Diana arches a perfectly penciled eyebrow. "On that, Sylvie, you and I can agree. Let's do it. You're tonight's Juliet."

Relief surges in me. "Really?"

"Don't be pitiful. Get in there and start rehearsing. You've got only a few hours to make something spectacular happen."

I head into the studio, my heart beating out of my chest, and walk toward the center of the room, where Alessandro still stands. Through my ringing ears, I can hear Diana announcing that I am Juliet.

I don't have time for nerves. I don't have time for doubt. I just have to do it.

CHAPTER TWENTY-TWO

NEW YORK CITY
NOW

Sylvie
Romeo and Juliet

I look down and take a deep breath.

Meditatively, I think, *I am in the right place at the right time.* Over and over, I think it.

"Okay, let's take it from the top of the balcony pas de deux," says Diana, her booming, cool voice echoing through the studio.

I walk over to where the balcony set is supposed to be. It's too close to the show time to use the real sets and the stage, so I won't have an opportunity to practice running down the stairs in pointe shoes.

Fuck, I think, *another thing that could go wrong. I better not bite it and roll down them.*

I shake off the thought, knowing it's not helping anything to think that way. I focus back on the task at hand.

Alessandro nods at me from across the studio. I beam from within, wanting to run to him, curl up into him, and apologize for blowing him off after Paris. I can tell he's holding back and trying not to cross my boundaries. I know he cares about me.

About what I think. I can tell he respects me. I can tell he's glad it's me playing Juliet.

I begin. A few moments into it, the door opens and Sebastian walks in. I look over to him and lose my concentration. Diana claps her hands to stop the pianist.

"What happened? That was good. Why did you stop?"

I see Sebastian from the corner of my eye as I try to avoid looking his way. He would rather make me look foolish than have a successful show. He crosses his arms over his chest.

"I don't know," I say, barely audible.

"Excuse me?" asks Diana.

"Give me a minute please," I say to Alessandro, and walk over to Diana and Robert.

"I can't concentrate with extra people in the room watching."

Robert looks at me and Diana turns around to see Sebastian.

"Well, you're going to have a lot of people watching you very soon, so I would figure out how to deal with it. You wanted the principal role so badly, you need to act like a principal."

Something boils deep within me. "You're right, Diana. Excuse me for a few minutes." Diana makes a face. "I know. I know. We have no time. I just need to do one thing, and then I'm all yours."

I walk in Sebastian's direction and then tell him with my eyes to follow me.

He does. Not because of anything but his own curiosity and I know it.

Once we are alone in the hallway, I say, "You need to leave. You're not directing me. You're not the ballet master. You're not wanted in that room."

"Oh, Sylvie, you surprise me. Come on, I was there for the beginning of this girl"—he gestures at me—"I want to be there at the end."

"You weren't there for the beginning. That started when I was four years old."

He laughs. "Sure. Okay."

"And it's not the end. This is me, dancing Juliet. At best, I am a principal who needs to do well tonight, and you're a factor that infringes upon that."

"You're not a principal, love—you're dancing a principal role."

I want to storm away, but instead, I get louder. "You already tried to fucking ruin me once. Why the fuck do you care so much? Why did you have to take me down so far before? You could have just denied we had a relationship. You didn't need to make me out to be a clinging freak when you know it wasn't like that."

"Wasn't it?"

"You fucking know it wasn't. I never even invited you to do anything. You invited me and Jocelyn over to your apartment, your hotel room, gave us wine, gave me drugs, took us to dinner, told me I was brilliant when I sucked your cock—even if I *had* been *obsessed* like you said, I was just a teenager. You were a grown-ass man. Ostensibly."

Finally, he looks speechless. He searches for words. But I keep going.

"You are fucked up, Sebastian. Deeply. Something in you needs something you should not have. You didn't deserve my attention. Or Jocelyn's. You didn't deserve to be attached to our success. And luckily, so far, you have only been attached to my failure. And I'm fine with that, you deserve that. But you will not be part of my success, not tonight, not ever. You fucked me in every sense of the word. Do you deny that?"

A beat. "No."

"Then leave me the fuck alone. Grow up."

I open the door to go back in and see a corps girl had been

filming, her face covered in a mask from the wardrobe, which is right next to her. I smile and point at her and her phone. He looks and she runs away.

There's no telling which girl that was—all the leotards and bodies look the same without the heads.

I let the door slam behind me and return to the studio alone.

CHAPTER TWENTY-THREE

Sylvie
Romeo and Juliet

Prokofiev's score echoes on the stage. It's dark as I take my place on the stairs that lead to the ballroom scene. The corps de ballet dancers take their places as the curtain is about to rise. Slowly, the lights come up and Lord and Lady Capulet will command the stage. I, as Juliet, am positioned on the grand staircase, a young observer until my turn to descend and join the ball. To start my future, as my character and as myself.

My heart is steady. My braids hang down my back, and my costume is perfect, adjusted to fit my frame after Victoria abandoned the role.

It is the role of my lifetime. Not because it is the best role. Not because I don't like other ballets more. But because this was the first ballet I fell in love with. The first role I dreamed of playing. The one I memorized by age thirteen. I had wanted it a few years ago, been excited to do it, but it hadn't meant everything to me the way it does now.

No. Juliet became something more iconic in my life than ever after everything happened with Sebastian. And Jocelyn. Because that had been a death. I had died then. I had died after coming so, so close to the love that I thought and knew I deserved. And I don't mean Sebastian. I mean ballet. I mean the NAB, I mean being here, and having my desires laid out in front of me, mine for the taking, and then having them mercilessly, needlessly taken from me.

And all because of a hierarchy I could not control, and communications I was too young to have.

But now I am Juliet. Reborn. And when I die tonight, it is not the end of something. It's renewal. It's rebirth. Every time I die as Juliet, I shed a part of myself and move closer toward my bliss. Whatever that is.

The curtain rises on the ball. Lady Capulet, Jocelyn, is poised at the very front of the stage. She turns slowly around and raises her arms. The stage comes to life. As she moves down the center of the stage toward the grand staircase where I'm perched, the other dancers waltz around her. Her walk is slow and deliberate. She looks more austere and mature than I've ever seen her.

The other dancers now bow as she passes them. Our eyes lock, and she does not release my gaze as she walks the length of the stage. I see only her in that moment, not anyone else. Her eyes are saying *You can do this, we can do this.*

Our connection is strong. I know just what she's telling me.

We break the gaze at the same exact second.

I look out at the packed audience. Here for me, whether they knew it or not. Here to share in the thing that I love too. It's my time now. I rise and run down the stairs as a giddy Juliet about to meet my first love.

Romeo.

I dance as Juliet that night, for the final show in this run, and when I smile, I truly smile. When I cry, I truly cry. I know Diana told me I was supposed to *hide* myself in my role. But I'm discovering that it's impossible, and the impossibility of it becomes frustrating. Maybe Diana doesn't know everything. Maybe my world will expand after this run. Maybe everyone will hate it.

No matter what, I am being myself.

The tomb scene at the end is famously easy to overperform. Incredibly easy to underact in an effort to not be *too much*. It's when my gift can really come to life.

When I find my Romeo dead, I—Sylvie, not just Juliet—am filled with such gut-curdling anguish and torment that I can hardly breathe.

On my knees over Romeo's body, I ball up my fists, the bone of my knuckle showing alabaster through my pink skin. With Prokofiev's help, I release years of anger and hurt and humiliation. I rise up on my knees and let my head fall back, uncurling my fists and opening my chest, my heart, to the world.

Even though there is no sound, everyone can hear the scream from within me. So loud in my own head that I almost want to cover my ears. I almost lose my absent voice.

My desperation oozes out of me as I try to move Romeo's lifeless body. The audience as a whole seems to lurch forward with a creak, wanting to help me.

But I am alone. Letting go of my broken self. Letting go of a version of the love I used to have. I am exhausted.

My Juliet cannot reawaken her Romeo.

I fold over him, finally crying. Really crying.

At the final bow, I hold Alessandro's hand and look out at the audience. Everything is in slow motion. Even the dust that dances in the stage lights. My body hurts, but in a way that seems like I haven't even noticed the pain in so long—and at last I can *feel* again.

I smile, looking out at the applauding audience, all of them standing for us. For me. For this. None of them can really know just how much true pain went into what they saw tonight. They can't know how long the road was to here. They can't know that they are standing at the finish line of a race that, for me, began twenty years ago. And none of us knows what happens after that finish line. It's as far as I ever hoped, and now it's here.

I see a face I recognize from a lifetime ago. Jordan, in the audience. The first time I've laid eyes on him since Vienna. I know that when Jocelyn sees him, she's going to be happy. Truly happy. Even I feel a strange sense of relief seeing him; as if things are falling into place, and not just for me. After the show, my old friend will have her life changed. I just know it will be good.

I begin to cry, and Alessandro turns to me.

"Are you okay?" he asks. The lights, the gaze of thousands still on us.

I nod. "I'm happy. I'm so happy. I forgot what it feels like."

He smiles. I don't know who initiates it, but before all of these people, we step toward each other, and kiss. This time as Alessandro and Sylvie.

He pulls away and says, "You know, little swan, I'd really like to take you for that date if you'd give me the chance again?"

I smile and kiss him again. Tears welling in my eyes. "I'm not little swan anymore, though, am I?"

He laughs. "Juliet. Will you go somewhere with me?"

I have never felt more like I was at the beginning of my story.

ACKNOWLEDGMENTS

To my mom and dad: Thank you for encouraging me to always follow my dreams and for supporting them fully. Love you.

To the coven: You know who you are . . . Thank you for your friendship, wild spirit, and laughter.

To Annelise: Thank you for believing in me and staying with me from the beginning.

To Paige: Thank you for helping to bring my vision to life.

FIRST
POSITION

MELANIE HAMRICK

Questions for Discussion

1. Sylvie joined a professional ballet company at the age of eighteen, which is very young but not an unusual age for many dancers joining their first professional company. Sylvie is legally an adult at eighteen, but do you think the company should have more formal oversight over the personal lives of their dancers?

2. Jocelyn is also eighteen but has had a very different upbringing from Sylvie. How do you think this shows in Jocelyn's personal and professional behavior?

3. It's common for many children to take ballet lessons, but not many decide to make this their career. Why do you think that is?

4. Do you consider ballet an art form or a craft? Both?

5. How familiar are you with ballet? Did you recognize any of the ballets mentioned throughout the novel?

6. Sylvie's ultimate dream as a dancer is to dance the role of Juliet on the stage. If you were a dancer, what roles would you want to dance?

7. Sylvie and Alessandro have an unconventional first meeting. Why do you think they decided to behave that way when they could easily have been seen?

8. Why do you think Sebastian seduced first Sylvie and then Jocelyn? Do you think his feelings for Sylvie are genuine?

9. How would you define the relationship between Sylvie and Jocelyn?

10. Why do you think Sebastian wasn't visibly punished by the NAB for his role in the affair with Sylvie? Although the relationship was consensual, do you think his behavior constitutes sexual harassment in the workplace?

Keep reading for a special peek
at the next novel by Melanie Hamrick.

I pinch the skin on my inner thigh between freshly manicured fingers. My legs feel like jelly as I watch the dancers onstage. As if he can read my tense mind, Jordan puts a hand on my knee and gives me a wink. He asked if I was sure I wanted to come to *The Sleeping Beauty* tonight and I acted like he was ridiculous for asking. But, as usual, it looks like he was right.

The scene ends and the curtains close to indicate intermission. I rocket out of my seat and say to our friends, "Anyone else feel like ditching the rest of the show and getting drinks instead?"

"Thank *god*," says Artie, leading the way out along the aisle. "I love being a person who goes to the ballet, but I hate *being* at the ballet."

"I've gotten my fill," agrees Jane. "I don't know how those girls do it, it looks like *such* hard work."

We burst out onto the street, fresh, cool air and dusty cigarette smoke draping around us. It's not until we're out there that I realize how claustrophobic I had felt.

"Can you imagine being a ballerina?" asks Artie. "I feel like your whole life just winds up being about sacrifice. Life is for buttered bread and perfect crème brûlée and wines as luscious as velvet, not for anorexia and discipline. Ugh, discipline."

"You poets drive me mental," says Jane. "'Wines as luscious as velvet,' I mean *really*." She lights a cigarette. "Not that I don't agree."

Artie bumps her with his shoulder.

I look at Jordan. His expression says, *You really haven't told them about your old life?*

I laugh as we start walking down the street. "You know I used to be a ballerina."

"Shut up. When you were a kid?" asks Artie.

"Oh my god, of course you were, look at you with that absurd waifish body of yours."

"I only left the ballet about six months ago."

"Eight months," corrects Jordan kindly.

"Eight?" I ask. "Huh."

I take a drag of Jane's cigarette.

She takes it back and says, "How do we not know this? We've all been attached at the hip ever since you two moved to London, and yet *this* didn't come up? I feel betrayed."

Artie is gaping at me. "I too feel betrayed. And guilty for saying how much I hate the ballet."

I laugh. "It's fine."

"Why did you quit?"

I feel Jordan's protective energy waft over me. "She's just on a break, I think. I think she'll go back when she's ready."

Artie and Jane have a hundred more questions as we walk down a cobblestone street lit by gas lamps, meandering in the lawless way we often do until we stumble upon some great little cocktail club or speakeasy.

Tonight, it's a cabaret that we find.

"Oh, let's go in here," I say. "I've been dying to go."

It's true, but I'm also feeling the heat rise in my cheeks as their questions threaten truths and feelings to rise up and take me over, and a cabaret is exactly the sort of distraction that can save me.

I'm absolutely right. As soon as we step through the doors of Josephine's, we are taken away to the rich, decadent world of America's Jazz Age. My vintage fur coat and beaded Oscar de la Renta dress are perfectly on theme, and I wish—not for the first time lately—that I really could travel in time.

My mind starts to wander and I desperately need to regain control of it. We need drinks. Stat. I still have a headache from last night's cocktails, but I don't care. I just need to feel less.

Jordan leans toward me. "You okay? We can always go back to our place."

"I'm fine," I say, with the biting tone I can't seem to leave out of my voice lately. I smile to lessen the impact, but I don't feel like it works. He gives me an affectionate squeeze anyway.

My phone buzzes in my clutch and I take it out to see a text from Sylvie. Sylvie, my closest friend, and the person with whom I've shared the most secrets and the most conflict.

I open the message.

Are you doing okay? I'm worried about you.

I write back immediately, irritable.

Why would you be worried?

"What would you like?" asks Jordan.

"Something strong. Old-fashioned."

He hesitates, but never tells me what to do, so he orders the drink. I notice he gets it made with the highest quality whiskey they sell, trying to save me from tomorrow's hangover.

I get another text from Sylvie.

Honestly, because all you're doing is partying and she only died two weeks ago. I just don't—

I don't even finish reading the text.

And then I hear my name. "Jocelyn?"

I turn to see the source, suddenly remembering with blistering clarity how I had heard of this club.

I smile and pretend that this is not the last person in the world I want to see.

MELANIE HAMRICK is a mother, a ballerina, a producer, a choreographer, and a writer. Born and raised in Virginia, Melanie began dancing at a young age. Her career as a ballerina spanned over sixteen years with American Ballet Theatre. While traveling the world with her family and for work, Melanie has always carried novels and notebooks with her. Melanie's passion for reading and dance inspired her to write her first novel, *First Position*.

Ready to find
your next great read?

Let us help.

Visit prh.com/nextread

Penguin
Random
House